I'm so Sure

A *Charmed Life* Novel

JENNY B. JONES

THOMAS NELSON
Since 1798

NASHVILLE   DALLAS   MEXICO CITY   RIO DE JANEIRO   BEIJING

© 2009 by Jenny B. Jones

Published in Nashville, Tennessee. by Thomas Nelson. Thomas Nelson is a registered trademark of Thomas Nelson, Inc.

Thomas Nelson, Inc., titles may be purchased in bulk for educational, business, fund-raising, or sales promotional use. For information, please e-mail SpecialMarkets@ThomasNelson.com.

Library of Congress Cataloging-in-Publication Data

Jones, Jenny B., 1975-
   I'm so sure / Jenny B. Jones.
      p. cm. — (The charmed life)
   Summary: When Bella's stepfather participates in a reality television show, the entire family gets involved, and as her less-than-perfect life goes on public display, she must rely on her Christian faith while she investigates a mystery involving the prom, deals with her returning ex-boyfriend, and negotiates an awkward relationship with the irritating yet attractive editor of the school newspaper.
   ISBN 978-1-59554-542-8 (softcover)
   [1. Dating (Social customs)—Fiction. 2. High schools—Fiction. 3. Schools—Fiction. 4. Journalism—Fiction. 5. Christian life—Fiction. 6. Reality television programs—Fiction. 7. Mystery and detective stories.] I. Title. II. Title: I am so sure.
   PZ7.J720313Im 2009
   [Fic]—dc22   2009027711

Printed in the United States of America

13 14 QG 6 5 4 3

Praise for Jenny B. Jones

"In *So Over My Head*, Jenny B. Jones hits a high note. You'll laugh, you'll cringe, you'll shake your head in wonder at the wacky but believable situations in which Bella finds herself. Grab anything you can by this author! The Charmed Life series is a great place to start!"

—Nicole O'Dell, author of the *Scenarios for Girls* interactive fiction series

"[So Not Happening] will certainly charm its way onto the bookshelves of any lover of chick lit and fun, light-hearted fiction.

—titletrakk.com review of *So Not Happening*

"Who wants to keep up with the Kardashians now that Bella Kirkwood is starring in a reality show? No need for Nancy Drew when Bella is on the case. This second in the Charmed Life series has everything: mystery, romance and comedic shenanigans. It's crazy, preposterous good fun! What's not to like?"

—*Romantic Times* 4.5 star review of *I'm So Sure*

"A novel by Jenny B. Jones isn't just good entertainment for your mind ... it's laughter for your soul. With unforgettable characters and a story to keep you turning pages into the wee hours of the night, the second installment in "The Charmed Life" is better than the first."

—deenasbooks.blogspot.com review of *I'm So Sure*

"Brilliantly written, charmingly witty and deeply emotive, this book is a treasure to be read many times over."

—RelzReviewz review of *Just Between You and Me*

Other Books by Jenny B. Jones Include:

Just Between You and Me

Young Adult Series

The Katie Parker Series
In Between
On the Loose
The Big Picture

The Charmed Life Series
So Not Happening

This book is dedicated to my super handsome nephew, Hardy. You are the sweetest, smartest, niftiest boy in the world. And I cannot believe your dad, who used to "accidentally" punch me in the nose and make me his wrestling guinea pig, could have a son as perfect as you. I love you!

chapter one

*T*hat dirty rotten cheater.

I lower my binoculars and swap them for a camera. A moment like this needs some megapixel proof. The lens zooms closer and closer on my target. I shove my way farther into the bushes of the Truman City Park and aim toward the old tennis court, where the loser twines himself around a girl who is definitely *not* his girl-friend. Leaning over and balancing on one leg, I angle my body and get the perfect shot. One more close-up to seal the deal.

"Hello, Bella Kirkwood."

With a squeal and a jerk, I topple over and crash into the shrubs.

Spitting dried leaves, I glare at the boy standing over me. "Hey, Chief."

As the sun shines behind him, the editor of the Truman High *Tribune* smiles, and for a moment I forget that I'm sprawled in a small tree with limbs poking me in very uncomfortable places.

Luke Sullivan is delish. Except for his attitude. And his arro-gance. And his broodiness. And his genius IQ that makes me feel like I have all the intellect of a gerbil.

"What are you doing?" With his hand on mine, he pulls me upright and I'm catapulted straight into his chest.

"Working." I take a step back. "Mindy Munson hired me to find out if her boyfriend was cheating." I jerk my head toward the couple making up their own game on the court. "I'd say we have a definite love violation here."

"So you're taking pictures of a guy without his permission. Don't you think that's a little creepy? A little unethical?"

I consider the idea. "Not so much."

"This has got to stop. Ever since we busted the football team, people think you're Nancy Drew."

It's true. When you get kidnapped by the leader of a deadly football gang, and said leader tries to permanently erase you from the planet, people think you're the stuff. And when you walk away from the attempted murder with your head still intact, folks start to think you're some sort of sleuthy hero.

Oh, the many perks of almost dying. I've spent the last two months tracking down stolen iPods, cheating boyfriends, a drill team stalker, and one lost bullfrog by the name of Mr. Toady Pants.

Not only does it keep me busy, it keeps me in shoes. Hey, the Prada fairy doesn't visit me like she used to. I do what I must.

"Did you finish the article I assigned?" Now Luke's all business.

"I'm working here. According to my watch the school day has been over for an hour, and believe it or not, I do have a life outside of the paper. What are you doing here anyway? If you're so hard up for female company that you have to follow me around, maybe you should give Mindy Munson a call." I throw a look at her loser boyfriend. "My keen reporter's instinct says she'll be on the market by tonight."

A corner of his mouth twitches; then he tilts his head and pierces me with those ocean blue eyes. "Who says I'm on the market?"

I blink. "Um . . . because I've never seen you with a girl. I realize I'm new to detective work and all, but unless your lady is invisible, she—"

"She's at Harvard." He picks a leaf from my jacket. "Freshman. And no, we don't see much of each other, but she should be in for Christmas."

Why do I suddenly feel like a deflated balloon? "You never mentioned her."

He grins, revealing perfectly straight teeth. "You never asked."

A chilly wind blows, and my chestnut hair reassembles itself into a new formation. Luke reaches out and tucks a wayward strand back into place, his fingers sliding across my ear.

"Get that shot!"

I jump as a flash explodes in my face. As three men surround us, Luke pushes me behind his back.

A squatty man sporting a Donald Trump comb-over steps forward. "Can we get another one of you and your boyfriend?"

I peek around Luke. "*What?* Who are you?" I shove Luke's protective hands away and plant a fist at my hip. "And this *isn't* my boyfriend." Why am I explaining here?

"Doesn't matter—just move in closer. These will be great promo shots."

"Drop the camera and leave her alone." Luke steps toward the guy. The boy may be tall and wiry, but he's a beast on the soccer field, so he's got some muscles on that frame.

"We just need a few more pics of the girl. Maybe you two could huddle up again?"

I gasp. "We were *not* 'huddled up.'" Though we have kissed once. But it was just to escape the deranged football players. I barely remember it. Just a dim, faded . . . totally hot memory. Donald Trump snaps another picture. "I don't know who you are, but how dare you spy on me and take my picture without my permission!"

Luke quirks a dark brow my way, then returns his stare to Mr. Comb-over. "Who are you?"

The short man shoves his card in Luke's hand. "Marv Noblitz. I work for WWT."

"Who?" No clue what that is.

Luke studies the card. "World Wrestling Television."

Though it's a vague fog swirling in my mind, I feel trouble beginning to take shape. "I think you might be looking for my stepdad." He's known as Captain Iron Jack on the amateur wrestling circuit. But I just call him Stepdaddy Spandex.

"We're looking for the entire family."

A horror movie soundtrack begins to play at full volume in my head. The kind of tune that pounds out right before things get ugly and the fake blood spews. "Look, Mr. Noblitz, Jake's the wrestler. Whatever you're working on, I didn't sign up for it."

"It's a reality show—*Pile Driver of Dreams.*" He chuckles. "And you didn't have to sign up—your stepdad did that for you."

"Huh?" My brain tingles with dread.

"Get ready, kid." He pulls out a cigar and sticks it in his mouth. "Hope you're prepared to live your life in front of millions, because we're going to follow you and your family for months. You'll barely take a tinkle that we won't be there with a camera."

I stand there mute. Frozen.

Luke pats me on the back, his face grim. "Looks like Hollywood's knocking on your door."

I sigh and close my eyes. "Yeah, well somebody needs to tell Hollywood Bella Kirkwood is *not* at home."

chapter two

With a camera crew on my tail, I speed through downtown, blaze through some dirt roads, and lose them with a couple of detours near Old Man Peterson's farm. It will buy me at least a few minutes.

I barely put my lime green VW Bug in park before I leap out, oblivious to the biting December chill.

"Mo-*ther*!" Ever since my mom moved us from Manhattan to marry her factory-working, wrestler wannabe, life has been nuts—at best. But *this* is going too far!

"Mom!" Touring the house, I find her, Jake, and my little step-brother, Robbie, in our newly remodeled kitchen. Laughing. Like life is fine.

Mom cuts into a roll of cookie dough. "Hey, sweetie. We were—" Her knife freezes. "What's wrong?"

Oh, the list. It's too long.

I try to break it down. "Um . . . Jake. Wrestler. Reality show. Surprise. Cameras. Me." Then I just wail.

Mom runs to me and pulls me into a seat. "Calm down, Bella. How do you know about that?"

My mouth drops. "The question is *why* didn't I know sooner?

Like *before* I got all Britney Speared with the camera crew?" Let the record show, I totally had underwear on.

"A few months ago I saw on TV where they were scouting for ten wrestlers for a reality show. So I sent in Jake's application."

Jake's arm slinks around my mom. "We had a one-in-a-million shot of making it."

My laugh is bitter. "With your luck with the odds, I wish you'd bought a lotto ticket instead. Your camera crew should be here any minute."

Jake lets out a shout, then grabs my mom and twirls her around the kitchen. My six-year-old stepbrother takes the opportunity to run circles around them, his Superman cape flying behind. Their whooping happiness makes me want to hurl.

Okay, so maybe most girls would think it would be nifty-cool to have a camera crew in your house and be on TV once a week. But not me. Not when it is centered around your stepfather's attempts at wrestling. The head of our household will be seen shirtless. In spandex. And a pirate costume. He says *aargh*, for crying out loud! I will never be able to hold my head up. And my own dad is going to flip. Though he's been a guest commentator on *E! News* a lot as a plastic surgeon to the stars, he's never been able to get his own show. And now my stepdad gets on TV—just for doing a really good body-slam.

The doorbell rings, and Jake and Mom rush to open it.

Budge, my other stepbrother, takes that moment to come down the steps. In his Wiener Palace sultan uniform, no less. "What's going on?" The feathers on his turban droop.

Budge and I were sworn enemies from day one. But ever since I lifted the lid on the craziness that killed his best friend last fall,

Budge has been extremely nice to me. We talk all the time. Like last week he said, "Hey, moron, can you pass the milk?"

That's some good progress.

"You'd better call the Wiener Palace and tell them you'll be late." I jerk my thumb toward the three men standing in the entryway. "You're not even going to believe this. Your dad's been selected to be on a wrestling reality show. And we're part of the deal. Basically our lives will be on TV for millions to see. No privacy. No control over their manipulative editing. The entire world watching our every move."

Budge shakes his head. "Dude, that is—"

"Humiliating, embarrassing, and intrusive?"

"Cooool." He scratches his red 'fro. "I'm gonna be on TV. Chicks *love* stars. This is gonna be awesome."

Awesomely horrible.

An hour later we're all stuffed into our outdated, 1970s living room. I sit on one end of the orange couch beside a beaming Mom and Jake.

"So I think we've got everything settled. Just have your management look over the contract and give me a call." Mr. Noblitz shakes Jake's giant hand.

"I need to talk to my family first," my stepdad says. "I'll let you know what we decide."

When the door shuts on Mr. Noblitz, Jake gets down to business. "Why don't we pray about this?" He reaches for my mom's hand. She reaches for Robbie's.

Budge and I stare at each other. *Fine.* I clasp his wrist with two of my fingers and bow my head.

At Jake's amen, Mom begins. "This is an amazing opportunity."

My stepdad beams. "Jillian's right. This could take me straight to the top in professional wrestling. But it's going to be an invasion for all of us."

"Who cares?" Budge says. "I'm in."

"Me too!" Robbie squirts invisible Spider-Man webs across the room. Though he leans toward Superman, my stepbrother likes to incorporate all superheroes in his daily routine.

"Bella?" Mom asks.

What else can I say? "I am not totally thrilled about this . . . but okay."

While my mother throws an impromptu party downstairs, I steal away to my room and shut the door on all the madness.

God, I know this is great for Jake's career, but what about me? What could possibly be the purpose in all this? Oh, sure, our family could be a witness to the wrestling community. But couldn't we just send them some tracts?

I fall back onto my bed and stare at the ceiling. My cat Moxie bounds onto my stomach and butts my chin with her face.

My phone rings and I answer without even looking at it. "My life just got flushed down the toilet, Bella speaking."

Familiar laughter fills my ear. "Bel?"

I sit up. *No. Couldn't be.*

He wouldn't dare.

"Bella, you there?"

He did. My rat-fink-cheater ex-boyfriend called me.

"What do you want, Hunter?"

"Don't hang up. I just want to talk."

"So talk."

"Wow. I've missed that sweet voice."

"Hunter, did you need something?"

Seconds of silence. "I miss you." He laughs. "I'm totally blowing this. I . . . just wanted to talk to you again. I miss, um, you know, hanging out. I miss us."

"Really? Every time I miss us, I think about you all kissy-faced with my best friend."

"That was just a moment of insanity. I was lonely when you left New York. Mia and I—we're over. We were never anything to begin with."

"Oh, okay. That makes it all better. Well, thanks for calling and telling me that. Gotta go—"

"Wait!" He sighs into the phone. I picture him in his room, running his hands through his thick hair. "I know I said too much. Look, Bel, I just want to be friends again. You have every right to hate me."

"I don't hate you." *I wish rabid pigs would carry you away, but there's no hate.*

"I have something else to tell you."

Oh, boy.

"I have, um, a disease."

"Ew! Well, that's what you get for being such a male ho."

"Not *that* kind of disease. This is . . . more serious. It's not good."

"What?" Okay, cancel the pigs. "Are you going to be okay?"

"It's treatable. But it's going to be a long haul and nothing is certain. Bel, I just . . . it's really important that I make everything right in my life."

"Hunter, I forgive you. We've gone over this."

"It's not enough."

I close my eyes and breathe. *Fine.* "Whatever you need, Hunter. I'm here."

"I was hoping you'd say that. I'll see you tomorrow."

"Tomorrow?"

"Bella, I'm in Oklahoma."

chapter three

"*H*appy Tuesday, Truman Tigers! It's time for your morning announcements!"

I tune out the student on the TV and doodle my name in curlicues on my notebook. I should be studying my notes, but I'm busy replaying Hunter's call in my head.

A movement catches my eye outside the door, and I see Lindy Miller, all wide-eyed and spastic hands, gesturing for me to come into the hall. Lindy ducks when Mrs. Palmer glances in her direction.

I make my way to the front of the classroom. "Um, Mrs. Palmer? Can I go blow my nose outside?"

She puts down her pen and frowns. "You can't do that in here?"

"I tend to make goose honks when I blow."

She waves me away and returns her attention to the student news program.

I grab a Kleenex and sail out the door. "What is it?"

Lindy looks like she just missed the game-winning shot. "I . . ." She covers her red face. "It's bad, Bella. It's really bad."

My heart drops to my toes. "Tell me."

"The class president moved today!"

Oh.

"Er, sorry." I pat her on the shoulder. "I didn't know you and Harry Wu Fong were that close."

"No!" she hisses. "Don't you get it? We have, like, three months until prom. The class president is in charge of that. With him gone, the vice president takes his place. And—"

"You're the VP." It all makes sense now. A few months ago, my tomboy friend Lindy got a total makeover. Kicky haircut, golden highlights, waxed brows, new clothes. All to impress her BFF Matt, who still has no idea she wants to be more than friends. Though she rarely wears the makeup I bought her, she still looks great. But she has *no* idea what to do with making anything pretty—like an entire prom. She hates froufrou stuff. Why she's friends with me, I'll never know.

"No, I'm not the VP. Now I'm the stinkin' president!" She wrings hands that can grip a basketball with no problem. "I don't know how to organize a prom. Harry Wu left me his notes, but aside from reserving the Truman Inn banquet room, there's nothing done, and prom is practically tomorrow!"

"Relax, would you? You have plenty of time. And you know I'll help you. Plus, I'm pretty sure you have a prom committee or something, right?"

"I have minions?" She relaxes a little. "This might not be so bad. I totally get to boss people around, don't I? How hard could prom planning be anyway?"

"It will be fine. I organized lots of formal events at Hilliard." That's my old private school in Manhattan. My former best friend, Mia, still goes to school there. This is the same *friend* I caught making out with Hunter not so long ago. I was always willing to share anything with Mia—purses, shoes, a new hat. But my boyfriend's lips? A girl has to draw the line somewhere.

Confident that Lindy is over her panic attack, I return to class. Mrs. Palmer lifts a brow as I pass by. "Took you quite a while."

"Major drainage."

On my way to journalism class, I make a pit stop at the girl's bathroom and touch up my face. It's become a ritual. Reapply gloss, give my hair a shake, and make sure nothing is dangling from my nose. It's not that I care what Luke thinks. Seriously, I don't.

Maybe a little. But I'd never go out with him.

Mr. Holman, the newspaper advisor, intercepts me at the classroom door. "In my office, please."

I trail behind him and find Luke already seated.

And ticked.

His arms are crossed, and he glares at me over his tortoiseshell glasses. His inky black hair is slightly mussed, like he's run frustrated hands through it.

I sit down in the vacant seat beside Luke, while Mr. Holman perches on the corner of his desk. "Bella, you've done some topnotch investigative reporting for the paper."

"Oh." I nod demurely. "Thanks." Take *that* Luke Sullivan!

Mr. Holman casts a furtive glance at Luke then continues. "I'd like to have you writing your own column. We decided that a regular feature on teen life in Truman would be a nice angle. Maybe start with a series on the life of a working student. We think that would be a great idea."

"*We* didn't think so. Mr. Holman did." Luke breathes through his nose like a bull ready to charge. "You've only been on staff since

August. You still need to work on the basics, in my opinion. You're not ready for your own column."

My spine stiffens, and I feel my cheeks flush pink. "I think I can handle it."

Luke rolls his eyes. "This will not be some fluff piece. It's serious. This isn't *Seventeen* magazine. We're a reputable paper. We have—"

"Colleges watching us. I know." Boy, do I know. I hear that mantra in my sleep.

Mr. Holman stands up and wipes at a jelly stain on his shirt. "We'll announce it on the morning news program and give the students an opportunity to e-mail you with their ideas and work stories."

I can't help but smile. "Sounds great. Thank you."

"Mr. Holman?" Another staff member sticks her head in the door. "I need you to check my copy."

He rests his hand on my shoulder. "We'll start this tomorrow. It will be a great addition to the paper. Really liven things up." Mr. Holman walks out of the office and into the small class.

The tension stays behind.

The fluorescent lights hum. The heater blows. The clock ticks.

But Luke Sullivan doesn't move.

I gather my things and rise. "Alrighty then. Just gonna get started on—" Suddenly he's at the doorway, blocking my exit. I catch a hint of his cologne.

"If you were truly interested in being a serious journalist, you would know that you need to stick with the basics and continue building your skills. This isn't like the little advice column you wrote at your old school."

Little? "Since when is helping people *little?*" Ugh, sometimes, this boy. One minute he's got my skin tingling with his charm, and the next he's barking orders like a drill sergeant, and I want to kick his shins. Jerk.

His eyes bore into mine. "I won't cut you any slack on your deadlines."

"Nobody asked you to."

"And you realize you'll need a job. A few of them, in fact. You'll need to make the arrangements and get local businesses to hire you temporarily."

"Yeah, I was totally going to work that angle. I know you're really busy with your Harvard girlfriend, so don't worry about me monopolizing any of your time." Omigosh! Did I just say that? Rewind! Rewind!

His left cheek dimples. "Are you jealous?"

"No, actually I'm sad." I give a slight smile. "For her. I can't imagine what it's like to go out with you. You probably tell her what to order on your dates. Or maybe you woo her by reading aloud from the *Wall Street Journal.*"

"Wouldn't you like to know?" Luke leans over me until there are mere inches between us. "Have fun joining the working class." And he walks out.

"I—I will!" *Take that.*

Okay, if it weren't for the fact that he saved my life last quarter, I'd really let him have it. But no, he simply *had* to show up at just the right moment and rescue me from a homicidal football player intent on killing me. I totally could've handled it myself.

All right, so I was drugged to the point of drooling and on my way to permanent nappy-time, but whatever. I would've figured something out.

Lunch rolls around, and before I can beeline to the caf, I hear my name on the school intercom. *Great. What now?* Maybe the principal wants to talk to me about my ideas to redecorate the building. It's in serious need of a makeover. A little style would help everyone's test scores.

I push through the office door and the secretary greets me. "You've got a visitor."

I turn around and there in a torn vinyl seat is Hunter Penbrook.

For a minute I remember what I first saw in him. His dashing good looks. His impeccable dress. His sense of fun.

But then he cheated on me. And now he's just a picture on my bulletin board for target practice.

He stands up. "Bella, it's good to—"

"What do you want, Hunter?" I grab his hand and lead him outside to the courtyard. I motion for him to sit on a picnic table while I remain standing.

"Thank you for meeting with me."

"Who are you staying with? Why are you here?"

"My dad had some business in Tulsa, so I took the rental car for the day. We're leaving tonight, but I had to talk to you."

"Uh-huh. So tell me about this medical condition you have."

He shakes his head and looks away. "I really don't want to talk about it. They think something is seriously wrong with my stomach, but don't have any clue what it is yet. I've been to the ER a few times. My dad is making them run every test known to man."

"But you could die?"

He shrugs it off. "There are a lot of things uncertain right now. But Bel, I want to make things right in my life." His hand rests on my arm. "I needed to tell you in person that I'm sorry for all the hurt I caused you."

Right now I'm kind of regretting the darts sticking out of his eyes on my bulletin board. "I've forgiven you." Okay, I haven't forgotten it, but when you see your best friend's face mashed to your boyfriend's, it's a little hard. "Maybe you just need to forgive yourself."

His smile is weak. "How do you do that? How do you just forgive somebody for totally devastating you?"

"I wouldn't say devastate."

"I cheated on you with Mia and ripped your heart open—"

"More like a slight snag. A paper cut."

"—and you just forgive me?"

I really want to roll my eyes here. "Yup. It's kind of what you're supposed to do."

Hunter's hand drops away, and he watches the lunch activity around us. Students play basketball. A couple shares a Powerade and some nachos. "I want that. I want what you have, Bel."

I snap to attention. "Well, you can't have it. Your all-access pass to Bella Kirkwood has expired."

He opens his mouth, then closes it, as if struggling for words. "I mean . . . I'd like to understand your faith better." Hunter meets my eyes. "I think I need that in my life."

I've made a lot of mistakes in my relationship with Hunter. One would be dating him in the first place. Hunter is not a Christian. I knew this. Knew I wasn't supposed to go fishing for a boyfriend in unsaved waters. And there might've been some other mess-ups, but if God can wipe my slate clean, why rehash?

"So you're here in Truman because you want me to tell you about Jesus?"

Hunter rubs a hand over his face. "Honestly, I don't know. I just felt compelled to see you. Like I've been led here this week."

"I don't really know what to say."

He tightens his jacket around him. "I know this is all really awkward. Maybe I shouldn't have come. I won't be back . . . I'm sorry." And he walks away.

Sometimes being a good person is a serious pain.

I run after him. "Hunter, wait." My arm reaches out, clinging to him until he turns around. "Don't go yet."

"I just need a friend, Bella. That's all I'm asking."

I slowly nod. "Okay."

And he enfolds me in a hug.

I allow myself the moment, remembering how I used to love these arms, these hugs. His smell. His strength.

Hunter breaks away, his eyes wide. "What is *that*?"

I follow the direction of his finger and blanch. "Nooo."

There across the street is a two-man camera crew.

"Bella, what is that?"

I give my back to the camera. "*That* is the end of life as I know it."

chapter four

*I*t's hard to have a mature conversation with someone in a spandex onesie.

"I have cameras following me around."

Jake looks up from his choke hold in the middle of the wrestling ring. "We've talked about this. Marv Noblitz told us what to expect."

"Hi, Bella. Good day at school?" This from the man whose head is trapped in the crook of Jake's arm.

"Hey, Squiggy." Squiggy Salducci is actually John Pederson, but that doesn't make for a good name in the ring. His persona is a nerd, complete with high-waisted pants and dork glasses. He calls himself "the intellectual wrestler."

"Jake, I just didn't expect it to be so intrusive."

He laughs as he pins Squiggy to the mat. "If you think that's bad, just wait 'til the crew sets up in the house."

Yeah, I have tried to block those details out. I'm in reality show denial.

"The main focus will be on me, Bella. Don't worry too much about it." Jake releases Squiggy from the floor. "Hey, Luke. Right on time."

Turning around, I find my editor-in-chief approaching. His eyes land on me briefly before turning their full focus on Jake. "Are you ready for the match this weekend?" he asks my stepdad.

"It's the first round of elimination for the show. I think I'm ready." Jake shakes Luke's hand.

"What are you doing here?" I ask.

"Covering the reality show for the local paper. Sometimes I work freelance for them. That way I can run the stories in the Truman High *Tribune* too."

"How convenient. Who called you?"

"Your mom."

Perfect.

"Who's the guy you were talking to at lunch?" he asks.

Oh, just my boyfriend. He goes to Princeton. "An old friend. Jealous?"

Luke smiles. "No. Just needed to know if this was someone of interest for the show."

"I'm headed to the diner. You boys have fun talking." I throw my bag over my shoulder and walk away. "And Jake, if you want a real writer, you know where I live."

I think Sugar's Diner was new sometime when Lincoln was in office and women still wore corsets. Any updates to the Truman establishment were made in the fifties, and things haven't changed since. Pink walls. Jukebox. Red barstools.

When I swing open the door of Sugar's, I find my mom on one of these barstools. She has a cup of coffee in one hand and a pencil in the other. My mother used to be a Manhattan socialite. That was before Dad traded her in for a newer model. She went from the country club in New York to the blue plate special in Truman.

I sidle up beside her. "Whatcha doing?"

"Hey, sweetie." She gives me a side hug and brushes the hair out of my eyes. "Just going over the family budget."

"Yeah, about that. No more off-brand deodorant please. My pits know the difference."

She laughs, but it's short-lived as her face grows serious. "Want a milk shake?"

Anxiety does the rumba in my stomach. "You only offer me a shake when something's wrong. Spill it."

Mom chews on the end of her pencil before tucking it into her blonde ponytail. "Talked to your father today."

That's never good. The two have nothing in common now but me. And Dad only calls Mom when there's something bad he needs to communicate to me but doesn't have the guts to do it himself. Dad is a brilliant plastic surgeon. But when it comes to parenting, he's as effective as a crooked nose job.

She blows on her coffee. "Your dad has run into some financial troubles."

"But he has an accountant."

"Not anymore. Seems she took his money and left for an undisclosed location. Your dad is in pretty hot water with the IRS."

"Didn't he check the accountant's credentials?"

"I think thirty-six–D was all he needed to know." Mom rolls her shoulders and looks me square in the eye. "This means no more under-the-table daddy payouts for you. Your days of visiting him and maxing out his credit card are over."

Mom believes we should *all* live on her and Jake's income, so my child support checks get put into a trust. I think it's the stupidest idea ever. But it hasn't been *that* bad because I do get in some serious shopping when I visit Dad once a month. I had high hopes for some splurging this weekend in Manhattan.

"Bella, you're seventeen. I think you know what this means. It's time to live like other people your age."

"I have to get my purses off eBay?"

"You need to get a job."

"I'm already on it."

My mom just stares.

"Seriously. I got my own regular feature in the *Tribune*, and I have to write a series of articles on the working teenager." I roll my brown eyes. "It should be one swell time."

"A little part-time work won't be so bad. Something to give you some spending money. Besides, it's going to be good for you."

"That's what you said about the Raisin Bran this morning." Ew.

"Logan works." She's referring to my stepbrother, who is also seventeen. Everyone on the planet calls him Budge but my mom.

"I'm not sure where I'll work, but I do know I am *not* serving hot dogs at the Wiener Palace." I have my pride. "But as far as Dad's money issue is concerned, I'm sure he will have this all cleared up soon." And I'll be back in business with the occasional shopping sprees.

Mom stands up and stretches her back. She grabs her order pad and sticks it in her apron. "You can talk to him about that this weekend."

Dolly O'Malley busts through the kitchen doors with an ample hip and an armload of shopping bags. Like my mom, she's a waitress. Unlike my mom, who still drips the occasional coffee and drops a plate a week, Dolly waitresses with as much finesse as a prima ballerina.

"What's in the bags?" I ask.

Dolly's face glows beneath her too-pink blush, and she looks to my mom. "I need your opinion. We know it's a boy, so do I go with a blue crib set?" She holds up a small quilt the color of a robin's egg. "Or maybe something more neutral like yellow?"

"Who's having a baby?" I reach for the yellow comforter as Mom hands me a chocolate-and-banana shake.

Dolly takes a deep breath and grins. "I am!"

I nearly spew ice cream out my nose. "What?" I look back and forth between my mom and her friend. "But you're single . . . and you're, like"—*fifty or something old like that*—"so mature."

Dolly gives her big, blonde hair a toss, a pointless act since it hasn't moved since 1985. "I'm only forty-six."

My mom swats my arm with a towel. "Dolly is adopting. A young woman at church contacted her last month about taking the baby."

"It was such a God thing. I wasn't even considering anything like having any more children." Dolly brushes her hand over a soft baby blanket.

Once upon a time Dolly was married to Mickey Patrick, who happens to be Jake's manager and trainer. Their two young daughters were killed in a car accident a long time ago—with Mickey at the wheel. He moved out not long after that, and let's just say Truman is too small a town for two ex-spouses to avoid each other.

I'm still trying to wrap my mind around someone offering Dolly a baby. "So this woman is pregnant and saw you one day, and thought you were the rightful mother?"

"I used to work with her mother here at Sugar's. The girl's only nineteen. She's got a long way to go before she gets her life together. The father's out of the picture, she's living with her mother, and she has no job. She's in no condition to raise a child."

"Congratulations," I say for lack of anything else. "You'll be a great mom. Hey, you know what else would be great?"

Both women raise their brows, suspicious of my segue.

I plunge on. "It would be supercool if you could get me an after-school job here, Dolly. Maybe you could talk to the manager?"

She cracks her gum. "Sorry, kid. We don't need any help. But I guess I could use some assistance out at my farm."

Dolly's farm is more like a ranch. It's a total mystery to me. She's worked as a waitress for years, yet she has a house and property any movie star would be envious of. She must make some really nice tips.

"Uh. Okay. I go to my dad's this weekend. Can I start next Monday?"

"I'll warn the livestock." She glances over the counter at my ballet flats. "And don't show up in those."

chapter five

~~Having a job can be so stressful for a teen. Last year I babysat for three hours, and I—~~

~~Most Truman High students know what it's like to chase that dollar. This past summer, I sold two pair of my Jimmy Choos to a less fortunate friend and~~

I delete my lame attempts at my first article on teen occupations. What do I know about working? Other than doing a little detective work for some cash, I've never had a job. This is not going to be as easy as I thought.

Luke walks by, and I try to look busy. "Are things not going well?" His face shows zero ounce of concern.

"Things are going fine, thank you very much. I am *loving* the idea of having my own weekly column."

He sits on the edge of the table. "Have you finished the other assignment I gave you? You know, the new weekly assignment doesn't replace the other reporting duties. Just adds to it."

"I'm aware of that." I plaster a smile on my face. "Check your in-box."

He leans a little closer. "You should be happy I sent you on assignment."

"Sending me to the band's oboe concert of Mariah Carey hits is not exactly what I'd call field reporting."

"Oboe players have a story to tell too. Speaking of stories, are you going to be at tonight's wrestling match? I wanted you to get me in to see Jake before it started. I have a few pre-match questions for him."

"I'm leaving for my dad's right after school." I click on the Internet and pretend to search for jobs online.

Luke peeks over my shoulder, blatantly reading my screen. "If you're lucky you'll find a job that utilizes your skills with hair, makeup, and shopping."

I bite back a retort as Mr. Holman approaches. But that *would* be totally cool.

"Just the two I wanted to speak with." He lays a hand on Luke's shoulder. "Luke, I looked over the preliminary notes on the wrestling reality show. I think it's going to be a great piece."

Luke sits straighter. "Thank you, sir."

"But I think we'd be remiss if we didn't take advantage of Bella's insight here. I mean she is *living* this reality show. Why not put her on the story too?"

Fiery blue eyes zero in on me. "I've got it covered, Mr. Holman. I can handle the story. Have I ever let you down?"

"Of course not. I just think we can run companion pieces here. Your take from the outside, and Bella's take from the inside." He slaps Luke on the back. "Okay, good conversation. Let's talk again soon. Bella, can I see you in my office?" Mr. Holman walks away.

You couldn't burn through the tension with a flatiron. I ease out of my seat and squeeze by Luke. "I guess he thinks I'm cut out for more than band recitals." And humming a Mariah tune, I go get the details on my assignment.

At lunch I take my tray and sit next to Lindy Miller and Matt Sparks. My salad tastes like grass, and I look longingly at Matt's cheese fries. The boy plays football and basketball and works out about four hours a day. He could eat a whole vat of cheese sauce if he wanted to.

I pick at a purple thing in my salad. "Did you guys know Luke Sullivan has a girlfriend?"

"Dude, she's hot." This from Matt, who probably thinks anything with boobs is hot.

"Did you know she goes to Harvard?" asks Lindy.

I stab a bite. "Yeah. Seems like I heard that."

"Luke said she's going to be in soon for Christmas break," Matt says.

"Hey, guys." Anna Deason slides her long, chocolate-colored legs into the last remaining seat at the table, her cheerleading skirt fanning around her. "Lindy, when are the nominations open for prom queen? I think this could be my year." Anna is a grade older than us and has been talking about her senior prom since August. Or maybe since kindergarten.

Lindy bites into an apple and shrugs. "I don't know. I, um . . ."

"The race for prom king and queen is not something to put off. It's important to this school. It's a long-held tradition that must be continued." Anna grabs a carrot stick. "Plus my Grandma Ruby's already bought me a dress."

Lindy looks to me for help. I focus on squeezing more ranch on my salad.

"We're having a class meeting next week. We'll get some prom details settled then. We have plenty of money to work with, so you know it's going to be a sweet event." Lindy proudly nods at her first official statement as class president.

"And make sure there's some good food there." Anna scrunches her nose. "None of the pizza roll things like last year. Those things are just nasty."

The entire cafeteria grows quiet, and I lower my fork. Mr. Sutter, the principal, walks down the rows of tables, eyeing every student.

"Uh-oh." Matt frowns. "He never comes in here. Somebody's in some deep dookie."

My pulse speeds as the principal comes closer and closer to where we sit. I scan my brain and review the last month. Does he know I used my cell phone this morning? Is calling Barney's in NYC to hold a pair of shoes really a crime? Because if it is, I would totally suffer detention for it.

Mr. Sutter stops at our table. He eyes every one of us, and I feel my skin grow hot. I might've clogged the toilet yesterday and not told a janitor. Sometimes I use too much toilet paper and don't know when to stop.

"Anna Deason, you need to come with me."

Anna's dark cheeks stain pink. "Why?"

"Because I asked you to, that's why. You have some explaining to do, young lady, and I don't think you want to do it in front of two hundred witnesses."

"Anything you have to say to me, you can say right here. I didn't do anything. I'm a straight-A cocaptain of the cheerleading squad. I don't do bad stuff." Her voice is rising. "I made a thirty-four on my ACT. I'm in select choir. I did *not* do anything wrong."

The principal lowers his voice to a growl. "Miss Deason, right now you are doing something wrong, and that is disobeying my directive. I have asked you nicely to follow me to the office. If you refuse again, my next option is to have you physically removed."

"Lead me there." Anna grabs my arm on her way up. "But I'm taking representation."

"Me?" I squeak.

"I have the right to my own counsel, and you're it."

The principal rolls his eyes and storms ahead.

"Sit down," he orders as we enter his cave-like office. You'd think the top dog of the school would at least get a window. No wonder he's in a bad mood all the time. He never gets to see the sun. He's like a character from *Twilight*.

"Miss Deason, the funds in the junior class account are missing. Would you like to tell me what you know?"

"How should I know? I'm a senior." Anna stands up. "They'd better find them though, because I've been waiting my whole life to be Truman prom queen."

Mr. Sutter drums his knobby fingers on the fake wood desk. "I had a nice long conversation with the president of the Truman National Bank this morning. He informed me that yesterday evening one of our accounts was cleared out to the tune of seven thousand dollars. And do you know where the money showed up?"

Anna and I both shake our heads.

"In a personal account under the name of Anna Deason."

"What?" she gasps. "That's a lie! How would I get the money out of the school account?"

"You did make a thirty-four on your ACT."

"It was luck! So did Brian McPhearson, and he wears his shoes on the wrong feet and drips snot!"

"The money was in your account only a matter of hours before disappearing."

Anna blinks a few times. "Where did it go?"

Mr. Sutter steeples his fingers. "I was hoping you could tell me."

Anna throws her purse on the desk. "You open that bag. I don't have any money in it. I can barely fit two lipsticks and a Summer Fresh pad in there."

Summer Fresh would be the local factory here in Truman. They make feminine products. I happen to be the proud stepdaughter of the maxi-pad line supervisor. Between his spandex tendencies and extensive knowledge of female business, some days I can hardly hold my head up.

"The bank says a girl went through the drive-thru and wrote a seven-thousand-dollar check on your account."

"Well, it wasn't me!"

"She was able to produce a driver's license."

I can't help but chime in. "What bank employee would be dumb enough to hand over seven thousand dollars in the drive-thru?"

Mr. Sutter shifts in his chair. "That's a detail we're also working on. The teller has since been let go. Her supervisor's in some hot water too. Anyway, Miss Deason, where were you at four o'clock yesterday afternoon?"

"I . . . um . . ." She turns tortured brown eyes to me. "I was at the coffee shop."

"Was anyone with you?"

"No. My boyfriend and I had gotten into this big fight, and I just needed to clear my head before I did anything drastic like punch his lights out."

"Or rob a school blind."

"I didn't do it! Somebody is setting me up—because I *have* my driver's license. Maybe the money will show up. It's a bank error! It's the Communists! It's aliens! It's those Scientologists!" Some of Anna's bravado slips, and tears begin to fall down her cheek. "I would never steal money. I don't know how to break into a bank account. You'd have to be a computer wizard for that."

Like Budge. My stepbrother. If I didn't know he worked every Thursday afternoon at the Wiener Palace, I'd have to wonder about his involvement. The dude is a serious genius. Not that you can tell by his grades.

"Is this your signature?"

Mr. Sutter passes a piece of paper across the desk. With trembling hands, Anna looks at a copy of the check from her account. "I didn't sign that."

"But is it your signature?"

Her bottom lip wobbles. "It looks like it." She drops the paper. "I don't understand. Is this some sort of sick joke? Because I am not laughing."

"And neither are we. You should probably clean out your locker, Anna. You might be staying home for a while. As in the rest of the year."

"But I have a game to cheer tonight!"

"And you probably should get that lawyer." Mr. Sutter's face softens just slightly. "This is a serious crime. I want you to think long and hard about this situation. If you have any information, you need to call me as soon as possible. If you're covering for someone, your consequences could be lessened if you just tell us the truth."

"I don't know anything about your money. All I know is that I'm innocent."

Our principal stands on his loafered feet. "Your parents are on their way. I'll just leave you two girls here until they arrive." He exits into the main office.

Anna melts into her seat and clutches my hand. "I didn't do it. You believe me, don't you?"

"Of course." Though it's all very weird. Too weird.

"I knew you would." She exhales a tired breath.

"You still need to get a really good lawyer."

"Lawyer?"

"Yeah, to prove you're innocent."

"I don't need an attorney." She slaps her other hand over mine. "*You're* gonna prove I'm innocent."

chapter six

At LaGuardia airport, I walk into my dad's waiting arms. I inhale his familiar scent and feel that old pang for how things used to be. Before Dad decided to give up family life for a dating marathon. Before Mom turned to the Internet to find her new husband—in Oklahoma. Before I found out my stepdad likes to body-slam people.

"So . . . money troubles?" I broach the topic in the cab, hoping Dad will laugh and tell me it's all a funny joke.

"Things are tight right now, but we'll find my accountant *and* my money. I will make a comeback."

My dad is *the* plastic surgeon in Manhattan. Through hard work, long hours, and the occasional butt implant, he has made quite a name for himself. But the fact that we're riding in a yellow cab instead of being chauffeured by his usual driver makes me wonder if Dad's financial forecast is gloomier than he'd like me to believe.

"Bella, your grandparents are in this weekend for a little visit." Dad doesn't even look at me. He *knows* how I feel about his parents. It's like God went out of his way to *not* give me any semblance of a normal family. My mom's parents died before I was born, but I hear they were amazing people. My dad's parents on the other hand . . .

um, amazingly obnoxious. Actually just Grandmother Kirkwood. My grandpa is okay. He can't help his weirdness—he has dementia. This means he's cuckoo in the cranium a majority of the time.

"Oh, well. How nice." This is all I can come up with. Last time I saw Grandmother Kirkwood, she eyed my chest and told me if I was lucky, I might get a boob job for next year's graduation. I wanted to tell her it was too bad Dad didn't have a machine that would suck out her horrible personality.

"We're having dinner at the house tonight. Christina is cooking."

I blink in the dark taxi. "Who's Christina? You didn't replace Luisa, did you?" Luisa was my nanny my entire life and pretty much raised me. Now she raises my dad.

He sighs. "I told you about Christina."

"No. You didn't." But Dad forgets a lot of things. Like calling on a regular basis.

"She's a friend—you'll like her. You'll meet her tonight. I think she's cooking some Brazilian food. Your grandmother will hate it." He laughs.

This would be girlfriend number 1,235,984,103 since my parents split. The ladies usually look like they're fresh off the stage of Miss USA and have an IQ slightly higher than a schnauzer.

Inside my room at the brownstone, Luisa waits for me. She hugs me in her ample arms and talks *muy rapido* in Spanglish. "Your father is very taken with this Christina de Luna." Luisa's brown face is impassive, but her voice carries an edge. "She could be the one."

I flop onto my bed and stare straight up at the angry cherubs painted overhead. One of my dad's old girlfriends called herself a decorator and redid his house with every room having a theme. Nothing matches or makes sense. Dad says it's symbolic. I say she must've hated him.

"You must change for dinner. Your grandmother will be rising from her evening nap any moment looking for you." Luisa clucks her tongue and mutters something about an old dragon.

I stay out of the kitchen and avoid meeting my dad's new girl until I go downstairs for dinner. I beg Luisa to join us, but this is bingo night at the Catholic church, and nothing comes between Luisa and her daubers.

"There's my girl." Dad beams at the head of the table. A tall, dark-complected woman stands at his side. Her black hair cascades down her back and stops at her small waist. Her sleeveless shift dress shows off her toned arms. Not only is she beautiful, but she works out. Ick. The worst kind.

"Bella, I feel like I know you already!" The woman comes to my side of the table and intercepts me, kissing the air beside each cheek. I resist the urge to wipe her fake kisses away. "Your father talks of you often," she says with a light accent.

"That's funny." I smile. "He hasn't mentioned you."

Dad pulls her back to his side. "I'm sure you're wrong, Bella. I've mentioned Christina many times." He smiles big, revealing his perfectly white teeth. "And this is Christina's sister, Marisol." Dad gestures to a girl who appears to be close to Robbie's age. "Christina and Marisol's parents died when Marisol was just an infant. Christina raised her all by herself."

Christina's manicured hand lands on my dad's chest. "That is what you do, no? You take care of your family."

He squeezes her tight. "Isn't she amazing?"

"She's something." I greet my grandparents, then pull out a chair and sit down. I don't get too wrapped up in my dad's girl-friends' lives. These ladies are just passing through. Next week he won't even remember Christina's name.

She claps her hands. "Sit, sit, everyone! Marisol and I will bring in the food."

Marisol bounds up with a cheerful grin.

"Such a delicate, graceful girl, that Marisol." Grandmother cuts her eyes at me.

"Like a fawn." I reach for my water glass and take a long drink.

"I used to have an old girlfriend named Fawn," Grandpa says to no one in particular. "She could dance the jitterbug like nobody's business."

Grandmother taps my elbow. "I see farm life has already influenced you."

I remove my arms from the table. "I hang out with cows a lot."

My dad clears his throat, a silent warning.

I try niceness again. "So, Grandmother, how was your flight from Connecticut?"

"It was bumpy, it ran ten minutes behind schedule, and the flight attendant did not have the brand of tomato juice I prefer."

"I hate it when that happens."

Grandmother purses her lips. Well, as much as one can purse with a face that has been nipped and tucked until it's stretched to the point of snapping.

"I used to be a pilot." Grandpa laughs. "Flew right over the president's house one day. Landed in his yard, and he said I had arrived just in time for his daily yoga session." He winks at me and pats my hand. "I can still do a mean downward dog, though your grandmother doesn't like me sticking my butt up in the air, as I'm a bit gassy."

"Here we are!" Christina enters the dining room carrying a big tray of meat. Her sister follows behind and sits right next to Dad. He squeezes her hand, and she beams. I get an icky feeling—like eating too many gummy worms and hanging upside down.

"That looks like roast," Dad says. "I thought you were fixing a Brazilian dish." He addresses the table. "Christina and her sister are from Brazil. As orphans, they were so poor, Christina hitched a ride on a pig truck, then stowed away on a boat to reach America for a better life for her infant sister. That was seven years ago, and now Christina is a talent agent with a prestigious firm."

Oh, boy. Angelina Jolie has *nothing* on this woman's international heroics.

My grandmother daubs at her eyes. My grandfather just stares at the roast.

Christina lays her hand on the back of Dad's chair. "Tonight we are having a traditional English dinner. I wanted to honor your parents' heritage."

My grandmother holds her hands to her heart. "My heritage. Isn't that wonderful?" I think her *father's* father might've been British. So it's not like Grandmother was Queen Elizabeth's best friend or anything. "Are those turnips I see?"

Ew. Seriously? Not touching those. Give me some fries.

"And we have a good horseradish sauce, of course." Christina takes her seat across from Dad.

Marisol grins at my dad. "Uncle Kevin and I made brownies yesterday."

Uncle?

"We sure did, sunshine." He kisses her cheek.

What? That was his pet name for me when I was little. I'm his sunshine!

"Marisol, why don't you and Bella get the other entrees?"

"Of course!" Perky Marisol all but skips back toward the kitchen. After an eyebrow quirk from Dad, I head that way.

"Here are the mashed potatoes. Not everyone can make them as good as I do." Marisol hands them to me. "For dessert we're having custard. I helped make that, too, and it's pretty much perfect."

Whoa. Girl's got an attitude. "The potatoes look great. I may have to pass on the custard." *Custard? A dessert where eggs are the main ingredient?*

Marisol's schoolgirl face slips. "My sister said you lived like a barbarian. Clearly they don't emphasize manners in your new home."

My mouth flies open. "You little—"

"We're going to be a family—the three of us. My sister's going to marry your dad."

I can't help but laugh. "No, she's not, Marisol. You should probably get that idea out of your head right now. I know *Uncle* Kevin is nice, but I wouldn't get too attached."

"They are too getting married! And I'm going to live here and probably take over your bedroom."

"You'll want to redecorate it then." I pat her on her delusional head. "I'm afraid my dad isn't the marrying kind right now, okay? Women like your sister just—"

The little brat swings her arm and knocks the potatoes right out of my hands. With a *splat* they land on the floor. "Don't you dare say anything bad about Christina!"

"I wasn't!" But since she's a lady, that's all the qualifications Christina needs for my dad to not commit to her. "Look, Marisol, I—"

She leaves me in the kitchen. Frozen to the spot. Potatoes on my shoes.

When I get the floor and myself potato-free, I return to the dining room. Marisol sits on my father's lap, bawling on his Armani jacket. He holds her and whispers low. Christina sits on his other side, patting her sister's back. *Oh, puh-lease.*

My dad's angry eyes meet mine. "Marisol didn't want to tell us, but we finally dragged it out of her. Do you want to tell us why she's crying?"

"Because she's a brat?" The words fly out of my mouth like my tongue is a catapult. "I mean *she* threw the potatoes on the floor!"

Grandmother rests her napkin in her lap. "She made them. I highly doubt she would then purposely ruin them."

I glare at a sniffling Marisol. She ought to be on Broadway with that act.

Christina holds up her hands. "Let's just enjoy a pleasant meal, eh? This is not a problem." She forces a smile in my direction.

Marisol jabs a finger in my direction. "Bella called Christina bad names."

"No, I didn't!" All eyes turn to me, waiting for an explanation. "I just, um, set her straight on a few things." I glare at my dad. "Things I will tell you about later."

"Kevin," my grandmother says, her eyebrows never moving from their locked position on her forehead. "Clearly your daughter has been under some unruly influences in Oklahoma." She shudders. "A farm. A wrestler. And who knows what kind of riffraff she's hanging out with in that public school."

"Riffraff? There is *nothing* wrong with my riffraff." What *is* that anyway?

"Apologize to Christina and Marisol." My dad pins me with accusing eyes.

Christina lays a hand on his arm. "It is okay, Kevin. I think you were right—Bella hasn't adjusted to all the changes in her life yet. It's normal for a young girl to act out."

I throw my napkin on the table. "If anyone acted out here, it's your psycho sister. I am seventeen years old. I do *not* throw food or insult my father's house *dates*." Even if they do come with obnoxious little sisters.

Christina stands. "We should leave. Marisol, get your coat."

An eruption of chairs scraping the floor, raised voices, and cries of "please don't go" fill the room like a derailed symphony. I bypass it all and head straight for my room, longing for the comfort of my bed and the evil cherubs.

Slamming my door, I grab my phone and with angry fingers begin a text to Lindy. My phone rings just before I hit Send on a message God would *not* be proud of.

"Hello?"

"Hey, Bel. It's Hunter."

I do a backflop on the bed and just breathe.

"I know you're in town this weekend. I was, um . . . wondering if you'd like to go get some coffee."

I've just had a horrible night with the Saint of Brazil and her possessed sister. Not to mention my dad seems to have a new daughter and didn't even take up for me tonight. The last thing I need is to hang out with Hunter, the guy who I caught tongue dancing with my best friend.

I roll over and grab my coat. "Meet me at Starbucks on the corner of Third and Ninety-Second."

chapter seven

The smell of mocha makes any boy more attractive, right?

That's what I tell myself as Hunter opens the door of Starbucks for me. The sharp winter wind ruffles his brown hair, and when he speaks his breath comes out in icy puffs.

"I'm surprised you agreed to meet me." He smiles, the corners of his eyes crinkling, and I feel some of my old resentment melt like whipped cream on a caramel macchiato.

"It's been a night of oddities." I give the barista my order, and before I can reach into my purse, Hunter has paid and tipped the lady.

"How's your dad? I heard about his financial troubles." Something in Hunter's expression stops me from telling him to mind his own business. "My dad had the same accountant. His money situation is pretty questionable right now too."

I take a sip of my mocha. "I had to get a job. On a farm." I think about my grandmother hearing this news and can't suppress a giggle.

Hunter watches me and smiles. "I can't compete with that, but my yearly Christmas trip to Europe got cut down to a mere week."

"Tragic." I wrap both hands around my cup and let the warmth seep through. "How are you feeling?"

Hunter shrugs. "I'm fine. I *will* be fine."

"Can't you tell me about it?"

"I don't want to burden you. I guess you could pray for me or whatever you do."

"Until a few weeks ago, I stuck pins in my Hunter Penbrook voodoo doll." I bite my top lip on a wicked grin. "I guess I could try some prayer instead. You know, I'm not leaving until Sunday afternoon. You could go to church with me." This was always a sore spot between us. I was into God and church. Hunter was into . . . Hunter.

"Okay."

I nearly spew the Starbucks. "Seriously? You know Sunday isn't Easter or Christmas, right?"

He twists a napkin in his hand. "I'm changing, Bella. I don't know how or why . . . but I am. I know I need something more."

I don't know what to do with this, so I leave it alone.

We finish our drinks, and Hunter insists on riding in the cab to see me back to my house. He walks with me up the steps, and we stop under the light.

"I've missed you." He reaches out and gives my scarf a tug.

"Thanks for the coffee." And before my brain can override, my arms are around him, pulling him into a hug.

Disengage! Disengage!

"See you Sunday." I pull away and rush into the house.

"I want to talk to you." My dad's voice stops me on the stairs. I turn around and find him standing below, his arms crossed.

Here we go. "Look, I didn't do that stuff tonight, Dad. Do you seriously not believe me?" Though I don't want to, I walk down and sit beside him on the first step. "I don't know what that little girl is up to, but she's as crazy as Grandpa."

"Bella, Christina is very important to me."

So were my shoes that got mash-potatoed. "You didn't even take up for me. Her little sister is screaming like a banshee, and you guys act like I had put her in a choke hold." Which I seriously considered at one point.

Dad studies his hands, hands that know precision and don't miss a single detail. "I'm sorry if things were blown out of proportion. It all looked bad from our end."

"If you think your end was bad, you should've been in the kitchen with the little freak."

"I'm going to ask Christina and the little freak to move in with me."

"What?" *No!* "But you're *my* dad. Er, I mean . . . that's wrong. You can't live with her. Is money so tight you need a roommate? I can loan you a few bucks." Just please don't move that Brazilian weirdo into this house.

"I really like her, Bella."

"I really like that guy who has the underwear ads on Times Square, but you don't see me asking him to shack up."

"I'm not sure what happened tonight or where the truth is. I don't know that it really matters—"

"It does. I'm your daughter, and you should trust me. No, you should *know* me. I wouldn't antagonize that little girl." Not to mention if my dad really knew me, he'd know I'd come up with something better than Marisol's amateur hour. Throwing potatoes. I'm sure.

"Those two are very important to me," Dad says.

It'll fade. I can speak from experience.

He runs his fingers through his short, spiky hair. "It's been a long night. We'll start again in the morning."

I wait for Dad to tell me he's sorry—that he was wrong.

He walks up the stairs and never looks back.

chapter eight

"unter went to church with you this morning?" My mom wheels into our driveway, ending the hour-long drive from the Tulsa airport.

"Yeah, he's been asking me about God and stuff." I tell her what I know about his illness. "He doesn't really talk about his condition, which makes me think it might be bad."

"Well, I think that's great he's interested. I know you don't really want to be around him after everything that happened, but, Bella, you could lead him to the Lord."

A few months ago I wanted to lead him off the Empire State Building. Now, I'm not sure about anything. The Hunter I was with this weekend . . . I liked him.

"Did you see anything fabulous while you were shopping?" Mom asks, that old gleam in her eye. The one that says, *I can spot Chanel couture from twenty paces.*

"Hermès had some of their new spring bags out already."

Her gaze turns dreamy. "I can smell the leather from here." She shakes her head as she turns off the Tahoe. "There have been some changes this weekend."

"Oh, more changes! Just what I wanted." Too much?

"The camera techs rigged up the inside of the house, like the producer talked to us about."

We climb out of the SUV, and I follow Mom inside. There are automated cameras set up everywhere. "This . . . is creepy." My skin tingles with goose bumps. People are watching me somewhere in a control room.

"The bedrooms and bathrooms are camera-free, but sometimes we'll have a real camera crew following us around in the house or in town."

"Perfect." The weight of the weekend sets in, and I climb upstairs to unpack.

When I get to my bedroom, I do a sweep of the area, searching every nook, cranny, and panty drawer for anything that looks like a microphone or camera. I come up with nothing. Thank God for small favors. That's all I need—to be changing bras and find I'm on a webcam in front of millions of viewers.

When my alarm sings the next morning, my eyeballs might as well be stuck together with Krazy Glue. I only travel to my dad's once a month, but that next Monday back at school always kicks my tail.

When I walk by Luke in journalism class, I offer one single crisp word, not sure where we stand. "Hey."

He lifts his chin in greeting and goes back to his conference with Steven Ludecky, our sports reporter.

Thirty minutes later when Luke stands behind me, I recognize his scent before he announces his presence. "Captain Iron Jack did a great job Friday night."

I swivel in my rollie chair. "Glad to hear it."

His eyes never leave the copy on my computer screen. "How was New York?"

"Cold."

He leans down until our faces are level. It's a contact lens day for him, and without the glasses his eyes are even more intense. "Is this how it's going to be? We're back to being enemies again?"

I survey the room, but everyone is busy working on their own stories. "I don't know. You're the boss here. I guess you set the tone."

He pulls out another chair and wheels it forward until we're knee to knee. "I'm sorry for the way I reacted. Sometimes . . . sometimes I get very possessive about this paper."

"*Nooo.*" My face is sheer shock. He is not amused.

"I'm trying to apologize here."

"And for your first time, you're not botching it up *too* much."

"Don't you have anything to say to me?"

How about when you sit this close to me, my heart races like I just finished the Boston Marathon? I still think about our one kiss on that crazy night we were running from football players. Sometimes when I close my eyes, I remember that moment in the cabin when we both could have died, and you pretty much saved me.

"Hung out with my ex-boyfriend this weekend." Did *not* mean to say that. *Bella, thy name is maturity.*

Luke's grin is slow. Sly. "This would be the boyfriend who cheated on you?"

Um, yeah. That would be the one. "So I gotta get back to my e-mails. Lots of work-related thoughts to write about. Job ponderings and occupational musings."

Luke stands up, but not before his lips pause near my ear. "I accept your apology too."

During fourth hour, the secretary announces a required junior class meeting at lunch in the library. When the bell rings to release us from calculus, I head down the hall to the meeting, knowing Lindy will be in a state of panic over having to preside.

Ten minutes later only a third of the class has shown up, and Lindy begins. "As you all know, Harry Wu Fong got accepted into some smart-kid program at Princeton University and is bypassing the rest of his high school years, so that leaves me as your president." A group of athletes cheer. "Unfortunately Fong had not done much in terms of prom planning. I guess he was too busy being a genius." She stops and stares toward the door. We all turn around.

Luke Sullivan walks in—holding hands with some girl. *Harvard* girl.

Lindy continues. "So not only do we need to hustle on making some prom decisions, but Friday we learned someone has wiped out our junior class account. So basically we're broke."

I so relate.

"We need a fund-raiser," someone yells.

"Yes, we do." Lindy chews on her bottom lip. "Does anyone have any suggestions?"

Mikey Sprinkle pushes up his bottle-thick glasses, then holds up a hand. "We could have a car wash and the girls could wear bikinis."

In your dreams, dude.

"We could sell pies." This from the guy in the back of the room who's as wide as a Dodge Ram. "I know I'd buy a few."

Luke's girlfriend is cute. And she looks disgustingly smart. That's a bad combination. I mean, I *knew* she'd be intelligent, but I was hoping she'd look like the butt end of a Doberman.

"Okay, so a bake sale." Lindy writes this down. "Who knows how to bake?"

Everyone just stares at each other. We're teenagers. We know how to eat pies—*not* how they're created.

"We have an idea over here."

I bristle at Luke's voice behind me.

He smiles at his girlfriend and she laughs. "Go ahead, Taylor," he says.

"Last year when I was in high school we did this thing for Valentine's Day. It was called Match-and-Catch. You fill out this personal survey, and it pairs you with your ideal match in this school. Everyone fills out the surveys, but you have to pay to get your results."

Four-foot-nine Will Newman pipes up. "Are you saying I could get a girlfriend out of this?"

"Yes."

Whoops go up all around. "Let's do it!" Dorks and athletes alike high-five and chest-bump.

Whoa, she said you'd get a match. She didn't *say you were guaranteed second base.*

Lindy whistles through her teeth and brings the meeting back to order. "Thanks so much, Taylor. That's a great idea."

Big deal. She's from Harvard. She's *supposed* to have great ideas.

"We also need to set up a Web site so people can start nominating seniors for prom king and queen. Who can do that?" Lindy asks.

As if on cue, all heads swivel toward Budge Finley, who does *not* look happy to be giving up his chicken nugget time for prom talk.

"I'm busy. I have a gamer's competition coming up next month." He sees our faces void of any sympathy. "December is a hectic month at the Wiener Palace. Wieners are in high demand right before the holidays." He crosses his arms. "Not gonna do it. Final answer."

Lindy looks like she's about ready to cry. "But you're the only one who can do this. Last time we needed a Web page for our class, Zach Dilbert created it and it somehow got hijacked by senior citizen nudists."

Petey Usher shakes his head. "Dude, I saw my grandma on there."

By this time I've made my way over to where Budge sits at a library table. "If you don't do it, I'm going to tell all these people that you have your own loofah and have taken over my cucumber facial scrub."

He sighs. "I can have it ready by Wednesday."

~~~~~~~~~

After school I drive my Bug ten minutes out of town to Dolly's sprawling property. Her house looks like a *Southern Living* centerfold, and she has it all decked out for Christmas inside and out.

She swings open the front door before I can touch a finger to the bell. "Let's go. Time's a-ticking. I gotta get back to Sugar's for the dinner crowd." She shoves me off the front porch and toward her Jeep. "Hop in."

"Where are we going?" She pulls back onto her dirt road and

into a field. I hold onto the handle above me as we jostle down the well-worn path.

"I have a little barn back here. Need some work done. I'll introduce you to Clyde, and he'll get you started."

"Started with what?"

Dolly only laughs, a throaty sound that probably sends men's hearts racing, but has me wanting to throw open the door and jump out.

A faint snowflake spits every few seconds as Dolly drives up to her so-called "little" barn.

"Do you keep Donald Trump's horses here or what?" I climb out of the Jeep and just stare, my mouth wide open in awe. Before me is a sprawling horse ranch. Five or six people mill around. There's an enormous barn with stalls. To my left is a giant tracklike area where a man is walking with a bucking pony. Horses are everywhere. And so is the Circle D symbol.

I turn in a full circle. "What is this, Dolly?"

She lifts a shoulder. "A little hobby of mine." Dolly gives me a light tap with her gloved hand. "What, you didn't think I built that house on what Sugar's pays me, did you?"

We walk together toward the man with the wild pony.

"After Mickey left me, I needed something. Everything in my life was gone—my girls, my husband. I sold our two-bedroom house, bought three acres out here, and lived in an RV. After three months of not even getting out of bed, I woke up one day and decided I needed something to do besides smoke and watch *One Life to Live*. I remembered when I was a kid I had a horse. So I bought one. Started working with it. Twenty years, two hundred horses, and a few acres later, I'm now a breeder. Waitressing—just a hobby."

"Are you any good?"

We reach the old man with the pony, and he stops. "Is she any good? Ever heard of Holy Smokes?"

It sounds familiar. "The horse that won the Kentucky Derby?"

"That was Dolly's third Derby horse. This lady here has the magic touch."

Dolly laughs and shakes her head. "This is Clyde Mullins. And he's been with me for fifteen years. Knows a horse farm like you know those fancy shoes. He's going to show you some of the most important jobs of running the place. Clyde, you take it easy on my girl here. I'm out." Leaving me with the white-haired man, she takes off in a loud roar.

"This way, girl."

"Am I going to brush some tails?"

"Nope."

"Dress some ponies?"

"Don't think so."

"File some paperwork?"

Clyde stops at the "little" barn and spits. "You ever seen horse poop?"

I swallow. "Never."

He grins. "You're about to make up for lost time."

chapter nine

*G*od must totally be mad at me.

I scoop up my last batch of horse manure and throw it in the wheelbarrow. I've been breathing through my mouth for the last two hours. During the first hour, I OD'd on the smell and had to put my head between my legs.

"Get the wet shavings now," Clyde calls out as he sticks his head in. "It's gotta be real dry."

"Do you have some potpourri or maybe a nice scented candle for the horse too?" Maybe a Jonas Brothers poster?

He laughs and keeps walking.

Ten minutes later I've swept the floor until my arms ache.

"Don't fill that wheelbarrow up with too much manure at once." Clyde walks by and throws out another helpful tip, and I find myself really tired of his Horse Crap Tutorial.

Swishing the broom across the floor one last time, I decide this is pretty stinking good. Seriously, this horse's bedroom has to be cleaner than mine.

Okay, now to wheel this pile-o-poo out to the manure area. Before today I didn't know people collected manure. I collect vintage Chanel bags, so I guess to each her own.

With gloved hands, I grab onto the wooden handles and drag the wheelbarrow around, pointing it toward the open stall door. *Okay, here goes.* Using all my upper body strength, I lift up on the handles and push it outside. And Clyde didn't think I'd be able to handle a full load.

This thing *is* heavy. Wobbly.

I look ahead the fifty feet it takes to get to the manure pile, and it stretches out before me like another continent.

Clyde ambles by again, his eyes on my progress.

"See?" I raise my chin. "This isn't so bad. Easy! A piece of—" The wheelbarrow pitches to the left. I suck air and lean to the right, pulling with everything I've got. Sweat explodes on my forehead, and my arms burn with the effort to right the wheelbarrow.

I run over a rock, and all control is lost.

The wheelbarrow goes left. The manure flies out in great, steaming globs.

And I fall right into it.

Face first.

I come up gagging and coughing. "Ew! Ew! Gonna die! Call 9-1-1! Get the fire department!"

When I finally clear out my eyes, I see two rough brown work boots.

"I wasn't doubting your muscles there, Wonder Woman." Clyde chuckles and flicks a piece of dirt off his pants. "The wheelbarrow gets unsteady if there's too much weight."

I continue heaving and spitting. "I'm gonna need some help here."

"You sure are." He holds out a shovel. "This ought to do the trick."

By eight o'clock it's dark, I reek like a sewer plant, and my left nostril is clogged with gunk from a horse's butt.

I catch a ride with Clyde to Dolly's house to get my car. He makes me sit in the back so as not to offend his delicate sensibilities. I bail out and watch him make a U and head back to the barn.

I open the Bug trunk and find a towel to throw over my seat. Easing into the car, I twist the ignition key. The engine makes a *thunk, thunk.* I drop my head to the steering wheel and bang it a few good times. This does nothing more than dislodge more dried manure. I give it another go, and the car still won't start. Maybe my smell killed it.

I dig for my phone and call Mom. No answer.

I call Dolly. No answer.

I try Jake, Budge, Lindy, Matt, and a few other friends—even the geek from American History who sends me messages on Facebook that border on sexual harassment.

Nobody is home! Is the whole world gone tonight? Did the rapture come, and I missed it? God thought I stunk too much to let me in?

I close my eyes and let out a whimpery mewl. I have one other person left to call. The last human being on the face of the earth I want to see me like this.

Fifteen minutes later I stare at the opened door of the green 4Runner and think walking back to town doesn't sound so bad. I probably need to burn off a few more calories anyway.

"Get in. I've got the seat lined with trash bags."

I bite back a curse as Luke Sullivan holds the passenger door open. "Thanks for coming. I know you were probably busy." *Talking to your Harvard girlfriend who would* never *be coated head-to-toe in horse business.*

"You smell different tonight. New perfume?" Luke coughs into his hand and turns his head away from me. I don't know if it's to hide his laughter or because he's about to gag.

"Funny. You're hilarious. You should have your own show on Comedy Central."

He shuts me in the SUV, and I hear him laugh it up as he walks around to his side.

I just want to die. To vaporize and disappear.

Even though it's cold enough to ice a pond, we drive with the windows down. I'm too tired and humiliated to even care that I'm freezing. There could be snot dripping out of my working right nostril, and I wouldn't even mind.

Luke stops grinning long enough to break the silence. "Can I ask what you were doing tonight?"

"Working. What does it look like I've been doing?"

"You really don't want me to answer that, little buckaroo." He flips on the heat, careful not to touch me. "You couldn't sling fries like the rest of our classmates?"

"Can you just drive please?" I hear him chuckle again, and it only fans the flames on my temper. "If you tell *anyone* about this, I will . . ." I can't think of a single, legal thing.

"Yes?"

"Tell the world what a horrible kisser you are."

Luke brakes right in the middle of the dirt road and throws it into park. In the dark I see his eyes trained on me. "Bella"—his voice is a gravelly whisper—"right now you are the most disgusting thing I have ever seen. You smell, you look like you got caught in a cattle stampede, and my vehicle will never be the same." He leans over the gearshift. "And if I wasn't so afraid of whatever's coating your lips, I would prove to you what a liar you are."

I stare at his mouth. "Liar?" My word comes out more like a breathy wheeze.

Luke eases forward an inch. "Don't tempt me."

I can hear my own heart beating.

Then he slings it into drive and tears down the road, a slight smile on his arrogant face.

We spend the rest of the trip without talking, and when he's almost to a complete stop in my driveway, I jump out like a stunt guy and all but crash through the front door.

"Your stink is overwhelming my superpower."

I glare at my little stepbrother and slam the door behind me.

Jake looks up from his newspaper in the living room. "Good day at Dolly's?"

"I see that smirk. I see it!" I point a dirty finger, caked with things I don't even want to think about. "Why didn't anyone *tell* me I'd be scooping poop today?"

Mom bounds down the stairs, a camera in hand. She snaps off a shot and smiles. "For your scrapbook."

"Yeah." I waddle toward the steps, leaving a trail of gunk. "Send it to Grandmother."

chapter ten

On Tuesday I shut my locker and come face-to-face with Anna Deason.

"What are you doing at school?" I cast a worried glance in every direction. "They think you're a criminal. Principal Sutter will have you led out in handcuffs." That would be totally embarrassing. And you *know* one of those yearbook staffers would be right there with a camera.

She shakes her glossy dark head. "Nuh-uh. My daddy's not only on the school board, but he's an attorney. And one mention of the word *lawsuit* got me back in school until I'm proven guilty. And right now the teller from the bank who cashed the check is AWOL."

"The teller is missing?"

"Yeah, gone. Victoria Smith's her name. She'd been at the bank for about six months. She's a senior here, but her locker's all cleaned out. The police said she left her mom's house. That's all I know."

"Are the police looking for her?"

"No. They got all the info they need. They have her sworn statement."

"But her story doesn't add up. Either someone posed as you or she knows the person she cashed the check to wasn't you." And I didn't get a chance to talk to Victoria yet. I have to find her.

"Love how all these people are looking at me like I'm a convict." Anna waves at someone passing by. "Listen, Victoria is not the sharpest eyeliner in the makeup bag, you know what I'm saying? The person who handed over the check might've had a mustache and she would've cashed it."

"Give me her mom's address, and I'll talk to her as soon as I can." Which will be hard to do since I now possess the world's worst job.

"My dad already tried talking to Victoria's mother. She wouldn't tell him anything. She said Victoria's leaving was a family affair and to butt out of it."

Then I guess I'll just have to get the information another way.

After school I call Dolly and tell her that I'll be a little late to the farm. Then with my newly recharged Bug, I drive to the industrial area of town and park in front of Mickey Patrick's gym, where Jake trains every day. That is, when he's not supervising the maxi-pad machine at Summer Fresh.

"Hey, Mickey." I nod to Jake's manager and trainer as I enter the gym.

He looks up from a stack of jump ropes he's untangling. "Jake said your evening at Dolly's kind of stunk." He winks like I don't get his pun.

"Couldn't someone have mentioned that Dolly has a multimillion-dollar horse farm behind her house?"

He lifts a bulky shoulder. "Thought everyone knew." Mickey looks uninterested, but I know it has to be a sore spot—that Dolly totally reinvented her life after he left.

"Hey, when's her baby due? She didn't really have time for details the other day."

"Whose baby?"

"Dolly's."

"What?" Mickey drops a rope. "She's—"

"Adopting, yeah." I watch Mickey's eyes round. "Oops. I assumed I was the last to know."

He runs a hand over his bald head. Mickey looks like a buff, middle-aged version of Mr. Clean. He's built, he's quiet, and he can intimidate the heck out of someone. Like now.

"I'm sorry, Mickey. I didn't know it was a secret or anything."

He looks through me. "I'm sure it isn't a secret. Just shows how out of touch I am." He throws the last jump rope into a pile and walks off, shutting himself in his office.

Jake flings himself from the ropes and smacks into his opponent, Mark Rogers. A two-man camera crew has lights set up and cameras rolling.

I tell myself to ignore the cameras and act natural as I walk toward the ring.

But it doesn't hurt to reapply my lip gloss.

"Dude, you're giving me razor burn. Isn't that a wrestling foul?" Mark rubs his arm.

The two guys laugh and Jake takes to the ropes again. I think wrestling is for boys who never grew up.

I clear my throat and Mark turns, moving out of the way just as Jake flies through the air. He lands a hard belly flop on the mat. "*Oomph!*"

Mark leans over the ring. "S'up, Bella?"

Mark is also a wrestler wannabe. He's pretty new at it, just like he's new at his job on the police force. He's probably been out of the academy a year or so, but ever since I did my own pile driver on some crime, he's been überhelpful.

"Gotta get some Gatorade." Jake climbs out and limps down the hall. The two camera guys follow.

"Whatcha got cooking?" Mark cuts right to it.

"I need an address. Victoria Smith. Where is she?"

"The bank teller in the missing school money case?"

I smile. "That's the one."

"I can't give you that."

"I have some homework to give her." Like twenty questions from me.

Mark zips his lip. "I cannot divulge that information." He wipes some sweat and coughs into his hand. "*Dad's house!*" He coughs again. "Sorry, sinuses."

"That's all you have for me?"

"Sure wish I could give you that address *in Tulsa*, but I can't. I'm a locked box. A sealed envelope. A safe with no key."

"Got it." I smile and hand him his towel. "If you think of anything else you can't tell me, let me know."

I pivot on my heel and run smack into Luke Sullivan.

His arms snake around and hold me steady. "Bella Kirkwood, you're up to something."

I wrench out of his grip. "I am offended. I was just here visiting my stepfather."

Luke crosses his arms and slowly shakes his head.

"Fine." I roll my eyes. "How long have you been standing there?"

"Long enough. I have dibs on a story for the missing junior class funds, so I hope you're not poaching on my territory."

"This isn't about the paper." But if I did solve the money mystery, it wouldn't hurt to write it up in a sweet little article with my name right under the title.

"Are you going to talk to Victoria?" he asks.

"She moved out of her mom's house."

"Answer the question, Bella."

"I've got to get to work."

Luke laughs, the sound rumbling low in his chest. "Call me if you need a ride—to find Victoria, that is."

~~~~~~~~~~

When I drive my Bug out to Dolly's horse barn, there's a man with a camera waiting. I ignore him and go find Clyde.

"You ready to muck out some more stalls?" He pats down an auburn-colored horse.

I'd rather eat my own socks. "Um . . ."

His laugh rumbles. "Relax, kid. Today I'm going to show you how to groom a horse."

"Like do hair?"

He doesn't smile. "Follow me."

Fifteen minutes later I'm standing next to Sundance Kid and combing her coat. Clyde assured me she was the gentlest of horses, but how do I know what's lurking behind this animal's large, black eyes? Could be an intense desire to karate chop me with a hoof.

I go through the whole grooming routine like Clyde showed me and then pick up a brush to tackle Sundance's tail. I stay to the side of the horse like Clyde demonstrated, working in small sections to ease out any tangles in the hair.

"Sundance, the bad news is you have some serious dead ends. The good news is you've got some great highlights."

Can't seem to get all the tangles. This one piece just will not come out of its knot. "Hang on, girl. I'll get it for you. I'm really good with hair." Need some detangler. I lean down a little closer. "Almost got it. Just a little bit more and—"

The tail lifts and a yellow stream shoots out like a Super Soaker.

I jump back. But not before I'm drenched in horse pee. At the sound of laughter, I look over and see Clyde and the camera guy watching me like it's a spectator sport.

"Hope you enjoyed that." I wring out my hair and wipe my hands on my jeans. "I think I'm going to cut out of here early, if that's okay."

On my way home, I call Dolly and tell her I've got all the info I need on farm life.

"That's okay, sweetie," she says. "It's not for everybody."

chapter eleven

$\mathcal{B}$udge, your Thursday night gamer meeting is going to have to wait. Jake said the *entire* family has to be home so we can watch the premiere of *Pile Driver of Dreams*." I'm just now getting to the point where I don't roll my eyes every time I say the show's title. It's a huge step in my path to maturity.

Budge readjusts his backpack over his shoulder and bumps knuckles with a passing friend. "So far this reality show crap is lame, man."

"Um, did they get footage of you getting bathed in horse tinkle? I don't think so." Who knows what else they have.

I stop in my tracks at the tap on my shoulder.

"Are you Bella Kirkwood?"

This question always fills me with dread. Especially when asked by a girl in a dog collar who clearly just escaped from a punk rock video. Or prison.

I turn around and hope my eyes are not bugging. "Yes, I guess I am."

"I'm Ruthie McGee. You might have heard of me."

I'm not sure what the right answer is here. "Uh ... no." The girl in front of me has the most remarkable hair of black and white, like an irate skunk roosted on top of her head. It stands in spikes that defy the laws of gravity.

I look back, thinking Budge took the opportunity to escape, but he stands behind me, frozen. Unable to move, suspended in a trance of hair and black leather.

"I need your help."

My next words take all the courage I've got. "I don't work for free." *Please don't kill me.*

Ruthie chews on a wad of gum, her black-lined eyes narrowed into slits. I take a step backward.

"Fine." She pops a bubble. "I'm willing to pay, but I don't want you to take on any other cases—just mine. And I'll make it worth your while, but only half now. The rest when the mission is accomplished. Here's my problem." She jerks her head toward Budge. "Is he just gonna stand there and eavesdrop?"

My stepbrother's mouth is open so wide, drool is bound to start pooling any second. I nudge him with my elbow.

"Ignore him. He won't repeat anything you say." Plus, I think he's too scared to move.

"I'm running for prom queen."

I process this. "Do you need assistance with your updo?"

She laughs, great rolling barks that come from deep within her throat. Then she sobers. "I need help clearing my good name." She shoves a piece of paper in my face. "This was on my bike when I got out of school yesterday."

"You don't really strike me as the ten-speed type of girl."

"My motorcycle."

"Right." I look the paper over. It has a color picture of Ruthie making out with a guy. I lift a brow in question.

"It's not me."

I check the paper again. "The face is kinda blurry . . . but that is definitely your hair."

"I'm telling you, that isn't me!" Ruthie reaches for her shirt-sleeve, where she's got a small box rolled up. She shakes her head and drops her hand. "No, I'm trying to cut back."

"Marlboros?"

"No." Her face scrunches. "That stuff will kill you. Breath mints. I eat 'em when I'm stressed. I went through twelve boxes just last night."

"There is a pleasant aroma of spearmint about you."

"The picture, Kirkwood. Focus on the picture. That is *not* me. Someone is trying to destroy my good name."

"Why would they do that?"

Her look says *are you stupid?* "Because they're jealous, that's what. I got the bod, the skills, the looks."

And a few tattoos.

"This note was with the picture."

Drop out of the prom queen race or prepare for the consequences.

I study the writing, but can't determine if it's from a male or female hand.

"Ruthie, it's not that bad. I mean, so you're kissing a guy here. Big deal."

"Big deal? This wacko is going to send this to everyone I know. The photo's been doctored, but no one will believe it."

"Who's the guy?"

"My best friend's boyfriend."

"Oh." Not good.

"My daddy's gonna freak."

"I'm sure he'll understand." *With a kid like you, he can't be expecting an angel.*

"Just tell me you'll investigate and find out who's doing this." She stuffs the papers in my purse. "You don't know my dad." And she stomps off in her black spike-heeled boots.

I laugh and look at Budge, who has at least managed to close his mouth. "Daddy must be rougher than she is, if she's scared. Do you know her?"

Budge swallows and nods. "That's the Baptist preacher's daughter."

"She's a nut job."

He dabs at some sweat on his forehead. "I think I love her."

~~~~~~~

After filling out a dozen job applications in town and dropping them off, I return home to the smell of steak.

I say hi to Mickey Patrick, who's perched on a chair in front of the TV. I know he's anxious to see how his star Jake is going to be portrayed tonight.

"Just in time to grab a plate," Mom says as I shuffle into the kitchen. Our kitchen suffered a fire a few months back and got a makeover, and it's the only room that doesn't look like 1975. Mom says we're going to slowly redo the other parts of the house, but so far we haven't even progressed to 1980.

"There's steak on the stove and salad on the table." Jake plops a baked potato on my plate. "Grab something to drink and let's settle in the living room."

We never know when the camera guys are going to be present,

so I'm thankful to see the house is free of them tonight. I count heads and find Budge in the living room already. Mom and Robbie in the kitchen. "Who are the extra plates for?"

"I invited Dolly. She's running late." Her gaze doesn't quite meet mine.

"Who else?"

"Luke Sullivan." Mom smiles and hands me silverware. "He said the paper wanted him to have as much access to us as possible, so I called him."

"Great. Perfect." Maybe he'll bring Miss Harvard. They can talk about super-smart things while we watch footage of Jake in spandex tighties. And if I'm really lucky there'll be footage of me with my head stuck up Sundance's butt while she's soaking me in urinary Mountain Dew.

"Excuse me." Robbie, dressed in his usual garb of a superhero t-shirt and red cape, moves in front of me to grab a baked potato.

"Hey, buddy, you've already got one on your plate."

Nervous green eyes look back at me. "I need to eat to build my strength. These are trying times for a superhero." And he zooms to the living room.

That was strange. The kid usually eats like a bird. But strange is the order of the day with him. It's like he has two personalities—one who believes he can fly. And the other part of him that is brilliant to the point of scary. I mean, when he's not watching Superman cartoons, he's watching the financial network on cable and taking notes.

The doorbell rings as I set my plate on the scarred coffee table.

Mom helps Robbie cut his meat. "Get that please, Bella."

With one dramatic sigh, I fling open the door with a look that's less than hospitable.

Luke smiles. He knows I don't want him here.

"Where's the girlfriend?"

"I'm working, so Taylor wasn't invited." He steps by me and greets the family.

"Luke, we have dinner for you. Bella will show you into the kitchen and get your plate."

Ugh. Seriously, Mom? I know I'm supposed to have a servant's heart, but I think the Bible mentions a few exceptions. Like arrogant, cocky editors. I think it's in Habakkuk. Um, forty-second chapter, two hundredth verse. Might not be in all translations.

Luke follows me into the kitchen. I plop a steak on a plate and let him do the rest.

He stares at the food. "You didn't spit in this, did you? Poison it?"

Hadn't thought of that.

"Any updates on the stolen class funds?"

I yank open the fridge. "What do you want to drink?" Maybe some Ex-Lax?

He moves in and reaches for a water. "You're dodging my question."

"I dunno. No new developments at this point." Unless you count the address for Victoria I got this afternoon from one of her friends.

He gets that look again. The one that makes me think he can see inside my head—and the contents amuse him. "Right." And he walks into the living room, settling in like he's part of our crew.

The only seat left is the space next to Luke on the couch. I consider standing, but I'm working on my maturity. I sit down and scoot so far to the edge away from him, the majority of my butt hangs off.

Dolly pops her head in the front door. "Hey, y'all." She enters the living room, dressed in sweats, Nike running shoes, and her ever-present big hair. She blanches when she sees her ex-husband. "What's he doing here?"

"What do you mean, what am I doing here? What are *you* doing here?" Mickey's cheeks turn pink.

Dolly stomps into the kitchen and returns with food. Jake brings in another chair from the dining room and places it in the space beside Mickey. Dolly stares at all of us, waiting for us to offer our own seats—away from her ex. No one moves.

"Fine." She sits down, her posture so straight it could snap.

As Mom and Jake talk, I hear Mickey mumble to Dolly. "You look nice tonight, by the way."

"I came here straight from the gym thinking it was just going to be a night with the Finleys. My Maybelline's all gone, I smell like sweat, and I just spent an hour in an aerobics class with twenty-year-olds."

His face falls. "I still think you look beautiful."

Oblivious to the Mickey and Dolly soap opera, Jake says a quick blessing and turns on the TV.

A familiar-looking man appears on the screen. He stands in the middle of a wrestling ring.

"*Tonight on* Pile Driver of Dreams, *ten people . . . only one will walk away with the chance to go pro and be a regular on World Wrestling Television's Friday Night Throw-Down. America, you will determine their destinies. Every week you get the chance to vote a wrestler off. We bring you live interviews and footage from their homes, getting up close and personal with their families. And we bring you the wrestling matches so you can decide if they've got what it takes to go pro. Ten people dreaming big . . . but is it big enough?"*

Mom's propped on the arm of Jake's recliner. She leans into him and squeezes his muscular arm.

"Careful . . ." Luke whispers. "You're smiling."

I guess I am. "This is a big deal for them." And it hasn't been this big life intrusion I thought it would be. I think the show is so focused on Jake, they pretty much leave the rest of us alone. I hardly ever see the camera crew. I think I expected my life to turn into *The Real World,* but it totally hasn't.

We watch as they do a brief bio on each contestant, showing video of wrestling matches, images of the family and the town each person is from.

The show begins with a guy named William Pearson, aka The Mutilator. In a brief interview, his son talks about what a great dad he is. His boss at Topeka First Federal tears up when he describes William saving the day when an armed robber held up the bank.

Another guy by the name of Sanchez the Snake discusses his mother while doing bicep curls. In the background his ex-wife quietly cries as he talks.

"Yeah, I want to be a wrestler . . . but mostly I want to save my mom. She's in Mexico waiting on a liver transplant. The only thing keeping her alive right now is the hope she has in me."

Oh, boy.

After three more men and two women contestants, Jake's face lights up the TV.

Next, Harvey Runnels, president of Summer Fresh, beams with pride. "In twenty years, this maxi-pad assembly line has never run smoother. Nobody knows feminine protection better than Jake Finley."

"It's true," Budge says from across the room. "Women owe a lot to this man right here." He and Jake do an air high five.

Luke's shoulders give a small jerk, and I know he's laughing inside.

Why can't Jake be a used car salesman like other stepdads I know?

The announcer's voice continues to narrate. *"A big man, big dreams, and a small town. But is there more to Jake Finley? Recently married to his online sweetheart, he added a stepdaughter to his family. While Jillian Finley appears to have adapted to Truman life, her daughter seems to cling to the drama of Manhattan."*

The steak becomes a tasteless wad in my mouth. I spit it out into my napkin and zone in to the nightmare unfolding on the television. I scoot closer to Luke to get a better look.

"Suffering a bad breakup when her boyfriend hooked up with her best friend, Bella found solace in the simple life of Truman, Oklahoma. Or did she?"

Video footage rolls of me at Dolly's farm. Me with my head under Sundance's tail, getting sprayed down in horse pee. Me dumping over the wheelbarrow of poop. Me screaming at dumping over the wheelbarrow of poop.

Budge and Robbie laugh until I can hardly hear the TV.

"I had no idea anyone saw that," I mumble. "Especially cameras." And my mom hasn't totally adapted to Oklahoma life either. Yesterday she sat at her computer and stared at a Valentino dress for forty-five minutes.

"Recently Bella Kirkwood's ex-boyfriend has returned to her life. Sources say he could be seriously ill and is searching for forgiveness . . ."

There I am, head-to-head with Hunter at Starbucks in Manhattan.

"... *or is the young couple searching for something more?*"

My dad's front steps. Me wrapped in Hunter's arms. It was such a simple hug, but the photo makes it look like ... so much more.

Beside me I feel Luke stiffen. I steal a glance at his face, but it reveals nothing.

I grab Luke's plate and stand. "This is ridiculous. Those cameras—they're everywhere. I had no idea!" I feel so violated. So exposed. So Lindsay Lohan'd. "This isn't fair. Can't we do something about this?"

Mom slowly shakes her blonde head. "We knew this would be intrusive, Bella. We talked about this. We agreed as a family."

"I thought they'd intrude on *him*." I point to Jake. "My life is one big tabloid now. This is crazy. Everyone knows my business. I feel like an Olsen twin!" I step over Robbie and his cape on the floor and take the plates to the sink.

I have to get out of here. I need some air. Some space.

Some Ben & Jerry's.

chapter twelve

After pulling Mom aside and assuring her I will be home by ten-thirtyish, I sneak out the back door and hop into the Bug.

I turn the key. And nothing.

"Come on. I don't have time to charge the battery. You can do it." I pat the car's dash in case she needs a boost of encouragement. I know sometimes I do.

I try a few more times, but the car is deader than my career as a horse groomer.

I jump at the knock on my window. Luke stands there with his arms crossed and that infuriating smile.

"Going somewhere?"

"Nowhere important. Just have to run an errand."

"Would this errand be in Tulsa?"

"Sorry!" I tap on the glass. "Can't hear you! You should probably go back in and take some more notes."

"Car won't start again?"

I roll down the window and feel the frigid December wind whoosh in. "No offense, but you're starting to annoy me."

He casually reclines against the car. "Face it. You need a ride."

"I don't need *anything* from you, Sullivan." I twist the key in vain. "How did you know I was going to Tulsa?"

"I have my ways." He dangles his keys from one finger. "We can stop at the Truman Dairy Barn on our way out of town."

"Like I'd be that weak." I'm sure.

"Double scoops?"

"Let's go."

~~~~~~~~~~

Luke knocks on the door of apartment 15B. A middle-aged man with three days' worth of stubble answers.

"For the last time, I don't want any Avon."

I turn my head and laugh into my coat. Luke selling Skin-So-Soft. That's a good one.

I nudge Luke out of the way and step into the light. "Mr. Smith?"

"Yeah?"

"We go to Truman High School. We were in the neighborhood and wanted to see Victoria."

"Make it snappy. *CSI* is coming on." He holds the door open. "Victoria! You got company!" He stomps down a small hall and shuts himself in another room.

When Victoria joins us in the living room, she wears a confused face. "Do I know you?"

"Hey, Victoria." I'm not really sure how to begin. "Um . . ."

"We're from Truman High. We work for the paper and wanted to ask you a few questions." Luke takes her elbow and the two settle onto a worn couch. "There's been a lot of rumors about the junior class funds being stolen, and we want to make sure you are accurately portrayed in this story and your side is heard."

I was going to go with "We work with the FBI, and we need information. Don't make us haul you downtown." Whatever.

Luke opens his mouth to fire off the first question, but I jump in ahead of him. Dude is *not* going to steal my case here. "Victoria, we'd like you to go back to that day you cashed the check and tell us about that moment from the time the car pulled up until the time it drove away."

She twists a piece of brown hair around her finger. "I've already told the police all this."

I paste on my kindest smile. "Can you tell us what Anna Deason looked like that day? Can you describe the person who presented the check? The driver?"

Her twirling finger stops. "It's all pretty foggy in my head now. Thanks for stopping by, but—"

Luke rests his hand briefly on Victoria's. "I know you've fielded a lot of questions. I can't imagine how stressful that's been for you."

Victoria's bottom lip puckers as she nods. "I ate a whole jar of peanut butter yesterday."

Hey, nothing wrong with that.

"Did you get a good look at Anna that afternoon?" Luke drapes an arm over the back of the couch.

"I—I thought I did."

"Was it an African-American girl? Can you say that for sure?"

I sit with my mute button on while Luke works his magic.

"Yes, I'm pretty sure. But it's hard to tell with our cameras. We see the driver's side clearly, but the passenger side can be kinda dark."

A small white dog lumbers into the room and rubs against Luke's leg.

"Oh, what a great dog. It's beautiful." Luke pets the wheezing mongrel, who sports random bald spots and looks like it's three barks away from keeling over. "What's your name?"

Victoria giggles and picks up her dog. "This is Maggie."

"Maggie, you're pretty cute. How long have you had the dog?"

I watch Luke turn on the charm and Victoria light up like the Las Vegas strip. I search the floor for a newspaper or magazine. Maybe there's a crossword or something I could do while these two totally ignore me.

"I've had Maggie since I was in first grade. She doesn't have a yard here, so she's mad at me." More giggling. More petting of the geriatric dog.

"Had you been planning on moving in with your dad?" Luke asks.

Victoria's hand stills on the dog. "Um . . . n-no. I guess not. I mean yeah, sorta." She sniffs and blinks out a tear. "It just kind of happened. My boyfriend broke up with me, and the bank fired me. I needed to leave town."

I try to move in with a question, but Luke holds up his hand. His voice is smooth as jazz. "You wanted to leave town or you *had* to leave town? Was anyone pressuring you?"

Victoria stares into Luke's blue sky eyes. The moment hangs there.

"I want my TV back! I'm missing *CSI*!"

She jerks her head as if waking from a trance. "It's my dad's TV night. Thanks for stopping by."

Luke stands and puts his hand on Victoria's back. "If you can think of anything else, please contact me." He gives her a card. "Sometimes stress does funny things. It's not uncommon to take a step back from the event and get a clearer picture. If that happens, if there's something you want to tell us—anything—I'd love to talk to you."

In the parking lot, Luke opens my door for me, and I flop my body into the seat and fume.

"I heard that sigh," he says, as he buckles.

"I'd *love* to talk to you." I clutch his arm. "Oh, Victoria, I *can't imagine* how stressful this has been for you!"

Luke starts the 4Runner. "Well, your interrogation tactics obviously weren't working."

"Her dad watches *CSI.* I thought she'd be used to it!" I roll my eyes until I fear they'll pop out the back side. "And it's a good thing her dad came out because you were seconds away from laying a big, wet sloppy kiss on that mutt."

He turns on a John Mayer CD. "Admit it, you needed my help tonight."

"I need your help like I need mono. Like I need zits on picture day."

A slow piano melody melts from the speakers, and John Mayer sings a husky song about love.

The entire tune finishes before Luke speaks again. "What do you think of Victoria?"

I exhale loudly and watch the barren trees lining the road. "I think she's hiding something."

"Me too." He taps his fingers on the steering wheel in time to the music. "I can ask around and find out who the boyfriend is. Might be useful information."

"Don't bother. I'll find out myself." But I know he's already got a plan brewing in that overly smart brain of his. "Hey, do you know you've made two wrong turns?"

Luke glances in the rearview. "Don't panic, but I think we're being followed." He hangs a stiff right. "Yep, we've definitely got company."

"Is it a cop?" I try to make out the vehicle behind us but can't see anything but headlights. "Maybe we should pull over."

He snorts. "Don't you watch horror movies? That's the *last* thing we want to do."

I say a quick, silent prayer and curl my fingers into the seat. *Lord, it would be supercool if I didn't die tonight.*

"Here it comes." Luke speeds up.

The headlights grow more intense as the car moves closer until it's beside us on the two-lane road.

I turn to get a good look at the vehicle. Four-door sedan. Heavily tinted. Can't see inside.

The car's engine roars, drowning out the sound of my heart pounding.

Time moves in slow motion. One second I'm checking out the car. The next I hear metal on metal, and I'm thrown into the door. The side of my head hits the window.

The sedan pounds into us again. Tires screech. The 4Runner swerves. Luke fights for control of the vehicle as it weaves left and right. A scream works its way up my throat. *Help us, God.*

Luke jerks the steering wheel to the right, and we sail into a ditch. Grass hits the underside of the SUV, and finally we stop—an inch away from a fence post.

The sedan races out of sight.

"Are you okay?" Luke throws off his seat belt. He flips the interior light, and his eyes and hands are all over me. "Bella?"

My body shakes like I'm chilled. My heart is lodged in my throat.

Luke's hands frame my face. "Bella, talk to me. Where are you hurt?" His fingers move across my cheek, my neck, my arms, my—

"Hey!" I slap him away. "Save it for Taylor!"

He leans back some and breathes a sigh full of relief. "So no injuries?"

"There's a distinct possibility I wet my pants."

His lips curl into a small smile. "You're gonna have a bruise here." He touches my forehead with feather-light fingertips.

"What about you?" I ask. "Are you all right?" He had to have felt the brunt of the impact.

Luke nods. "I had the steering wheel to hang on to." His eyes assess me again before he starts up the SUV and slowly backs up and steers us out of the ditch. "Did you see the driver?"

"No. Too dark. Did you ID the car?"

He shakes his head. "I couldn't even tell what color it was. Not a light-colored vehicle. That's all I know. I was just focused on keeping us on the road."

"You did a great job." I slouch deeper into my seat, letting some of the tension go.

His hand reaches out and rubs my arm. "Are you sure you're all right?"

My hand rests over his, and I nod my head. Our eyes meet and hold. I feel my pulse accelerating for reasons having nothing to do with the wreck.

Luke's phone rings, and I'm snapped back to reality. Hero's syndrome. That's all it is. The guy saved us tonight, and I'm just feeling gooshy inside because of it.

Luke checks the display, silences the phone, then rests it on the console. I glance down at the name. *Taylor.*

I look up and find Luke watching me out of the corner of his eye. "I'll call her later."

"She's a cute girl," I say, for lack of anything significant to add. "Hope there's not trouble in nerd paradise."

His laugh is brief. "Not at all. Speaking of paradise, how's your ex? Hunter, is it?"

I chew on my lip and scan my brain for a snappy comeback. A poison dart of a barb. "He's fine." Seeing my life flash before my eyes has somehow robbed me of anything remotely smart. "We've had some great discussions about God lately." Why am I telling him this?

"Do you think God would want you to be romantically involved with someone who cheated on you?"

I eye my purse and envision myself whacking Luke in the head with it. But it would knock him out, and I'm too wired to drive. "I think I read somewhere we were supposed to forgive." My voice is ice. "I could be wrong. Sometimes I get my Bible mixed up with my *Seventeen.*"

"Yeah, there's forgiveness and friendship, then there's stupidity in hooking up with the guy who didn't even respect you enough to be faithful the first time. And with your best friend, right?"

I rub the tender spot on my head. "Thanks for the morality lesson, Mr. Judgmental." Like I'm even considering getting back together with Hunter. At least, I'm mostly not. Pretty much not. More than likely *not* considering it. "Hunter needs a friend right now. And I'm going to be that friend no matter what happened a few months ago."

"I guess it makes for good TV."

"What does *that* mean?"

Luke frowns behind his glasses. "I don't know."

The next ten minutes pass in silence. When I can't take it anymore, I voice the thought that's been running laps in my head. "Are we agreed this wasn't a coincidence?"

I hear Luke's deep exhale. "We'll see what the police have to say."

"But what do you think?"

His gaze is wary. "I think someone wants us to mind our own business."

chapter thirteen

Though my mom wanted to keep me on lockdown this morning, I convinced her I was okay enough to go to school. And with finals next week, I really can't afford to miss a single class.

During lunch I search the parking lot for cars that have some dents and extra paint, but only find one possibility. Call it a gut feeling, but I don't really think Mrs. Brunstickle, the eighty-one-year-old janitor, is our prime suspect.

Grateful my Bug starts, I follow Luke to the police department after school, where we give our statements and file a report.

"Where are you off to?" Luke opens the door to his 4Runner, and it creaks in protest.

"Pancho's Mexican Villa."

He lifts a brow. "Do you have a lead you're not telling me about?"

"No." I feel my cheeks flame. "A job interview." I shut myself in the car before he has a chance to retort.

The owner called and left a message a few hours ago, saying he'd reviewed my application and liked what he saw. I guess listing "I Heart Salsa" as a qualification was a good move.

I park the Bug and take in Pancho's in all of its glory. Thumbing its nose at the principles of architecture and curb appeal, the restaurant is shaped in the form of a sombrero. It sits directly across the street from the Wiener Palace, and word is the competition between the two eateries is fierce.

The door jangles as I enter the building. "Welcome to Pancho's Mexican Villa," three workers call out. They don't look up from whatever it is they're doing, and if they got any less excited, I'd think they were unconscious.

"Um . . . thanks." I approach the one most likely to have a pulse. "I'm here to speak to the owner. Is he here?"

The girl rolls her eyes. "Manny's always here." From beneath her red poncho, she lifts her hand and points to the office. "In there."

"*Qué pasa?*" a deep voice bellows when I knock on the door.

I ease into the room and blink. "Manny?" I had expected a man of Latin descent. We have a decent-sized Hispanic population in Truman, so surely the owner of the sole Mexican joint in town would *not* look like a lower-class Jersey boy with a beer gut and gold chains.

"Wassup?" He holds out a fist, and I hesitantly bump mine to it. "You must be Bella Kirkwood, right?"

I think I might want to be somebody else. "Er, yes."

"I'm Manny Labowskie. Come on. Let me show you around." He stands up, and I get the full view of the ensemble. Shiny navy running suit, jacket zipped a quarter of the way down. Hairy chest in lieu of a shirt. A thick rope chain hangs around his neck like a memento from a rap star's garage sale. His high-tops squeak as we tour the restaurant.

"Now when people come in the door, you gotta say, 'Welcome to

Pancho's Mexican Villa!'" He scratches his extended belly and grins. Capped teeth smile back at me. "Go ahead, give it a try."

"Now?"

"Sure!" He lowers his voice to a whisper. "I can tell a lot about a person by the way they call out the Pancho greeting. Let's hear it."

I nervously scan the room. Besides the workers, there're only two customers, and luckily I don't know either of them. So far, my reputation is safe. But as soon as I get my own sombrero and poncho, I can kiss it good-bye.

I cup my hand around my mouth. "Welcome to Pancho's Mexican Villa." I sound like a ticked-off cheerleader.

Manny slaps me on the back, nearly sending me to the other side of the room. "Good stuff, Kirkwood. That was sheer poetry. Now let's visit the kitchen."

I follow him behind the counter. "Shouldn't those guys have gloves on?" I point to two high schoolers who are elbow deep in refried beans.

Manny's eyes go all shifty. "Um, right. Definitely. Junior! Chris! If I see you without gloves again, you're, like, fired. What do I tell you about the gloves?"

The two guys exchange confused looks. "That we only had to use them if we saw someone with a health department badge?"

Manny erupts in laughter. "Oh, those kidders. Those nuts." He smacks one on the back of the head, sending a sombrero into a vat of salsa.

"Now, Kirkwood, my life's work is to make the best taco in the whole town of Truman."

Shouldn't be too hard since this is the only place that even offers tacos.

"We make them good, and we make them fast. You have about ten seconds for each taco."

Yikes. "That's pretty fast."

Manny covers his heart with a big, hairy hand. "Do you believe in the Lord, Kirkwood?"

I nod.

"The town of Truman is my mission field. And I'm reaching the people . . . one taco at a time."

"Touching." I think somebody's eaten too many pinto beans. "You do understand this is temporary and for the Truman High *Tribune?*"

Manny's gold-ringed hand waves away this idea. "People don't stay here long anyway. I'll take what I can get."

Thirty minutes later, I've been shown how to operate the two main assembly lines—the burrito and the taco. I've learned the order of operation and exactly how much of each ingredient should go into the food. I think I've got it.

"Well, what do you think? Are you ready to join the Pancho's Mexican Villa team? We only pay minimum wage, but unlike the Wiener Palace, I can offer you all the chips you can eat."

"I was hoping for a little more."

"Fine. Half off *queso.*"

"I'll take it."

"*Muy bien!*" Manny spits on a finger and rubs a spot of dirt off his Nikes. "That means very good. You should probably write that down. You don't know when I'll just bust out the Spanish on you. Now, come with me."

He leads me back to his office and squishes a giant sombrero on my head and drapes me in a poncho marked XL. "Can you start immediately?"

"I guess. I'll need to call my mom." I try to adjust the shapeless poncho, but it's no use. I'm tall, but it still hangs long and offends every fashionable bone in my body.

"I can tell you are just what I need for a very special job. Not anyone can do it, but I trust you with it." He pats his heart again. "I feel like I know you already, and the Lord has spoken to me and said, 'Manno'—that's what he calls me—'Manno, this is just the right person for the job.' Are you ready for that special assignment, Kirkwood?"

I bob my head weakly, knowing doom is about to rear its ugly head.

Manny slides a giant sandwich board over my coat. I readjust my hat and look down. *Pancho's for Your Luncho. Wieners Give You Gas.*

"Clever."

Manny winks. "I know, right?"

Three minutes and seven seconds later, I'm planted by the side of the road, waving a giant taco and wondering what my chances are for an apocalypse.

"Hey!" Budge yells from across the street. "What are you doing?"

"Ruining my odds for ever getting a date!"

He storms over to where I stand guard, his giant Aladdin pants swishing in the brisk wind. "My boss sent me out here. She's warned Manny about that stupid sign."

"I don't think his sign is illegal." Stupid. Humiliating. Possibly a big joke from the dark side, but not illegal.

Budge opens his mouth, then stops. He digs into his silky back pocket and pulls out a phone. "Smile! This baby's totally going on Facebook."

I make a grab for the phone, but the sandwich board slows me down. "You jerk! When I get home, I'm going to—"

I'm interrupted by the rumbling sound of a motorcycle. Budge looks beyond my shoulder, his mouth gaping. "It's—it's her."

I swing around as Ruthie McGee pulls her bike next to us. She kills the engine and whips off her helmet, her spiky hair miraculously bouncing right back into its place.

She reads my sign. "Nice motto. Catchy."

"Is that tobacco in your mouth?" I stare at the wad she's got between her cheek and gum.

"Beef jerky."

"Classy."

"Someone's hacked my MySpace page and sent out all these bad notes about me—complete with pictures. Are you on the job or aren't you?"

It's really hard to have an intelligent conversation with someone when you're wearing a sign about the farting dangers of wieners.

"Look, I've had some developments with another situation. I haven't forgotten about you, Ruthie."

"Someone's out to destroy my reputation. Someone with killer computer skills."

My eyes shift to Budge. "I know someone like that."

"I'm not an evil mastermind. I use my skills for the good." Budge's face softens as he gazes at Ruthie. "I can't imagine anyone hurting you."

She switches her jerky wad to the other cheek. "Really?"

Budge nods. Then nods some more. "T-t-totally. Maybe I could help you?"

"What'd you have in mind?"

"I'd have to take a look at your computer, but we might be able to trace the hacker back to his or her own computer. I get off work at seven."

She turns the key on her bike and revs the engine. "Be at my house at eight." She jabs her gloved finger in his vest. "And don't be late. This is the night I reserve for my flute practice and poetry reading."

Ruthie zooms away, and I don't have to look at Budge to know he's slack-jawed and moon-eyed.

I sigh and straighten my hat. "She could've at least bought a taco."

chapter fourteen

Good morning, Tigers! This is Megan for Tiger TV with your Monday announcements."

I read over some vocab words in English class, wishing I had studied more over the weekend. Between church, calculus homework, and a call from Hunter, I just ran out of time.

Hunter is being so incredibly nice. He always was a good boyfriend—well, minus the cheating part. But now he's practically dream boyfriend material. Like he's a little less self-absorbed, a little more humble, and . . . I have to admit I like the new Hunter. When I told him what I had going on at work and school, he actually listened.

". . . And don't forget to pick up your Match-and-Catch forms. Junior class officers will be passing them out in the caf during lunch. To get the results of your perfect Truman High mate, just pay ten dollars . . ."

I lean across the row and poke Budge in the shoulder. "Are you going to do that?"

He huffs, sending his red 'fro bouncing. "Dude, do I have *loser* written across my forehead?"

"So that's a yes?"

"The day I fill one of those out is the day I wear girl's underwear."

At lunch I go find the Match-and-Catch table, knowing Lindy will be there.

"How's it going?" I ask.

"We're being stampeded. Pass these out." She shoves a stack of forms in my arms. "Don't forget tonight's the FCA ice skating party downtown."

"Yeah, I have to work, so I'll be there pretty late." Tomorrow is dead day—a day to review in every class before finals start Wednesday. So to let off some steam before all the cramming begins, we're having a Christmas party.

"Hey!" Ruthie McGee shoves her way to the front. "Have you seen Budge?"

"No, I—"

Ruthie spots him walking by, grabs him by the collar, and yanks him into the crowd. "Did you find anything out yet?"

Budge blinks a few times. "Um . . . I . . . haven't really found much information for you. I'm still working on it."

She tweaks a form out of my hand. "My boyfriend broke up with me when he saw the incriminating photo. I need a new man." She stares down Budge. "Are you going to fill one out?"

His mouth opens like a fish. "I . . . was just coming here to get one. Bella, give me a Match-and-Catch form."

I pass it to him. "Victoria's Secret makes a nice panty, by the way."

I return from my second night on the job smelling like one big taco. It's saturated my hair, my pores, and permanently stuck up my nose. My fingers hurt from rolling burritos, and my poncho looks like I bathed in salsa. The working world is vicious.

I walk into our living room and find Moxie staring at a wall. She attacks an invisible prey, then walks away purring, her job done. Moxie doesn't do higher-level thinking. We're not real sure that my cat thinks at all.

After I shower off all the greasy gunk, I kiss Mom good-bye and drive downtown to where the ice rink is set up. Though it's nearly nine, the party should still be in full swing.

I hear the Christmas music before I even shut off the car. Carrie Underwood sings about a winter wonderland. I shiver into my coat and find my friends.

"Bella!" Anna intercepts me as I pay for my skates. "Big news."

"You were on *America's Most Wanted* last night?"

Her scowl is filled with attitude. "Real cute. The charges were dropped."

"Are you serious? That's awesome."

"They finally confirmed my alibi."

"How?"

"Your brother took my laptop into the police station and was able to show them I was using the Wi-Fi at the Java Joint."

"You mean Budge?"

"Yeah, I owe that boy. I mean, I knew we could prove I was there, but finding witnesses was going to take a while."

"Who asked him to look at your laptop?"

"It was Luke Sullivan's idea."

"Really?" Why didn't he mention it? "Um, I'm happy for you. I'm glad I didn't go ahead and get you that nail file for Christmas."

"You're really cracking me up tonight, Kirkwood."

I laugh at her sour tone and leave her to join Lindy and Matt.

"Hey, guys." I sit down at a bistro table as Lindy and Matt sip hot chocolate. "How's the rink?"

I peer over the edge to take it all in. Christmas trees stand all over the grounds. Chairs and tables sit under a row of canopies, with tiny white lights twinkling overhead. The oval rink glistens in front of us, and everyone from grandmothers to toddlers spin across the ice.

"Oh. I see Luke and his girlfriend are here." My editor-in-chief skates next to his college girl. A silly stocking cap sits on her head, and her hair sprouts out in two juvenile pigtails.

She looks totally cool. And I want to thoroughly dislike her for it.

"Something wrong?" Lindy follows the trail of my stare.

I force my attention back to the table. "No." I hope this smile is believable. "I'm just impressed with the rink. It's cool the town creates this every winter. I mean, it's no Rockefeller Center, but it's pretty close."

The up-tempo song ends, and a slow one takes its place. Couples filter onto the rink. I see Taylor rise up and kiss Luke on the cheek. They laugh, and he escorts her off the ice.

"You guys should go skate." I nudge Lindy with my knee.

"I don't know." She braves a look at Matt. "Um . . . do you want to?"

He shrugs. "I guess."

"Well, you don't have to sound so excited." She huffs and walks away.

Matt stands up, ready to follow. "What was that about?"

"I don't know," I say innocently. "Maybe you shouldn't sound like you'd rather eat live worms than skate with her."

"We skate together every year. What's the big deal?"

Boys. So dumb, yet so necessary in our world.

Matt joins Lindy on the ice, and after lacing up my skates, I make my way there as well. Sure it's mostly couples, but who cares?

My blades wobble as I step down, but soon I'm steady and gaining speed. I weave through the crowd, the wind catching my hair. Tilting my head back, I fill my lungs with the crisp winter wind. A snowflake falls, then two. I stick out my tongue to catch the next one. After a few minutes, I hold out my arms and skate backwards, and when the speed feels right, I twist my body and pop into a jump.

I turn at the sound of clapping behind me.

"Is this a one-girl show, or can anyone join?"

"Hello, Luke." I face forward again, skating on as if he's not there.

I hear his blades slice to catch up. "You're pretty good."

I wave at some friends we pass.

"I said—"

"I heard you."

His brow furrows. "Are you mad at me?"

"Why would I be mad at you?"

"Because you're a girl, and that's what you do."

I know he's just baiting me for a response, so I smile and hum along to the music.

"Do you know there's a guy with a video camera over there?" He points across the rink where a man stands with a lens trained on me.

"Just ignore him. That's what I do."

"Like you're ignoring me?"

I slow my skates. "Look, I've had a hard day of slinging tacos. Why don't you go find your girlfriend and talk to her?"

That annoying smile returns to his face. The one he always gets when I mention Taylor the Genius Girlfriend. "She just left to meet some friends."

I return to ignoring him. Doesn't the Bible say if you don't have anything nice to say, don't say anything at all? No, wait. Not the Bible. My mom? The fortune cookie I ate last week?

"Bella." Luke's hand on my arm stops us both.

Couples swish around us as I study Luke's face. There's something there I can't define.

"I'm not mad at you, Luke. I just wanted some time to skate." I stare up at the sky and let the flakes collect on my lashes. "This makes me miss Manhattan, and I want to soak it all up."

"I saw you talking to Anna."

"You could've told me you were working with Budge and the police."

He runs a hand through his black hair. "This isn't your mystery to solve."

"She asked me to clear her name."

"I should think that car running us off the road would be enough motivation for you to stay out of it."

"What, so you can be in danger, but I can't?"

"You almost got killed the last time you stuck your nose in something here at Truman High."

"Luke Sullivan . . . I think you're worried about me." Now it's my turn for the sly grin.

His face is impassive. "You have a new assignment for the paper. I want you to interview sophomore Tracey Snively. She was student of the month."

"No! You're just trying to weasel me out of the missing funds story. Besides, Tracey Snively is that girl who has like thirty cats. And she smells like yams."

"I'm the editor, and right now we have no missing funds story. And last time I checked, we still had a paper to publish."

"Don't shut me out of this. Anna came to *me* to clear her name. Ruthie came to *me* to get to the bottom of this. Not you."

He pulls us to the side of the rink. "Ruthie McGee? What does she have to do with this?"

"Oh, gee. I'm sorry. But that's something I'm working on all by myself." I bat my lashes. "Can't tell you."

I skate away and rejoin Lindy and Matt. Since they aren't in the throes of one big make-out session, I assume that Lindy didn't declare her true feelings to her BFF, and Matt didn't tell Lindy she's the milk in his Cheerios.

An hour later, much of the crowd has gone home. I say good-bye to my friends, grab my purse, and walk to my car.

The Bug glistens with a diamond frost, and as I stick my key in the door, I notice it's unlocked.

That's funny. I always lock it. No, this isn't the backstreets of New York where they'll strip your car down to the caps, but still, a girl has to be careful.

Suddenly I'm very aware of how alone I am out in the gravel parking lot. Just me and a few cars.

I quickly open the door, and there on the seat is a piece of pink paper. The type is in a jagged font.

Bella,

>*I'm warning you to mind your own business. I'd hate to see*

you get caught in the path of what I want. Nothing will stop me—not even you.

A chill snakes down my spine.

And a hand settles on my shoulder.

I scream into the night air and jump straight up, my hands slapping out. "Back off! I know Pilates!"

"Bella." Luke grabs my hands and pins them to his chest. "Bella!"

I melt into him and sigh in relief. "I totally knew it was you. I did." Raising my head, I step back and put some distance between us. "What are you doing out here? I thought you'd left."

His forehead wrinkles. "I was talking to some friends when I saw you walk off by yourself. Thought I'd make sure you got to your car okay." His blue eyes zone in on the note. He takes it from me, and I notice my hands are shaking. So much for acting unaffected.

"How many of these have you received?" His gruff voice is like sandpaper to my nerves.

I snatch the note back. "I'm not feeding you any more information just so you can cut me out and get the story for yourself."

"An answer, Bella."

"Fine." *Why are boys so annoying?* "This is the first. But it's none of your concern."

Luke's fingers latch onto my shoulder again. "*You're* my concern."

I'm pulled in by the intensity of his eyes. He draws me closer to him, and my hands rest on his jacket.

His eyes drop to my lips.

I hold my breath, afraid to move.

Afraid he's going to kiss me.

Terrified he's not.

Beside us a car alarm wails, and we jolt apart.

I pan over Luke's shoulder to see a black-haired man backing away from a Honda, his video camera drooping. "Shoot. I really needed that footage. I don't suppose I can get you two to move in close again?"

We both stare.

"I didn't think so."

chapter fifteen

*M*rs. Palmer hasn't even started reviewing for our lit final, and I'm already counting the minutes. Why is it they have to ruin the few days leading up to break with finals? Forcing me to study until my brain oozes out does *not* make me want to break out in some "Deck the Halls." But come Friday, I'll be Manhattan bound and far away from tests and report cards, spending an early Christmas with my dad.

Budge lumbers into English class, his red curly hair shielding half his face. He glances around for a seat, and knowing the only one open is behind me, I wave my hand and pat his desk. With our work schedules, I haven't gotten to talk to him at all. And stepbrother has some explaining to do.

I pounce as soon as he sits down. "Why didn't you tell me you were working with Luke Sullivan?"

Budge picks a piece of lint off his "Frodo for President" t-shirt. "I didn't know I had to report to you."

"I was taking care of clearing Anna's name. And Ruthie's. I don't need Luke's help."

He pulls a pencil from his fro. "I don't do turf wars, but Luke has my loyalty."

I gasp. "He paid you!"

Budge's stubbly jaw drops. "That offends me, Bella. I am wounded to the core. My mind is just reeling. In fact, I might have to look over your shoulder and copy off your final tomorrow just to ease my pain."

I do a partial eye roll.

"*Good morning, Truman High! This is Tiger TV with our last announcements for the semester.*"

"I was in the process of getting witnesses to confirm that Anna was at the coffee shop at the time the check was cashed."

"I'm sorry, Velma. I didn't mean to get in the way of you and the Mystery Machine."

I narrow my eyes. "If you don't help *me* out and keep me in the loop on Ruthie McGee, I'll . . ." Thinking, thinking. "Tell her something that would destroy your reputation forever." I lift my chin. "I know things." Other than the fact that he has one Justin Timberlake CD hidden in his room, I've got nothing.

"Oh, I'm so scared."

Maybe it's the lighting, but I think I see a flicker of doubt.

". . . *The finalists for your senior prom queen are Anna Deason, Felicity Weeks, Ruthie McGee, and Callie Drake. Your prom king candidates are . . .*"

I tune in to the announcements long enough to make a list on my notebook and reread the names.

"*Get online and exercise your American right to vote. Results will be announced at prom in March.*"

"Your girlfriend made the cut."

Budge flushes red. "She's not my girlfriend. And she scares me." His mouth lifts. "I kinda like it."

At lunch I'm supposed to meet cat girl Tracey Sniveley for an interview, but she doesn't show. I fix a salad, buy a water, and walk toward my friends. As soon as I sit, everyone quiets.

I glance at the faces of Anna, Matt, and Lindy. All guilty-looking.

I spy a flash of white. "What's that behind your back there, Anna?"

"This?" It remains out of sight. "Nothing. Just, um, *Sports Illustrated.*"

"Really? Who's on the cover?" Though she's a cheerleader, Anna knows nothing about sports. Even less than I do.

"Uh . . . Tiger Sharapova."

"Hand it over."

With a worried glance at Lindy, Anna puts the magazine in my hand.

"The *Enquirer?*" I read the cover. "The Olsen twins are in secret negotiations with aliens from Mars. Cameron Diaz dates ninety-year-old men. Bella Kirkwood—" *What?* I pull the magazine closer. "Bella Kirkwood: Can This Wrestler's Daughter Juggle Her Two Loves?" And there on the cover is a picture of Hunter with his arms wrapped around me. And another of me standing next to my car, staring into the eyes of Luke Sullivan, his hands on my shoulders.

"It's okay, Bella. It's just a tabloid."

I glare at Matt. "Of *my* life! How can they print this? And why would anybody care?"

"Are you kidding me?" Anna takes back the magazine. "People can't get enough of *Pile Driver of Dreams.* Even my grandma watches it."

"But I'm no celebrity!" What if Luke's seen this? Or his girl-friend? *Okay, calm down.* Nothing's happened between us. No big deal. And do I even care what Hunter thinks? But then again, if he's sick, does he need this kind of stress? I know I don't.

"The pictures . . ." I search for words. "They're not what they look like. I promise. No hanky-panky on my end. I've totally kept my lips to myself." Tragic, but true.

"Heyyyy." I turn at the deep voice. Ruthie McGee sets her tray beside mine. "Nice pics." She elbows me in the ribs. "Juggling two guys. Atta girl!"

"But I'm not!" I take a long drink of Dasani. "Um . . . did you need something? I've got Budge doing his computer magic, so hopefully we'll get to the bottom of who took over your MySpace and sent that picture."

"Well, let me know if you need my help," she says. "I have distant mob connections."

After school I drive to my taco nightmare.

"Um, Manny, my cat kind of chewed a big hole in my sombrero. Do you have another one?" *Please say no. Please say no.*

"You got it, *señorita.*" My boss holds up a meaty finger. "Wait here." He goes back into his office and returns with a hat bigger than the last. "You'll grow into it."

"Only if my head swells," I mumble. I slip on my poncho, flop on the sombrero, and take my place behind the counter.

Two hours later the dinner rush is in full swing.

Two men walk in and I give them the standard greeting. "Welcome to Pancho's Mexican Villa!" We serve tacos and humiliation.

"I'll have a Nifty Nacho and a Mucho Munchie Burrito. Sam,

what do you want?" The taller of the two steps back to let his friend order.

"You," I hiss. The black-haired guy with the camera. "You work for the show. And you sold the pictures to some *trash* magazine!"

His grin stretches wide. "I got a kid to support. Nice shots though, eh?"

My mouth opens and closes. I filter all the words I *want* to say, but know I shouldn't. "This is my life you're distorting. I have friends, a family. People's feelings are getting hurt." Like mine.

He shrugs. "Who cares? That's the biz, baby. If you were smart, you'd work it. You could have all of America involved in your love triangle. That sells."

"I am *not* for sale. And there is no love triangle."

Chris Stilwell hands me the first order.

"Get used to it, babe," the photographer says. "I'm not going anywhere. And it's okay to be a girl who plays the boys. Keep stringing them along, I say."

Oh!

As if my hand disconnects from my brain, I reach for the salsa and throw it on his shirt. "I am not some cheap skank."

The tall one laughs. "You don't have to be. That's what Photoshop is for."

I turn around, grab the refried bean dispenser. I pull the trigger and bean burrito innards squirt all over my target.

"Dude." Chris twirls two cheese shooters like pistols and hoses the photographers down. "Right on!"

A table of teenagers in the back joins in, throwing *queso* and chips clear across the room.

A woman screams and holds up her tray in defense while her husband grabs three tacos and flings them like grenades.

The air is filled with hamburger meat and other lardy delights. I lunge for the floor and crawl military-style toward Manny's office.

I knock on the door, and it opens. Manny looks side to side, then down. "Did you lose something?"

A tortilla smacks him in the face.

"My job?"

~~~~~~~~~~

Why is it lately when I come home at night, I need to be hosed off?

I guess tonight is the last night for smelling like a nacho platter. I think I got all the research I can from Pancho's. And Manny agreed. I try to focus on something more positive, like getting out of school a day early and leaving for my dad's Friday. I can't wait to get out of town.

With the beans out of my hair, I step out of the shower and into some clean clothes. A little quality time with Robbie will cheer me up before I cram for finals.

My towel still on my head, I walk down the hall to Budge and Robbie's room. Hearing the TV blaring and someone singing, I know Robbie's got to be in there. I knock once and then shove open the door.

My brain shudders as I process the sight before me. Budge screams and flies off the bed. With his bulky body, he shields me from the TV.

"It's not what you think!" His face is white as a tortilla.

"Let me see what you're watching there, stepbrother." I smile.

Whatever it is he's hiding, I have a feeling I'm going to be able to use it.

"Just walk away and pretend like none of this ever happened."

"I heard singing."

His Adam's apple bobs. "Radio. It was the radio."

I glance at the stereo sitting quietly in the corner. "Nah. And the tune . . . it kind of sounded familiar."

Budge closes his eyes. "Leave my room!"

I'm in a scrappy mood tonight, so I do what any stepsister would do. I get a running start, leap into the air, and tackle him. He spins around and around, and I hang on for dear life.

"Aughhhh!" With a battle cry, he flings me across the room, and I land on Robbie's bed.

Where I get a perfect view of the TV. "Hannah Montana!" I dissolve into giggles. "Budge watches *Hannah Montana!*"

"No!" he shouts. "I was just flipping channels!"

I roll off the bed. "It's okay, Budge. I've watched a lot of her too."

He stares back toward the screen. "Really?"

"Yeah, when I was like twelve!" I barely dodge a pillow and run out of the room.

I search the rest of the house and finally find the brother I actually wanted to talk to in the living room. He's sprawled on the floor, tongue stuck out and crayon in hand. An empty bag of chips is nearby.

"Hey, Robbie. Nice picture. What is it?"

He doesn't even look up. "It's a pastel representation of my feelings on the corruption of our legal system."

"Oh." Why can't he draw puppies and smiley faces like other

kindergarteners? "Hey"—I crouch down beside him—"are you feeling okay? You seem a little down lately."

Robbie spins on his stomach, drags his art with him, and faces the other direction. "I'm fine."

"Robbie, what is going on with you? Is it school?"

Robbie's sienna-brown crayon pauses. I watch as his eyes lift to mine and his chin quivers. "I can't tell you." He reaches his small hand into the chip bag, pulls back some crumbs, and licks them off his hand.

"But maybe it's something I could help you with."

"Nobody can help me. Superheroes work alone. We're destined to walk this earth in solitude. If anything's wrong, only I can make it right."

Seriously, the boy watches way too much of those TV shows for smart people. His vocabulary is crazy. I should probably let him take my English final for me.

"You know you can tell me anything, right?"

"I don't want to talk about it." He picks up his crayons and paper, and his feet make slip-slap noises up the stairs.

Hearing my mom talking in her bedroom, I follow her voice while I take the towel off my wet head. She sits on the bed with her cell phone to her ear and waves.

"Dolly, that's great news. Keep us updated, no matter the time."

Mom shuts her phone. "Dolly's about to be a mom! The girl's in labor right now."

"That's awesome." Dolly deserves some happiness.

"Hey, aren't you home from work kind of early?" She leans over and stares at my hair. "What is this?" She picks at my scalp.

I study the red thing in her hand. "Could either be a pepper or a tomato. Hard to tell." I fill her in on my evening of projectile food.

"Bella—"

"I know." I slip off the bed. "It was stupid. But I promise not to shoot beans on my next job."

chapter sixteen

~~~~~~

I wake up early the next morning, and before my feet touch the floor, I have a chat with God about parents, boys, and burritos. Seeing I still have plenty of time, I crawl over an unconscious Moxie and go to my desk to catch up on e-mail.

There's one from Dad with a picture of him, Christina, and Marisol at Rockefeller Center. Marisol gazes at my dad like he's king of the world or something. *Delete.*

I click on the next one, which has my own e-mail address as the sender.

> *Dear Bella,*
>
> *You don't know what you're dealing with. Take my advice and mind your own business. Next time I might not be so nice. You're pretty when you sleep, by the way.*
>
> *Your friend.*

Chills flitter across my body as I click to open the picture in the attachment.

I clutch my chest. "Oh my gosh!" It's me. Asleep. Someone was in my room last night!

I force myself to take some deep breaths. Okay, this is not funny. I'm totally creeped out. How did this perv get in? And why? I live with a wrestler, for crying out loud. Who would be stupid enough to break into *our* house?

An hour later, Officer Mark leaves the house after getting all the information he could. The kitchen is almost silent, yet the air is heavy with all the unspoken thoughts.

"You are not to go anywhere alone." My stepdad rubs his face with his giant hand. "If you need to go anywhere, you call one of us. You can reach me anytime."

"I'll be fine. How about if I just let you know where I am at all times? I'm sure it's just someone trying to scare me. He's probably harmless." I hope.

"So it's a he, huh?" Budge asks.

I work up my first smile of the day. "This is the work of an idiot, therefore it has to be a guy." Actually, I don't know. I have no idea who it could be.

My mom stands behind me and wraps me in a hug. "Jake will call the security system company today."

"I won't let anything happen to you." His expression darkens. "But you really do need to back off your investigative pursuits. Let someone else handle it."

"Like the police," Mom says as she walks to the fridge. "Robbie, why are there five Twinkies in your lunch sack?" She holds up his black Batman bag. "That's not what I packed last night." She takes them out one by one.

I watch my little stepbrother slide lower in his seat. "I dunno. Guess I thought I'd get hungry."

Jake reaches out and tussles his son's hair. "If you want to be a big, strong man like me, you can't eat all that junk."

"Yeah, you should drink raw-egg smoothies like your dad." I'll take my Pop-Tarts any day. After a family prayer, we all head our separate directions.

"Budge will be following you to school in his car." Mom hands me my purse as I open the door.

"Well, my cool factor just took a nosedive." I kiss her on the cheek and step outside.

"Bella?"

I glance back.

"I know you're not going to let this go, so just promise me you'll be careful. Trouble seems to have a way of following you."

"Me?" I smile, but Mom doesn't return it. "I'll be fine. Maybe just say a prayer for me."

Mom rolls her eyes heavenward. "If I prayed any more for you, I'd have to quit my job at Sugar's. So stay safe or else you'll be spending some extra time with your grandmother." Mom's face is all innocence. "For safety purposes, of course."

Before first hour at school, I close myself in a bathroom stall and take a moment to clear my head. *God, this is so not cool. I need some heavenly pit bulls of protection to guard me. This is something I need to do, but between you and me, this morning I was so scared I nearly peed my Victoria's Secrets.*

"I'm doomed." I hear a voice from the next stall. "I'll go down as the worst president in history. They'll impeach me!"

I know that voice. I stand up on the toilet lid and peep over. "Lindy?"

Sad eyes look straight up. "Oh, hey. Just, um, studying for a final."

Right. "Everything okay over there?"

"Last night I shot a game-winning three-pointer. Why can't being in charge of prom be that easy? No wonder Harry Wu Fong moved away."

"You're doing a great job. We're making a ton of money on the Match-and-Catch fund-raiser. What's the problem?" I haven't turned in my personal interest survey, but I'm going to. Eventually.

"Somehow the reservations for the caterer got cancelled. Where are we going to get food now? They said someone called yesterday and told them we wouldn't be needing their services. And now they're booked up!"

"It's going to be okay, Lindy." Um, not sure how. But it sounds nice. "Did they say who called? Guy, girl? Did you get a name?"

"Oh, so now I'm not only a horrible president, but I'm not smart enough to ask the obvious questions!"

In journalism class, I pull up the threatening e-mail and read it until I've memorized every scary word.

"What do we have here?"

I startle at Luke's voice. "Nothing. Just working." I minimize the screen. "I'm so diligent like that."

"Wow, kinda jumpy this morning." He props a hip at my work-station. "Anything new you'd like to tell me about?"

I try to pull up another file, but my hands can't seem to steady the mouse. "Nope. Can't think of a thing."

"You know, we are supposed to be working on this missing funds story together."

"We've already gone over this. You expect me to keep you in the loop, but you don't return the favor."

"I'm sorry, Bel." His voice is low and sincere. "I haven't been acting fairly."

I study his face. No sarcasm present. "Are you feeling okay today? Running a temp?"

"I've been praying about our situation."

I swallow. "What situation would that be?" *The one where we're in a race to see who can solve the mystery first* or *the one in which I find myself sniffing your Abercrombie-scented air?*

"Us." Luke takes off his glasses. "Circling each other like alley cats whenever we have to work on a story together. I'm the leader of this paper, but I haven't been acting very . . . um, leadery."

"I don't care what Mr. Holman says about you, Luke. I think you have a great vocabulary."

He laughs and the tension between us dissolves like melting icicles. "Look, I know you've probably got some news. And since you're going to be headed out for Christmas break, you can't follow up on your leads. We can either work together and solve this *or* we continue in our stubborn pride and flush it down the toilet."

Toilet. "Before you break out in an inspirational show tune, let me take a wild guess here. Someone overheard Lindy and me talking this morning in the bathroom and came straight to you?"

His grin is nothing less than Big Bad Wolf. "I meant the other stuff too."

"Sure you did." I roll my eyes and give him my shoulder. He totally had me there. And part of me wants to tell him about the e-mail and get a little sympathy. But he'd just take me off the story. And that is *not* going to happen.

"I'll check with the caterer and find out what I can about the phone call. You know if we let that go too long, our chances of getting the caller's number are slim."

He's right. And with a psycho lurker out there, the sooner we get this wrapped up, the better. "Ughhh," I growl. "Fine. But you better keep me updated. Text me over the break. No, actually I want phone calls." I jab my finger into a chest made solid by years of soccer. "Don't let me down."

"*Me* let you down?" He captures my finger. "I'll leave that to your friend Hunter."

I sputter like there's fuzz in my lip gloss. "What is that supposed to mean?"

He drops my hand. "Nothing." He shrugs big. "I just think you should watch yourself around him. Okay, let's review what we know about the stolen money."

Though I go all blinky-eyed at his topic change, I let his cryptic statement go and show him my notes instead.

<hr />

By the end of the day, my mechanical pencil is out of lead and my brain is devoid of working cells. Finals are straight from the dark side. Not to mention I stared at every single person I came across today, wondering if anyone fit the bill of maniac night stalker.

I blow a kiss to the two camera guys in the car across the street and hop into my Bug. This is Jake's day to train with Mark Rogers, my friend with the Truman PD, and I want to pick his brain.

Swinging open the doors of the gym, I wave at Mickey.

"Hey." He motions me into his office. "I heard what happened last night. I want you to know there are a lot of eyeballs in town watching you." He frowns. "That sounded creepy, didn't it?"

"Little bit."

"You know what I mean. We look out for our own here in Truman." He takes a drink of Gatorade. "Uh . . . so how was school?"

"Fine. My finals are over." I can tell this isn't really what he wants to talk about. "Mom called me at lunch today. She said the baby was born this morning. A healthy boy."

His head lowers in a slow nod. "A boy."

"Dolly's taking him home tomorrow."

Mickey sits up straighter. "Well, I was just asking about school. But I appreciate the update. I . . ." He pauses, and it's like I can feel the words crashing to the surface in his head. "I hope everything goes okay for Dolly. She was meant to be a mom."

And once upon a time, he was a father. "Mickey, I think—"

"I better get back to work." He restacks some papers. "Lots to do before this week's show."

I back out of the office and follow the trail of grunts and yells.

Jake is in full pirate gear today. He has the patch over his eye, tall black boots, and something that's painfully close to a Speedo with a skull and crossbones on the rear.

Mark sees me approach and takes his eyes off his opponent. Jake uses the opportunity to hoist him up and give him a spin.

"Hey, Bella!"

"Hey, Mark," I yell as his feet go swinging by.

My stepdad throws him to the mat and mutters something about making him walk the plank. Stepping back, he breaks character. "How were your last finals?" Jake reaches for a towel from the ropes.

"More fun than a girl has a right to have." And my brain is still mush. "Have you noticed anything off with Robbie lately?"

Jake pats the towel to his face. "Not really. But I've been so busy, I haven't spent as much time with him as I'd like."

"Ah, the price of fame." Mark rolls to a standing position, his hand massaging his back. "I really need to work on my landing."

"I know that look on your face, Bella. I'll take a water break so you can talk to Mark."

I smile at Officer Mark as my stepdad climbs out of the ring. "I think you're making great improvements. You could've totally stopped him from picking you up. I know you like to go easier on Jake because he's older."

Mark crosses his arms. "What do you want to know?"

"Just wanted to check if there'd been any developments on the missing junior class funds."

"No. Your friend Anna was absolved. And Victoria Smith simply made a dumb mistake." Mark sits back into a stretch. "All we know is she saw a guy and girl in the bank drive-thru. We can't even tell what kind of car in the bank's surveillance video. But Bella, until this morning, this case really wasn't on our list of things to be concerned with."

I grab his water bottle from the mat and hand it to him. "What would be a motive for harassing two seniors? And me?"

He shrugs a big shoulder. "Jealousy, a bitter ex-boyfriend, the geek girl who never gets noticed. And no doubt, this person thinks you're getting close to something. I think we can now tie the threats you've received to the night you got run off the road."

"And I just need to find the connection." I pin him with my best serious-girl stare. "What are the chances you'd use me on this case?"

"Less than zero." He takes a drink. "After today's development, you have no business sticking your nose in it."

I smile and dig my car keys out of my purse. "I'm just asking for the sake of the paper. Don't worry about me. I don't have my nose stuck in the case."

Though the rest of my body has plunged right on in.

chapter seventeen

I'm so glad your father suggested I pick you up at the airport," Christina says on Friday as she gives the cabbie directions to the house and settles back into the seat. "He's in a meeting but will be home later."

Her hair is perfectly highlighted, her nails flawlessly manicured, and she has the newest Chloé bag. The one I've been saving for. The one I'm still $1900 away from getting, which is like a million in teen-job dollars.

Christina's hand touches my coat sleeve. "I feel that we got off to a rough start last time you were here."

"Are you living with my dad?" I know the answer. I just want to hear her say it.

She presses her rosy lips together. "Yes. When two adults care about one another—"

"Spare me." *Pull over, driver. I need to puke.* "Will you be celebrating Christmas with us?"

Her smile is as fake as the collagen in her lips. "Yes. Your father thought it would be a nice way for us to spend some more time together." Christina folds her hands in her lap. "Bella, I think you should know that I love your father. So does little Marisol. And we're not going anywhere, so it would be helpful to all of us if you could just accept that."

I stare out the window and watch the snow blanket my city.

The cab lets us out, and I politely refuse Christina's help with my bags. Luisa meets me in the foyer, and I let her smoosh me in a hug. She smells like snickerdoodles and old times.

"How were your finals, *niña*?" Luisa sees my look of stress. "Why don't we get you settled in your room?" She gives me a playful whack on the tush, and we make our way upstairs, leaving Christina alone.

"Tell me she grows on you." I flop on the bed and stare at the psychotic cherubs overhead.

Luisa begins to unpack my suitcase. "Did you bring something nice to wear for Christmas dinner?" She stares at me over the hanger of a dress.

"That bad, huh?" I get up and help her unpack.

"Your grandmother loves her. That is all I say."

That pretty much says it all. Grandmother also likes the idea of boarding school, weak tea, and wearing lots of purple.

"What is this? Bella helping her old Luisa?" My former nanny smiles. "I think Oklahoma has been good for you. I like this new Bella."

We turn at a knock on the door. "Where's my girl?" Dad walks across the pink carpet and pecks me on the cheek. "Good flight?"

Much better than the drive home.

"I guess Christina told you that they're all moved in here. Marisol is visiting friends for the next few days but will be here for Christmas dinner on the twenty-third."

"You know I don't agree with this."

"You always were my little worrier." He tweaks my nose.

Behind him Luisa rolls her dark eyes and files out of the room.

"Tonight I have a dinner meeting with some clients at Tao. It will be outrageously boring, so I invited a friend of yours to keep you company."

They all pretty much stopped talking to me after I found my best friend with my boyfriend. As if I were the guilty party. I don't really have any friends left in Manhattan.

"Who?"

"Well, I ran into Hunter Penbrook at Starbucks the other day. So I invited him."

"Oh." Contemplating this. "Okay." I guess.

A few hours later, Dad, Christina, and I are dropped off in front of Tao. It's a great place to spy some celebs, but as we're led to the table near Buddha, my eyes zoom in on Hunter. He pulls out a chair for me, and I sit.

Dad introduces me to everyone at the table. They nod politely, then jump into business. Hunter and I fade into the background.

"How are you feeling?" I maneuver my chopstick and take a bite of sushi.

"We just ruled out leukemia, so that's a relief," Hunter says.

"That's great."

"Now they're checking on my liver. But enough about that." He smiles. "I have good days and bad."

"And what's today?"

His grin widens, and his eyes sparkle into mine. "Definitely good."

"How is your dad's business?"

Hunter's expression darkens. "He's not faring as well as your dad since the accountant took off with the money. He just can't seem to bounce back."

"I'm sure that doesn't make your health issues any better."

His warm hand covers mine. "I don't want to talk about depressing things tonight. I'm happy to be here—with you."

I'm ten minutes into the main course when I notice the guy in the corner with the small video camera.

"I'm going to slip out," I whisper to Hunter and jerk my chin in the cameraman's direction. "Lately I can't go anywhere without an audience."

"Yeah, I saw the tabloids last week. I hope that didn't bother you."

I try to read Hunter's face. Is he glad the tabloid thought we might be a couple? Or is he smiling because it was kind of funny in a twisted, drama queen sort of way?

Hunter stands up. "Want to grab some coffee?"

I say good-bye to Dad, Christina, and his business associates.

Not wanting to tax Hunter with a walk, I hail a cab to the nearest Starbucks. We walk in and I inhale deeply. I love that smell. If there was a way to safely stick coffee beans up my nose, I would.

Hunter gives our order. "One caramel macchiato and one soy vanilla latte no whip."

"You remembered my favorite drink." There's something nice about a person really knowing the small details that make you who you are. I miss that.

We take our drinks and walk outside into the cool air. It hasn't snowed for hours, yet the sidewalks are still slushy. Times Square looms before us, and I link my arm into Hunter's and lead him that way in a leisurely stroll.

My pocket buzzes. "It's a text from Mom." I pull up the message. "Jake made the cut tonight!" I clap my hands and laugh. "I really hated to miss *Pile Driver of Dreams* tonight, but I recorded it. Have you been watching the show?"

"I'm familiar with some of it." Hunter stops and covers his face with his scarf.

"It's cold, isn't it?" I button up his top coat button. "Are you feeling okay?"

I look over his shoulder and my heart sinks. Mia. She walks toward us, a group of my former friends trailing behind her like faithful troops.

"Hello, Mia." My voice is even. Controlled. Yet I want to scratch her eyes out. "So you've decided to apologize to me?"

"I'm sure." She laughs. "Besides, it looks to me like we're even."

My head bobs with attitude. "I didn't steal *anyone's* boyfriend. Let's get that clear right now."

Mia holds up a hand. "Whatever. When his weird phase wears off, he'll be crawling back to me. And it *will* wear off, Bella." Then she lasers Hunter with her glare. "I don't know what this is all about, but I know you, Hunter. Something's going on. And maybe I won't be there when you snap out of it."

She and her Bratz doll posse saunter down the sidewalk until they're swallowed by the crowds of people on Times Square.

"She is a piece of work." I shake my head and laugh. But Hunter isn't laughing with me. He stands frozen to the spot, staring in the direction of Mia's retreat. "Hey, you okay?"

"Why did you forgive me?"

"Because you asked me to."

"That's all it took? But I don't—didn't deserve it."

A few snowflakes pepper down, and I catch one with my glove. "Nope. You didn't."

"Is this one of those God things again?"

"I guess so."

Hunter wraps an arm around me, and we walk again. "If you weren't a Christian, what would you have done?"

"Kicked you in the giblets."

He rests his head on mine and laughs. "Jesus *does* save."

chapter eighteen

~~~~~~

On December twenty-third I bow my head and give thanks to God. As in, *Thank you, Lord, tomorrow I'm going home.*

I have managed to stay out of Christina's way, minus one shopping trip in which she thought she could buy my affection with a new pair of suede boots. It did not work. But when she added the new Burberry coat, I did almost bust out some love poetry on her behalf. Seriously, I'm pretty weak. And the coat is to die for. And I guess Christina's not *that* bad. She seems to care about my dad.

I slip into my dress for Christmas dinner and take a turn in the mirror.

My phone rings, and I skip across the room to get it. Probably Hunter again. We've talked every day that I've been here.

I read the display. *Luke.*

"Do you have news?"

"Hello to you too." His voice sounds good to my ears. "How is Manhattan?"

"Cold. What did you find out?"

"I couldn't get a phone number from the caterer. But they said it was definitely a female who called them and cancelled."

"I guess that's a start. Is that all you dug up?"

"Bella, you should have more faith in me. I'm pretty good at this." I hear the smile in Luke's voice. "Whoever made the call said she was Lindy Miller."

"Why would someone try and sabotage prom?"

"That's the part we'll have to figure out when you get back."

I sigh and slip my feet into some heels. "I can't get back soon enough."

"Missing me that much?"

This makes me grin. "I'm missing Truman, believe it or not." A few months ago I wouldn't have thought it was possible. "I miss my family, my friends." And Luke?

"I saw your picture in a paper today. Looks like you're keeping busy in New York."

"What do you mean?"

Knock! Knock!

Luisa sticks her head in the door. "Time for dinner. The old bird can't wait much longer."

"You fixed turkey?"

She pulls me to my feet. "I was talking about your grandmother."

I press the phone back to my ear. "I'll talk to you later, Luke."

But he's already gone.

~~~~~~~

I pass the creamed corn and wish for the millionth time that Christina's sister, Marisol, came with a mute button.

"And then I want a new iPod phone. And a MacBook. And this dress I saw at Barney's. And these Prada boots. And tickets to . . ."

Dad catches my eye and winks. He leans down and plants a quick kiss on Marisol's nose.

"Isn't she adorable?" Grandmother beams.

Grandpa's hearing aid whines. "She's giving me gas."

Me too. I mean, first Mom got replaced and now me. *What, am I not cute enough? Not bratty enough?* I think more angry thoughts and chug my water, wishing it was some good Southern iced tea.

When Luisa brings in dessert, a chocolate trifle, it's everything I can do not to jump out of my chair and dive in headfirst.

"Luisa, please stay." My dad stands up. "There's something I'd like to share with the family."

Oh no. No way.

I watch in horror as my dad goes to Christina, bends on one knee, and reaches for her hand.

"Dad, can I talk to you in the kitchen?"

"Not now, Bella." His eyes never leave Christina. "I've made a lot of mistakes in my life. And I've lived a long time as a selfish man. But this lady right"—he holds her hand over his heart—"this special lady here has changed all of that. She's seen me at my lowest, and I hope that she'll join me on my way back to the top."

"Dad, I don't feel so good." A slick sweat explodes on my forehead.

"Later, Bella. Christina, would you do me the honor of becoming my wife?" He slides a ring on her finger.

Little Marisol claps her hands in glee. I want to hurl my fork at her.

Christina lifts her hand up to the light. She laughs and wipes away some tears. "I would be honored to be—"

Blughhhh! I puke in my dessert plate.

"Ew!" Marisol wails and bursts into tears.

"Well, I never!" Grandma holds her napkin over her taut face.

Grandpa pats me on the back. "One time I puked for two days straight. Come to think about it, it was right after I married your grandmother."

My guts feel like they're splitting in two. I'm hot. And cold. And—

"Bella, are you okay?" My dad puts his hand to my head. "Say something."

"Congratulations." And clutching my stomach, I race to the nearest bathroom.

chapter nineteen

Only twice in my life have I wished for death. The first time was in the second grade when Brian Wickham pulled down my skirt in front of the entire Sunday congregation and everyone saw my Care Bear underwear. And the second was last week when somehow I contracted food poisoning and heaved my guts up for a solid day.

Dad repeatedly said he was sorry.

Christina said the salmon dip I'd grazed on before dinner had gone bad.

Grandmother *tsked* and said that would teach me to snack before meals.

And I think I said something like, "*Ack! Gag! Barf!*"

After that everyone pretty much left me alone. How was I supposed to know the dip was out so it could be thrown away?

Because I was hugging a toilet when my flight left on Christmas Eve, I couldn't get back to Truman until days later. I missed Christmas with the family, but Mom made everyone rewrap their gifts and have a do-over for my benefit. Robbie loved it, but Budge practiced his twenty-five-variations-on-eye-rolls the entire time. The camera crew filmed every second.

Between Christmas vacation and missing eight days of school for snow, January evaporated like a snowman in Arizona. *Pile Driver of Dreams* exploded into a reality show hit. Everywhere I went people were talking about it. Jake even started getting fan mail. He had some close calls in the show, but is hanging in there. *US* magazine called him a fan favorite in its review.

The snow days also gave our prom wrecker little time to stir up any more trouble. And lots of time to think of new catastrophes for February.

———————

"Robbie, make sure you take all your stuff with you from the bus. Don't leave anything behind." Mom Velcros Robbie's lunch sack closed. "It's just Tuesdays and Thursdays. You can handle that, right?" She ruffles his hair and puts a kiss on his sad face before he shuffles to the living room.

Mom now has an early morning class at the Tulsa community college. And Tuesdays and Thursdays are the days Budge and I both have to leave early, me for chemistry tutoring, and Budge for a meeting with his dork gamers, otherwise known as future million-aires whose money will one day make them hot.

Mom rests her hand on my shoulder. "Bad news, Bel. Jake got a good look at your car last night. You need a new alternator."

Perfect. "How much is one of those?"

"More than you've got. So until you save up, you can catch a ride with Budge."

I sigh into my bite of oatmeal. "I'm broke. Christmas wiped me out." And this job-a-thon for the school paper isn't helping. I totally need to clear Ruthie's name and get the rest of her payment. "Mom, don't you ever just miss money? You always act like it's so easy."

"Easy?" She snorts. "Do you know how long it's been since I got a new pair of shoes? Me, who used to attend Fashion Week? I have friends in Manhattan eating lunches that would take my whole week's paycheck. So, no, it's not easy. But I told you it would be an adventure." Her face softens. "And can you imagine life without Jake and your stepbrothers?"

"No." Except when Budge hogs the bathroom.

"I know you've been looking for another job, but you know who's got openings, right?"

I blink. "I'm *not* working at the maxi-pad factory." My dad wouldn't stand for that, would he? "Besides, job hunting is just part of teen life—good material for the column. I'll find something soon." I look toward the stairs and yell. "Let's go, Budge!"

Robbie returns and gives Mom's skirt a tug. "I think I have a fever."

Mom touches his head. "Nope. Feel okay to me."

"I think I have food poisoning like Bella."

I turn to my stepbrother. "Does it feel like a hand is reaching into your stomach and trying to French-braid your intestines?"

"No."

"Then it's not food poisoning." I flatten out some wrinkles in his Superman cape. "Are you sure everything's okay at school?"

"It's fine." He shoves away from the table and grabs his backpack. "I'm gonna watch TV until the bus gets here." He slinks out of the kitchen and back into the living room.

I stand outside in the backyard as Budge pulls his car out of the garage. Though the initial shock has worn off of having a stepbrother who drives a hearse, it still appalls me to have to ride in it. I mean, *dead* people were in this thing. Their germs are soaked into the steel gray lining of the car. I don't want gross corpse-y germs up my nose!

I get in the car and immediately turn down his screamo. "I need an update on Ruthie McGee."

Budge jumps, his elbow hitting the horn. A foghorn sound follows. "W–what do you mean? There's nothing to talk about. Nothing."

My eyes narrow. "First of all, I *know* you went over to her house Friday night. But I mean what's going on with tracing the anonymous e-mails she's gotten?"

"Dude, I've tried for over a month. I can't crack it. It's like some wizard sent those e-mails." He turns onto David Street, running over a curb. "I have to pick up my friend Newton."

Budge pulls into the drive of a small white house. An old dead Christmas tree sits with the trash at the curb.

Newton Phillips slams out of the front door, yelling back at his mother. "I'll do the dishes when I get home! When I'm rich, you'll be sorry you bossed me around!"

I watch him stomp to the hearse. "Newt's got attitude."

He hops in the back, greets me, then does some secret handshake thing with Budge that only techie dweebs can follow.

Budge looks in his rearview. "Dude, I totally found out how to create a multileveled vortex in that second dimension."

The rest of the ride consists of me humming along to screamo so I don't have to pay attention to gamer talk. By the time we get to school, I want to cut off my own ears and stuff them down Budge's throat.

Walking into journalism later in the morning, my eyes are automatically drawn to Luke, who has his shirtsleeves rolled up and is already in work mode.

"Your interview with sophomore Tracey Snively was riveting stuff," he says as I sit down at my Mac.

I look up from my screen only long enough to glare. "Yeah, your idea to visit her in her home of thirty cats was sheer brilliance. Really gave the article a special edge. Plus I horked up fur for days."

"Well, something has increased our sales." He throws a paper down on my table. "Maybe it's this."

I ignore his sarcastic tone and pick up *Entertainment Weekly*, and there's another picture of me and Hunter from my Christmas visit in New York. It's a close-up of the two of us in front of the Buddha at Tao. This instant celebrity business is so weird.

"Thanks," I snap. "I'll add it to my growing scrapbook." What's his deal? It's not like Hunter's my boyfriend. He's totally not. Actually, I don't know what he is. We've called each other almost every night since Christmas. He seems so different. Changed. And he says he's gone to church a few times by himself.

"Was there something else?" I ask.

"As a matter of fact there is. Why don't we step into Mr. Holman's office for a moment?"

"Fine." I follow him into the empty room. Luke shuts the door. *Uh-oh. This isn't good.*

He rolls up his sleeves, as if taking the time to sort through his thoughts.

"What did I do this time?" I laugh.

But Luke is not smiling as he lifts his head. "When exactly were you planning on telling me that someone broke into your house before Christmas break and e-mailed you another threat?"

"Oh. That."

He closes the small space between us. "I don't even know what to say to you right now."

"Maybe your feelings could best be expressed in show tunes. I know when I get upset, I like to sing some old Broadway favorites."

Luke's left eye twitches. "Number one, we are friends. And friends share things with one another. You couldn't trust me with that information? I had to hear it from Officer Mark."

"I'm not going to ask what you were talking to him about," I snap. "Probably doing your own investigation into our case, so you could take the lead."

"He approached me." Luke's words are short, crisp. "He wanted to make sure I was keeping an eye on you after everything that had happened."

"So you're mad that I made you look foolish in front of him."

Luke pinches the bridge of his nose. "I'm not mad, Bella. I'm furious." He leans down and puts his face level with mine. "If you don't keep me updated on everything that happens, you will be off this paper. Permanently. I don't work with rogue reporters seeking glory and their face on the front page."

"I'm not—"

"I work with team players. Right now, you are a committee of one. And that arrogance is going to get you hurt."

"Arrogance?" *Why, you little pea-brained, chess-playing—*

"I care about everyone on this staff, and that includes you." Luke's voice is calmer. More controlled. It sets my teeth on edge. "From now on, if *anything* out of the ordinary happens, you are to call me immediately. Consider it another assignment." His eyes connect with mine. "And if you don't follow through, it will be your last."

"I am so tired of my life being everyone else's business. What's wrong with keeping one thing to myself?"

He reaches out like he's going to touch me, then drops his hand. "Because the thought of anything happening to you makes me want to tear someone apart."

I swallow.

"Just tell me your solo days are over. *And* you won't be anywhere by yourself. We're working together. It's you. And me."

I fumble for the doorknob, unable to take my eyes off him. "I . . . I have an article to finish." And I run for the safety of my computer.

When I arrive at lunch ten minutes late, I get a good look at our table and realize we've become quite a motley crew. We have Ruthie, the biker chick. Me, the Manhattan transplant. Anna, the ever-enthusiastic cheerleader. Lindy, the stressed-out class president. And Matt, the jock who just sits there and eats his sub sandwich and chips.

"Lindy, are you okay?" My friend is facedown on the table, her salad shoved to the side.

"I was not meant to be a leader. What's Donald Trump's secret?"

I pluck a tomato off her tray. "Bad hair?"

She sits up. "First the banquet hall at Truman Inn. And now . . ."

"Acid rain?"

"It's not funny, Bella. I just got a call from the Truman Inn. They wanted to let me know that when we cancelled the reservation for prom, we lost the five-hundred-dollar deposit."

I open the wrapping on my sandwich. "When was *this* reservation cancelled?"

"About five minutes ago." Lindy holds up her hand to stop my next question. "It was a female who called them. The person pretended to be me. Again."

Matt bites down on a chip. "Did you tell them you still wanted the banquet hall?"

Lindy stares at Matt with her *you idiot* face. "They had a waiting list. So now the Truman Men's Association is having Pedicures and Polish Sausage Night there."

We all take a moment to think about that one.

Ruthie stretches out her arms and then cracks her knuckles. "Well, that makes me want to hit something. Some idiot is ruining my prom."

"I'll be back." Leaving my lunch, I grab my purse and head through the double doors to the courtyard. I call information. "Truman Inn, please."

"Please tell me you aren't making reservations for a romantic getaway."

I swivel around. "Luke." I smile into the winter sun. "I was just checking on something for a friend."

He crosses his arms. "We said we were going to work together. And you're not to be anywhere alone."

"I don't recall ever agreeing to that." I press my ear to the phone and jot down the number.

Luke's hand wraps around my arm. The other reaches for the phone. "I'd be happy to dial."

I roll my eyes. "Fine." And I fill him in on the latest cancellation.

Luke calls the Truman Inn and works his magic. Charm oozes out of his every word. "Write this down." And he reads off a telephone number to me.

When he calls the new number he smiles. "Voice mail."

"Whose?"

"One of your prom queen candidates—Callie Drake."

"Let's go get her." I step forward, only to be snatched back.

"Not so fast. Doesn't this seem wrong to you?"

I stare at Luke's hand on mine. "Oh, I don't know. Doesn't seem too bad. Kinda nice and tingly actually."

"I'm talking about Callie."

Oh. Me too. "I don't even know who she is."

Luke drops my hand. "Before we run to the principal with this, let's do a little surveillance. Unless you have to work after school, that is?"

"Um . . . work? I guess I could squeeze you in."

―――――――

I meet Luke at his 4Runner after school.

"I don't have a lot of surveillance experience," he says.

"Me neither. Wait here." I run across the street and through some bushes. I find two of the *Pile Driver of Dreams* camera guys. "I need to follow someone. Gimme some tips." For two minutes I take mental notes of everything they say.

"Good luck!" one yells as I walk back to Luke.

"Well?" He starts the SUV.

"Larry said to park a half a block away and get a good pair of binoculars. Doug said to bring lots of snacks."

"Where are we going to get binoculars?"

I fish through my purse and hold up a small pink pair.

Luke shakes his head. "Why am I not surprised?"

"Nosiness." I smile. "It's my spiritual gift."

"I asked around today, and Callie has a boyfriend. There's a good chance she's at his house. She doesn't work." He hangs a right.

"Nothing wrong with that."

With one hand on the wheel, Luke reaches around his seat and picks up a yearbook. He hands it to me. "Page forty-two. You'll see her picture."

I flip to the page. She's cute. In a natural sort of way. Long hair, no makeup. I thumb through the pages as he drives. "Hey, here's a layout on the Miss Truman High competition. Lookie here." I hold up the spread. "'Girls protest beauty pageant,'" I read. "And there's Callie front and center. Says the protesters claimed it devalued women."

Luke points at the contestants in bathing suits. "I see all sorts of valuables there."

We both laugh, and I smack him with the book. "Maybe our girl Callie wants to be prom queen so she can bring it down. Probably wants to expose it for the ridiculous popularity contest it is."

"Obviously she's working with someone," Luke says as he stares at a house we drive by. "She can't be doing it all alone—running us off the road, magically transferring money, sending untraceable e-mails, harassing you." He pulls onto Main Street. "That was her boyfriend's house. Nobody there."

"Let's move on to her house."

An hour later I've got a crick in my neck, I've eaten all the mints at the bottom of my purse, including the fuzzy ones, and all we've done is watch Callie's silver Focus.

"Let's just talk to her about the call, Luke. I'm tired."

"I'm going to get out and look at her car. Make sure there's no scuff marks on it—in case she's the one who sideswiped us."

I press a button and my chair reclines. "Okay. See you in a bit."

"I need you."

My hand jerks, and my chair sits straight up. "What?"

"I need you to distract Callie while I go check." He opens the car door. "You drive. Pull right up next to her car."

We swap places, and I cruise us to her house. "What will I say?"

"I don't know. You'll think of something."

"Well, it's not like we can talk makeup." I say a little prayer as I hop out of the SUV. *Dear God, please give me guidance in my moment of deceit.*

I look back with dread and Luke motions me on. With a shaky hand, I knock on her front door. Yippy dogs go off like obnoxious, fuzzy alarms.

"Yes?" Callie answers the door.

"Um, Callie? I'm—"

"I know who you are. I've seen you on TV and in the *Enquirer*."

"Oh." *I've seen your picture too.* "I, uh, am working on a piece for the Truman High *Tribune* and wanted to talk to you about"—*Don't say anything that will tip her off*—"the rumor that they will soon be enforcing a dress code at school."

"They will?"

"Yes." I am *so* uncreative today. "I'm getting some quotes from departing seniors."

"What's the dress code going to be?"

"Er . . ." I watch a kid in a wife-beater sail by on his bike. "Tank tops and skirts. School colors."

"How short are these skirts?"

"Short?" It comes out as a question. "Yes, very short." I point to a spot way above my knee. "They said it will be good for ... circulation." I look over my shoulder toward her car. I see the faintest hint of a coat. Hurry up, Luke!

"Well, we have an all-male school board. What do you expect?"

"Huh?" I turn back around. "Right! What do you expect?"

"My boyfriend would never allow *me* to wear skimpy clothes. He thinks it takes the focus off my brain and character."

"Uh-huh."

"In fact, he'd probably beat up anyone who even glanced at my legs."

This snaps me to attention. "Oh, is he the jealous sort?"

She smiles like this is cool. "Very. We both just believe in shining with our inner lights and not being judged by outward appearances."

"Yeah, yeah. Lights. Shining. So then how does he feel about your being a contender for prom queen?"

She sighs heavily. "He's not happy. At all. We fight about it a lot." Her voice drops. "But all principles and values aside, sometimes a girl just wants to be the one wearing the tiara, you know? Just once in my life, I want a tiara moment. Does that make sense?"

I smile. "Yeah, it does. I hope your boyfriend comes around."

"I don't know if that's going to happen." Her face darkens. "My friend Felicity Weeks told me that he's been going around *encouraging* people not to vote for me."

"Felicity's one of the other queen candidates, right?"

"Yeah, we're totally BFFs. Joshua—my boyfriend—he doesn't

like Felicity much. He says I need to find some new friends. I just think he's jealous of any time I spend away from him."

I have to ask. "Callie, why are you dating this boy?"

Her brown eyes go all dreamy. "He truly is a great guy. He just has these . . . triggers. But he really does want the best for me."

"Yeah, that sounds really *encouraging*."

"Looks like *your* boyfriend is ready to go."

I glance back at the 4Runner, and Luke waves from the passenger side. "Uh, thanks for the quotes. And good luck on your run for the tiara."

"Luck?" Callie laughs. "If I get queen, it won't be because of luck."

I say good-bye and hop in the SUV. "Did you find anything on her car?"

"Nothing but a few door dings." Luke stretches and rests his fingers on the top of my headrest.

"Whoever ran us off the road has had plenty of time to repair her vehicle." I tell him everything Callie said.

Luke's brow furrows. "If she wins, it won't be because of luck? At this point, I don't know whether that's inspirational or ominous. Hey, where are you going?"

I pull into the Dairy Barn drive-thru. "I need to talk to the ice cream lady. Last time I was here, she looked very suspicious."

Luke laughs. "I respect your commitment to the job, Kirkwood. You do go above and beyond."

chapter twenty

So since this Thursday is Valentine's Day"—Lindy shuts her locker and sneaks a glance at Matt—"we're passing out the Match-and-Catch results today at lunch."

Ruthie bites into a Pop-Tart as the first bell rings. "So I can find out who's the best guy in the school for me?"

"Did you fill one out, Matt?"

He looks away from Lindy and shrugs. "Yeah, I mean I guess so. It was for a good cause and all."

"Aren't you the least bit curious who it paired you up with?" she asks.

"I gotta go to science class." He waves absently and joins the downstream flow of the hall.

Callie Drake and her boyfriend walk by. He's got his arm anchored around her neck, and the two are laughing. I zip up my backpack and fall in behind the couple.

"You're going prom dress shopping *again*?" her boyfriend says. "What's the big deal? Pick one out and be done with it."

"I did pick one out—with Felicity. You said it was too revealing. I'm having a hard time finding one with a turtleneck."

I bite my lip on a smile.

"And I don't want you going over to Felicity's anymore. Not while her little boyfriend's there." His voice is angry.

"Him? Are you jealous of him? You are so ridiculous, Joshua. This is out of control."

"I'm not jealous, Callie. He's . . . weird. I don't like him. Why can't you hang out with some new friends?"

I inch up closer, straining to hear.

"There's nothing wrong with—"

"Kirkwood!"

Ugh! I slow down as Ruthie catches up with me.

"What are you doing?"

I bite back a sigh. "Eavesdropping, if you must know."

"You got someone you want me to bug? I can totally set you up. Say the word."

"No!" Tempting though. "No bugs."

"Hey, um, will you tell Budge that my computer has a thingie, and I need him to take a look at it?"

"You got another bad e-mail?"

"No."

"It has a thingie?"

She averts her eyes. "Yeah. On the dooma-flachie. It's broken. It's making it hard to—"

"Print do-hickies and send dealie-whoppers?"

"Exactly."

"Sounds serious. I'll pass that on. But you know, you could talk to him like he's just another boy. He could be interested in you as more than just a computer to fix."

She stiffens. "I didn't say I liked him."

"Right. Okay, I'll pass on the urgent computer request." Sometimes I think she's had one too many piercings.

At lunch I'm called into the office and find I have a huge floral arrangement. I open the card, half expecting to see another scary note.

New York is less without you. But my life is more with your friendship.

See you soon,

Hunter

Aw. Isn't that sweet? I smell the roses and lilies and grin. Plucking one of the blooms, I leave to find Lindy so I can help her pass out the Match-and-Catch forms. She hands me a single envelope.

"What is this? I'm not getting one." I don't have ten extra bucks.

Lindy refuses to take it back. "It's on the house. You've been helping me with all of this, so consider it a thank-you."

"Oh." My fingers tingle to open it. But I can't. I don't want to know. Oh, yes, I do.

"Looks like you don't need Cupid's help."

I set all my stuff on the ground and look up to find Luke. "What are you doing here? Don't tell me *you* paid to get matched. That probably wouldn't thrill your girlfriend."

He lifts and lowers a brow. "Lindy asked me to come and help."

"Oh. Right." I'm an idiot. Why do I always come off sounding like a jealous harpy? I'm not. I'm totally not. I'm sure if his Harvard girl and I got to know each other, I'd love her and want to be her very best friend. We'd probably wear each other's clothes and do each other's hair.

No, actually I want to rip her hair out. She's so stinkin' smart! And pretty! And—

"Luke, here's your Match-and-Catch results." Lindy passes him an envelope.

He stares at it like it's a tarantula. "Um, you can just keep it. I'm really not interested."

"Suit yourself." With a shrug Lindy returns to handing out envelopes and collecting money. "It's in appreciation of the articles you did in the paper on the fund-raiser. It's helped a lot."

"Just take it," I say. "I won't tell Taylor." Oh! There I go again. *God, what is wrong with me?* I've been watching too much *Gossip Girl*. Reading too many snarky books. Maybe I should listen to a bunch of Christian music or watch some *Hannah Montana* with Budge. I know, I'll view *VeggieTales* until the evil is purged out of me, and all that comes out of my mouth is goodness, light, and songs about cucumbers.

Luke just smiles and grabs some Match-and-Catch results to hand out.

"Lindy!" Felicity Weeks shoves her way through the crowd, her blonde curls jiving all over her head. "Guess what! My dad found us a place for prom."

The entire crowd stops and cheers. Two girls burst into tears. Luke and I lock gazes and share an eye roll.

Felicity high-fives a senior. "My dad's rented some huge event canopies. We can have it outside at our house."

"She has a huge home." Luke whispers near my ear. "We could probably have prom in her living room."

Lindy resumes her work. "We can't pay for that. Except for the wad in my hand, we have no money. Zero. Nada."

"But that's the best part. It's free! Daddy's footing the bill. He *wants* to help us."

More *woo-hoos* from our growing audience.

"Felicity, that's awesome." Lindy looks at me. She's beaming, and I can see a load of stress has been relieved.

"Gimme my results." Anna Deason holds out her hand, and I dig through my stack. "This better be good. I want to see if my man's name is on here. Plus, if things don't work out, I'll know who the alternates are."

"Did you hear we have a prom location now?" I ask.

She sniffs. "Whatever. I could've found us another location. I don't know what everyone is so excited about. It's not like she donated a kidney."

Before I can respond, something catches my eye. "Luke, look."

Mr. Sutter stands across the hall with Callie. She's agitated. Red-faced. Her hands move at warp speed.

"Let's take a walk." His hand moves to my back as we migrate to a spot within hearing distance of the principal.

"—but I didn't call the Truman Inn. *Why* would I do that? I'm a senior, for crying out loud. Of *course* I want prom."

"Miss Drake, the inn gave us your phone number. That's where the call came from. They have a record of it."

"Well, they're wrong. Someone probably got into my purse at lunch. I'm in the running for prom queen, Mr. Sutter. Think about it. Why would I do such a thing?"

He crosses his arms. "Last year's Miss Truman High comes to mind."

"Hey, I protested peacefully. I'm not the one who brought the eggs and the squirt guns."

"Unless you can prove someone used your phone, I have no choice but to suspend you for a week."

Mr. Sutter escorts Callie down the hall, and I turn to Luke. "When did you tell the principal?"

"This morning. I talked to some people, and the Miss Truman High wasn't the first pageant Callie protested. I think she's our girl, but we still need to find out who's working with her."

"The boyfriend?"

He nods. "It's definitely something to pursue."

An odd silence falls between us. Like neither one of us wants to move.

"So do you have your prom date?" Luke asks.

I pull a ponytail holder out of my pocket and make a loose knot. "I'm keeping my options open."

Luke tucks a rogue piece of hair behind my ear. "Hunter?"

I struggle to focus beyond the chills on my neck. "What if I do bring Hunter?"

"What if you do?" His face is impassive. "Do you really think that's a good idea?"

"He's changing, Luke. I can tell. He's just . . . different."

"How convenient."

"What is that supposed to mean? What's with all these cryptic comments about Hunter?"

"I just think you should be cautious is all. It wasn't so long ago that you thought he was a total snake."

The crowd around Lindy grows, nudging me and Luke closer.

"Like I said, I've forgiven him."

"Forgiveness doesn't have to mean blind trust."

"Look—" Someone bumps my shoulder, and Luke reaches out to steady me. I stare back into his piercing eyes.

What was I saying?

"Yes?"

"Um . . ." *He has a girlfriend. He has a girlfriend.* "How about you take care of your relationship, and I'll take care of mine."

"I'm just concerned. I would hope by now you consider me a friend."

"I don't get in fights with my friends. My friends don't boss me around."

An arrogant smile tugs at his mouth. "Then what am I?"

I can't read his signal here. Is there an innuendo? A current of something? Is my brain malfunctioning due to lack of lunch?

Luke removes his hands and checks his silver watch. "I have to meet a senior for an interview. Think about what I said."

"Which part?"

But my voice gets lost in the roar of students as he walks away.

When I rejoin Lindy, a cloud of gloom hangs over her brown head. "Hey, why the sad face, madam president? You have one less thing to worry about with Felicity's dad coming through for us."

She hands a classmate the last envelope, then drags her hound dog eyes back to me. "What did your results say?"

"Um, haven't read it yet." Not sure I want to.

"I opened mine. Matt Sparks and I are a match."

"Lindy, that's so totally cool. Do you think he's read his yet?"

"Yeah. Read it and laughed about it. He said, 'Can you believe this thing says we'd be perfect together?'"

"Oh. I'm sorry."

She throws hers in the trash can next to her. "I give up, Bella. I'm done. It's time to start looking for a prom date instead of just hoping Matt will wise up. Do you have any ideas?"

"Um . . . Budge has this brainy friend named Newton."

She nods once. "I'll take him."

chapter twenty-one

I can hear it now.

"*How did you spend your Valentine's Day, Bella?*"

"*At Mickey Patrick's gym with thirty grown men and a roomful of Lycra, watching my stepdad pound someone into the ground. Gosh, who needs a date?*"

"Isn't Mason the sweetest thing?" Mom holds Dolly's sleeping son in her arms. "Robbie, can you believe you used to be this small?"

My stepbrother sits between us and nods his head absently.

"How's my little guy doing?" Dolly stops by for the hundredth time in five minutes. "Are you sure you don't mind holding him, Jillian? I've got to bring in ten more cheesecakes, then I can take him."

"I'll help you, Dolly."

The room goes into a shocked silence as Mickey stands by the door.

Dolly lifts her chin a notch. "Fine. They're in the Jeep."

They return carrying handfuls of food, but neither says a word. A few minutes later *Pile Driver of Dreams* starts.

"*It's down to five wrestlers, America. Your vote tonight will put one more down for the count. This week we begin announcing the elimina-*

tion at the weekly wrestling matches. *So cast your votes this evening,
and tune back in tomorrow night as we announce who's getting a permanent body-slam.*"

The show begins to highlight the remaining lady wrestler, and
some of us get up to fill our plates. Not surprisingly, most of the
men stay planted in front of the TV as they show pieces of
Cinnamon's life. Especially those pieces in the leather bustier. Her
boobs are like weapons barely contained in her top. Who needs
wrestling moves when you could knock someone out with those?

As a favor to Mom, Dolly agreed to cater the event. She has
tables set up with a Mexican food theme. Honestly, I haven't so much
as touched a nacho since my last night at Pancho's Mexican Villa.

"Just put the cheesecake there." Dolly points to the few empty
spots on the tables.

Across the room little Mason whimpers. Then it crescendos
into a full-scale wail. Mom stands up and pats his back. "I've tried
the bottle. I checked his diaper." Mason's tiny arms flail, and his
shaky cry even gets the attention of the guys watching Cinnamon.
Mom brings him over to Dolly and places the baby in her arms.

"He's been so fussy all week, and I haven't slept in days. I think
he has colic." Dolly says sweet things to Mason in hushed tones.

"Can I try?"

My eyes bug at Mickey's hesitant request.

Dolly starts to wave him off, but the baby doubles his volume.
"I guess. But be gentle with him."

"I know, Dolly."

"Well, it's been a long time since either one of us has had a baby
to hold." She sucks in her lips like she wants to stop any more words
from escaping.

Mickey extends his sinewy arm and places the baby on it like a cradle. He gently rocks Mason, singing a lullaby so low I can't make out the words. The baby peers up at Mickey but continues to yell.

"Maybe you should give him back to me." Dolly holds out her arms.

"No." Mickey continues to rock. "He just wants a different song, don't you, Mason?"

Mickey starts a new tune, and though I still can't hear it, I'm mesmerized by his expressive face. And so is Mason. The baby's volume descends until it's just a whimper. Then nothing. We all stand there and watch as Mickey rocks and sings Mason to sleep within minutes.

"Thank you." Dolly studies Mickey's face for a brief moment, then returns to gazing at her son.

"What was the lullaby you were singing?" I ask as Mickey continues to rock.

"AC/DC."

A cold blast of air filters though the room as I see Lindy, Matt, and Ruthie come through the door. Budge glances their way, then does a double take. He jumps up to the food tables and butts in next to me.

"Did you invite her?"

I ladle out some *queso*. "Who?"

"Ruthie, that's who." His face burns barn red.

"You invited your friends, and I invited mine." I glance at his posse of gamer geeks, who are all but drooling at Cinnamon on the screen. Newt's drink is spilling onto his shirt, and he hasn't even noticed.

"You could've at least warned me." Budge runs a hand over his stubbly face. "I didn't even shave."

I sniff. "You don't smell. Nothing's hanging out of your nose. I'd say that's a pretty good day for you."

Budge looks to Ruthie, who's chatting with my mom. He looks back to me. "I—I . . . Bella, this may come as a huge surprise, but as much as I talk about chicks, I'm actually not very, um, good with them."

"No?"

"Yeah, I know. I really haven't had all that much experience."

"Shocking." I throw on some jalapeños. "Well, here's a tip. Girls do not find talk of vortexes and bump-mapping the least bit romantic."

He shakes his head. "You and your kind are like from another planet. What do I talk about?"

"You've been to her house a few times. What did you talk about then?"

"She did all the talking. I just worked on the computer."

"Talk to her about her bike. Her church. Her . . . addiction to hair products. Just be yourself. Look what you have in common— school, um . . . and school." I wave at Lindy and Matt. "Hey, Budge, does Newt need a date for prom?"

"I guess. Newt said he was waiting for this girl to be his date, but I don't know that it worked out. I do know he's not going without a date."

"Send him over to the food table."

Across the room my mom calls out a greeting as my editor slides through the entryway. "Luke!"

"Your boss is here." Budge snorts and walks back to Newt and his friends.

Luke high-fives and fist-pounds all the guys. He's become a regular, and I can't figure out if I like that or not.

As he walks toward me, I can't help but admire his slightly faded jeans and the steel gray Henley that lightly clings to the muscles beneath.

I mentally shake myself. *Focus on the fajitas.*

"Happy Valentine's Day," he deadpans.

"Yeah, sorry you're here." I hand him a plate. "And not at a candlelit dinner for two."

"This is exactly where I want to be." His frown is slight. "I wouldn't want to miss this."

I feel like our conversation just forked in two different directions. In lieu of a response, I move on down the food table.

Newt chooses that moment to stomp over, his Vans heavy on the concrete. "You wanted to see me?"

"Yeah, Newt, I was wondering if you'd be interested in escorting my friend Lindy to prom." I point in her direction.

"Is she the one in the pink sparkles and mustache?"

"No, *he's* Betty the Bulldozer."

Newt squints behind his glasses. "Does he wrestle in those heels?"

I grab Newt's chin and angle his head toward Lindy.

"Ohh." He nods. "Uh-huh."

That's his only response? How about, thank you. She's *so* much hotter than any other girl I could get on my own. "Are you interested?"

"I don't know. I do want to go to prom . . ."

"What's not to know? Do you already have a prom date?"

"I might have an option."

"Prom's in six weeks. Do you have a date yet or not?"

He scuffs the toe of his shoe. "I guess not."

"Do you have transportation?"

"I should by then. I gotta get my mom's car fixed."

"Tux?"

"I'll get one."

"Lindy has a strict no-hands, no-alochol policy. Can you adhere to that? Raise your right hand and repeat after me: no kissy, no drinkie."

"I got it, Bella."

"And don't you get anywhere near *her* vortex."

With a glowing blush, Newt all but races back to his seat.

Luke coughs to cover a laugh. "What was that about? He looked like he was about to cry."

"Just business."

"Want to go to the basketball game with me on Saturday?"

I drop the ice tongs. "Game? Go? Together?" *Dear God, please anoint me with the power of complete sentences.*

"Yeah, Anna Deason said she tried to call you tonight. She got some threatening e-mails."

I was on the phone with Hunter after school. "E-mails like Ruthie's? Doctored pictures?"

"No, as in telling her that if she doesn't drop out of the prom queen race, she'll be sorry. Two nights ago she was at a game and her shoes got stolen. Could be just coincidence, but I thought we'd go to the game and watch her cheer. Keep an eye out for anything suspicious."

One of the ever-present camera guys darts across the room and trains his lens on me. These guys are like roaches. They're everywhere and impossible to get rid of. I turn around and give him my back. Which puts me right up in Luke's space.

"Yeah, I'd love to go with you. Er, I mean, love to go to the game. But I kind of need a ride."

"Still don't have an alternator?"

"My mom's making me pay for it myself." I see his lips twitch.

"Summer Fresh is looking for part-time help."

"Oh, wouldn't you just *love* for me to be elbow deep in panty liners. Well, no thanks. There is *nothing* that will make me work there."

chapter twenty-two

"You're not going to buy me a prom dress?" I clutch my phone with both hands.

"No, honey. Your mother and I both think you need to learn the value of money."

"But Dad, I do value money. A *lot*."

I hear him laughing. "Get another job, Bella. And save your money. Besides, you have tons of formals from your Hilliard school days."

"Both those are *so* last year, and I have to pay to get my car fixed."

"Christina and Marisol said to tell you hello."

Ugh! Is he even listening to me? Does he even care that I'm wearing last year's dress *and* riding to school in a funeral hearse?

"Christina wants to know how you feel about a summer wedding?"

"Remember how I felt when I got food poisoning and yakked all over dinner? *That's* how I feel."

"Yes, sweetie, your cookies are excellent." He laughs into the phone. "Sorry, Bella, I was talking to Marisol. She made me peanut butter cookies. Isn't that adorable? Now what were you saying?"

"Nothing." *Like it would matter to you and* sweetie. "I have to get ready for the wrestling match in Tulsa. I'll see you soon, Dad. Love you." *God, I seriously need some help dealing with my dad's new life. This is not going well. And I thoroughly dislike that cookie-making little girl.*

I grab my purse and coat and head down the hall. When I hear noises from Budge and Robbie's room, I decide to backtrack and peek in.

Robbie's cape is gone and he's in regular clothes. A flannel shirt replaces a superhero t-shirt. He pushes a button on a remote and a kung-fu guy repeats a move on TV. Robbie attempts a karate chop, then plays it again.

"Whatcha doing, buddy?"

Robbie jumps, hands ready to chop.

"Whoa, don't hurt me." I hold up my arms in surrender.

"I wouldn't hurt you, Bella." He bows like a *sensei*. "I know these hands can be lethal weapons."

I take a seat on his bed. What happened to the Spider-Man sheets? "Where's your cape, Robbie?"

"It's in my closet."

"Why?"

He shrugs and turns his attention back to the TV. "Maybe I want to be a superhero in disguise."

"Why are you watching martial arts movies?"

"Because Dad wouldn't teach me any of his moves."

"And you have to know how to hurt someone *because* . . . ? Robbie, look at me."

He pivots back around but stares a hole in the shaggy carpet.

"Superman and Spider-Man know how to defend themselves. It's part of the job."

"Says who?"

He lifts his head. "Because I—" He shakes his carrot-top head as if erasing the sentence on his tongue. "Because that's what happens in the movies, of course."

I drop to my knees and get eye level. "You'd tell me if anyone was picking on you, right?"

Jake chooses that moment to stick his head in the doorway. "Let's go, guys." He winks at his son. "Daddy's itching to gut-wrench someone tonight."

Used cars. Why can't he sell used cars?

"Are you nervous, Daddy?" Robbie asks, totally disconnecting on our conversation.

"Nah. If I win tonight, I win. If not, that's in God's hands too. It's been a great ride being on the reality show, eh?"

"Oh, it's been a blast." I force a smile. "The camera guys are just like family now." A family of rodents.

Four hours later I've had popcorn, a burger, a candy bar, an extra large Sprite, and six trips to the bathroom. Jake did a great job this evening, and I hope at least for his sake that it's not his last week on *Pile Driver of Dreams*.

"Laaaaddddies and gentlemennnn!" The announcer moves to the center of the ring. "Tonight we have Oklahoma's own Cap-tain! Iron! Jack!"

The entire crowd squints an eye and growls, "Arrrgh."

"Many of you have watched. Many of you have even voted." The screens around the arena change to satellite feeds of the four other contestants in their own venues. "I have the distinct privilege of sharing the results. Will Captain Iron Jack be returning next week to *Pile Driver of Dreams* or is he down for the final count?"

Mom and I scream with the rest of the fans. There has to be at least a couple thousand here.

"The remaining contestants will be in Nevada next Friday night as we move the semifinals to Las Vegas! Our wrestlers will meet *and* compete for the first time!"

"Go Captain Iron Jack!" Budge yells. "Sin City, here I come!"

"Are you ready, Tulsa?" The announcer opens an envelope.

Jake stands in the middle of the ring next to the announcer. Mickey stands below, his hands clasped like he's praying.

"Captain Iron Jack"—the announcer wraps his arm around Jake's shoulders—"I'm afraid I have some bad news for you."

Groans ricochet all over the arena. My heart plummets.

"The bad news is Vegas ain't Oklahoma, but Captain Iron Jack, that's exactly where you're headed! You're going to Vegas, baby!"

The crowd erupts and the four of us jump up and down, screaming. He did it! Jake really did it.

I reach into my purse and grab my phone. "Luke? Jake made it. He's going on to the next round."

He laughs. "That's awesome. Wait just a sec, okay?"

I hear a beep.

"Taylor?"

Ugh. "Nope. Still me. Bella."

"Must've lost her. Tell Jake I'm really happy for him."

I struggle to hear him with the noise around me. "Yeah, I'll do that. Bye."

"Hey, Bella?"

"Yes?"

I hear him breathe deep. "Thanks for calling me."

Silence. "That's what friends do." And I hang up, a little sadder than I was only one minute ago.

chapter twenty-three

ut I'm really qualified. Nobody knows ice cream better than me."

The owner of the Truman Dairy Barn shakes her white poodle-curl head one last time, and I leave. I've been all over Truman today. *Nobody* is hiring.

I hop in my mom's Tahoe. Times are hard. I need my car fixed and I need a prom dress. And prom shoes. And prom earrings, lipstick, hair, nails, perfume, necklace, and matching handbag. The five dollars in my pocket is *not* going to cover it. I miss my dad's credit card.

This morning in my quiet time I read a devotional about pride. It said that God dislikes it so much, he gives us the cold shoulder. I certainly don't need that. And I know I'm supposed to resist pride, and it's wrong. But I have yet to find anyone in the Bible whose only job option left was cranking out maxi-pads. Who needs a car anyway? I'm doing fine catching rides in the hearse.

Okay, actually, no I'm not. I'm forever thinking I smell formaldehyde. *Fine, God. I'm ready to suck it up and gain some humility. I can't afford you being mad at me. Not with a maniac at large.*

Taylor Swift blasts from my phone, and I pick it up.

"Hey, Hunter."

"What are you doing?"

"Deciding whether I want to give up my car or give up my dignity. I have to get a job, and the only place that's hiring is the factory where Jake works."

"Doesn't he make—".

"Yes!"

Hunter's laugh does not make me feel like turning the car toward the industrial park to Summer Fresh.

"These are desperate times, Hunter. You have no idea."

He laughs again, but this time it's bitter. "Oh, I know more about that than you think. At least you have prom to look forward to."

"I don't know. Maybe I should just skip it until next year. It's going to be really expensive, I don't have a job, and I don't even have a date."

"I'll go with you."

I chuckle. "I'm so sure."

"Seriously. Dad has business in Tulsa in March. I'll just see if he'll postpone it until your prom weekend."

"You'd do that for me?"

Hunter's voice is soft and familiar. "I'd do anything for you."

"And I won't find you outside making out with my best friend under a tree and some twinkly lights?"

"I thought you had forgiven me."

"I have." Forgetting seems to be another matter. "Hunter, I would love it if you'd go to prom with me. It would mean a lot."

"Then it's settled."

I balance the phone between my cheek and shoulder. "So how are you feeling these days?"

"I'm okay." His tone says to drop it.

"Any updates?"

"They've ruled out a few more things. I've got more tests this week. Don't worry about it. You have enough to think about."

"Knowing the doctors can't figure out what's wrong with you and it could possibly be fatal is not something I can just push out of my mind."

"I never said I was dying." I hear him clicking on a keyboard and know this topic has probably lost his attention. "I just said it was severe, and I wouldn't be sure of the outcome. Nothing has changed. But talking to you always makes me feel better. And I know you're praying for me and stuff. It's like sometimes I can feel your faith, you know?"

Being Hunter's friend is the so the right thing to do.

As I end my call, I realize in the last few minutes I've driven the Tahoe to Summer Fresh. The entrance to the sprawling concrete building looms before me. If Hunter sees Christ in me, then what would Christ do? Probably move to the next town.

No, he'd suck it up, go in, and fill out an application. *God, give me strength as I walk through this dark, dark valley of life.*

Here goes nothing. I jump out of the SUV, call my overly protective mom to check in, and head toward the Kotex Compound.

"I'd like an application for a job. Part-time."

A gray-headed woman eyes me over the top of her bifocals. "You look familiar."

"I'm Jake Finley's stepdaughter." Throwing around a shift manager's name ought to mean something.

"Nah. That's not it." She opens a drawer and rifles through it.

"Yessiree. Here we go." She pulls out an *Enquirer* and pokes her nail at a picture. "This is you, ain't it? I love this show!"

"Can I just get an application?" I'm not sure if I'm having a moment of maturity or insanity, but it could wear off at any moment.

"I know this is you. Says here you've got two boyfriends."

"I really don't—"

"Says here you solve local crimes."

"It's not like—"

"And you've secretly been dating Prince Harry of England?"

I step a little closer at the clearly doctored picture of me and the prince. Nice. "Just between you and me, it's all true. But if Harry finds out I told, he'd stop buying me diamonds, so let's just keep that one on the DL."

She nods her gray head vigorously. "Look at me—buttoning my lip." She presses her mouth together. "Mmmmmm."

"Great. I knew I could count on you. Um, application please?"

She makes some more muffled sounds and hands me a blank form and a pen.

"Ginger, do you have those accounts ready?" A man lays some manila folders on the receptionist's desk. "Hey, aren't you Jake's kid?"

Behind him Ginger makes fish lips and shakes her head.

"Yes, I'm his stepdaughter. I'm, uh, filling out an application. He said you were hiring."

"Reuben Pierce." We shake hands, then he grabs the form. "You're hired."

"Just like that?" No. That was too quick. "I'm working on a

story on teen jobs for the school paper, so I might not be around too long." *Please tell me that's not acceptable and to go merrily on my way.*

"I can tell a good pad maker when I see one. And we here at Summer Fresh always like to help out Truman High."

Oh. How generous.

"I want to see you here Monday after school. Can you handle that?"

"I'm not sure."

"What's that?"

"I mean, yes. I'll be here." We shake hands again, and I wave good-bye to Ginger, who now is doing the lock-and-key number and pointing to her lips.

Outside, I spy a familiar white van across the street. "Yes!" I yell. "I'm going to make feminine products! Stick *that* on your TV show!" And I peel away.

A couple of hours later, Mom knocks on my bedroom door. "Luke's here, honey."

I save the article I'm working on and skip down the stairs in my jeans, Chucks, and bobbing ponytail.

He sits in the living room and talks to Budge.

"Just gonna grab my coat," I yell and detour into the kitchen where I left it. I wander into a serious heart-to-heart between Jake and Robbie.

"I'm going to ask you one last time, Robbie. Why didn't you finish any of your schoolwork this week?"

As I reach for my jacket on the back of an empty chair, my little stepbrother shrugs. "I dunno."

Jake holds a note with the school letterhead. "Until your teacher calls me with a positive update, no TV."

"But Dad, I *have* to watch my superheroes. And I got some judo DVDs."

"You'll be doing homework, son. No TV this week."

There's a cramp in my heart as little Robbie snivels into his shirtsleeve. What is going on with that kid?

Luke stands up as I enter the living room. "You look nice. Very casual and sporty."

At least he didn't say I look like a good pad maker.

Luke holds an umbrella over my head as we walk outside into a growing rainstorm. As usual, he opens my door and shuts me in. Has Hunter ever opened a car door for me?

"Lindy said to tell you she has your Match-and-Catch envelope. You left it the day we passed out the results," Luke says.

"I've been too busy to even think about it. I guess I'm just hanging in the wind—not knowing who my true love might be."

"Your prom date could be in that envelope."

"Already have one," I blurt without thinking. A full minute of silence ensues. Then another. "You're not going to ask me who it is, are you?"

Luke takes his eyes off the road long enough to look at me with bland eyes. "Let me guess. Hunter called and said *just* the right thing, and you're convinced even more that he's changed, and now he's going to ride up in a white Hummer and escort you to prom."

"Somebody did *not* put on his happy pants today." I stare out the window at a slice of lightning. "I suppose your girlfriend is perfect?"

Luke turns his 4Runner into the gym parking lot and finds a spot. "Have you prayed about jumping back into a relationship with Hunter?"

"Yes." Sorta. Maybe. Pretty much no. "And for your information, Pastor Sullivan, I'm not *jumping* into anything."

We walk into the gym and flash our press passes, which is pretty cool. I feel like a cop on TV when I do that.

I follow Luke to the concession area. "Are we going to interview some people? Take some pictures? Get some quotes?"

"We're getting nachos."

A few minutes later he turns around and hands me cheesy nachos with some canned chili on top. It looks disgusting. And I can't wait to dig in.

"Your Sprite." He extends a bottle, and I'm oddly touched that he remembers these little things, like my favorite drink.

"Luke, do you know what my favorite color is?"

He leads me up the bleachers to find a seat. "Pink. And black." He smiles at my cotton candy–colored scarf.

I settle my food in my lap as we sit. "And on what side do I usually part my hair?"

He focuses straight ahead on the ball game already in progress. "The left. But tonight you've flipped it to the right."

"You do have good reporter skills."

His intense blue eyes leave the court and fix on my face. "What does noticing things about you have to do with me being a good reporter?"

I don't know how long I stare at him, but a blast from the scoreboard snaps me back to the game.

After the junior high game ends, the Lady Tigers take the court, and the cheerleaders line up under the basket. Lindy spots me in the crowd and waves as she sinks a warm-up shot.

"Hey, guys." Matt Sparks climbs the bleachers and sits down

beside me in his team sweats. "Glad you could make it for the games. Bella, good article in the paper about the high cost of prom."

"Thanks." I beam. "Who knew it could be so expensive, right?" But come Monday, I'll be working toward a paycheck. One pad at a time. "Are you taking a date?"

"Nah." Matt looks to the court as the two teams take their places for the tip-off. "I'm sure I'll just hang out with Lindy like usual."

I nearly choke on a chip. "Didn't she tell you? Lindy's going to the prom with Newton Phillips."

Matt blanches. "Who?"

"Newt. He's a friend of—"

"I *know* who he is." Matt's fingers tap the seat. "When did this happen? Is it like a date?"

"Um . . ." What do I say here? "You'll have to talk to Lindy. I didn't mean to spill the beans. I just thought you'd know." *Hope you weren't planning on coordinating your tie with her dress.*

"I need to go stretch." He stands up. "I'll see you guys later."

"That went well." Luke watches him leave.

"How was I supposed to know she hadn't told Matt?" My grin spreads slowly. "His reaction was interesting though, wasn't it? So what about you? Is Taylor coming in for prom?"

He claps when the Tigers score. "She'll be staying at school."

The buzzer sounds for a time-out, and the cheerleaders take center court. I watch Anna smile her peppy smile and lure the crowd into a chant. I scan the audience for anyone even remotely suspicious. Aside from two guys in twin mullets, I see nothing unusual. No one that screams, "I stalk potential prom queens."

"There's Dolly." Luke waves toward the end of the gym, and

Dolly starts walking our way. Baby Mason is held tight to her chest by some sort of sling contraption.

"What are you doing here?" I ask as Dolly sits in the spot Matt vacated.

She lets out a breath, sending her big bangs up even higher. "Mason and I needed to get out of the house for a while." She strokes his sleeping head. "And I have season passes. I love me some basketball. And I figure it's never too soon to introduce a boy to sports, right?"

Mason looks like he's unconscious, so I doubt he'll be absorbing much of the game tonight.

At half-time I'm about to go to the concession stand for some Skittles when the cheerleaders take the court again. They spread across the floor, and music begins to pump out of the speakers. I sit back down to watch the show.

"Wow. They're really good." Dolly pats Mason's back. "They just shot that one girl up like a torpedo."

That one girl is Anna Deason. Though she's incredibly tall, she's slender and light. As a techno mix of a song plays, she and a few other girls do backhand springs across the floor as the other cheerleaders begin to build. The song speeds up, and Anna runs to the center of the formation. Two cheerleaders form a basket with their arms, and Anna is thrown straight into the air as the music crescendos.

My eyes follow her straight toward the ceiling.

The music stops. And the gym goes black.

Shrieks come from all around.

Then a loud thud from the gym floor.

Luke's hand finds mine as I get to my feet. "Don't move."

"But Anna—she could be hurt."

"Must be some storm out there," Dolly says as Mason begins to fuss.

"What's going on?" Did the lightning knock the electricity out?

"Call a doctor!" someone yells from below. Anna. She must be injured. And maybe others, if she fell on them.

Though it feels like an eternity, only two minutes pass before the lights flicker back on. Someone in the press box picks up a mic. "Just the weather, folks. I guess the lightning flipped a breaker. Please stay in your seat until we can get these two young ladies safely out of the gym."

Anna hangs limp over her dad's arms as he carries her out. The cheer coach follows behind, helping another girl hobble toward the exit.

Luke stands. "Let's go check it out."

I trail behind him into the gym lobby. He peruses the anxious crowd that's gathered. "Let's go talk to Hank Gates."

"Ben Gates's dad? Why are we talking to the point guard's father?"

"Because he's the fire chief." Luke slips through a knot of people, then pulls me through, his fingers wrapped around my hand.

He stops in front of a middle-aged guy in a Truman Fire Department cap. We wait until he finishes a conversation with the school superintendent.

"Mr. Gates?" Luke steps forward and engages the man in small talk about the game, his son, and some random current events. "So lightning knocked the lights out, huh?" he finally asks.

"Yep. Looks that way. We've had some wild storms the last few nights, but luckily no damage."

I join the conversation. "Did it just affect the gym?"

He scratches his beard. "Yeah, kind of crazy. It didn't trip any other breakers in the high school but the main gym area. Even the locker rooms had power." He shakes his head. "Mother Nature's just full of mischief tonight."

Luke catches my eye, and I know we share the same thought.

Mother Nature?

Or someone a little more sinister?

chapter twenty-four

Happy Monday, Truman Tigers! This is Melanie Coulson for Tiger TV with your morning announcements. It's not too late to cast your vote for prom king and queen. Hop online today and . . ."

Budge sits sideways in his seat, ignoring the TV. "I'm so sick of all this prom stuff."

I dig through my backpack until I find our novel for the month, *Heart of Darkness*, and barely resist the urge to chuck it across the room. More like *Heart of Pukeness.* "Why don't you just ask Ruthie to prom? What's the worst thing that could happen?"

"She'd put me in a choke hold and laugh in my face."

It is possible. "I don't think so. But she is a little untrusting of guys right now. Her last boyfriend dumped her over those doctored pictures."

"What a jerk."

"If you don't ask her, someone else will. What if a biker family moves into town today, and some dude with chaps and a leather vest steals her heart? Do you really want to risk that?"

His head droops. "I could never compete with someone in chaps."

I pat his shoulder. "Seize the day, Budge."

I barely stay awake through the lecture on the novel. When the bell rings to end class, I'm the first one out the door.

"Did you get my message about Anna?" Luke asks, as I sit down at my computer in journalism.

"One broken arm, one concussion, and one surly attitude. Yeah, it was the talk of church yesterday."

I scroll through my e-mails to check for any possible job offers or other miracles.

Wait—what's this?

Bella,

> *You don't listen very well, do you? You have no idea what I'm capable of. Nobody does . . . but you're about to find out.*

I hit reply to see if the address is legit, but it comes back to me rejected. Big surprise.

"What is that?" Luke hovers over me, and I can smell the clean detergent of his shirt.

"Um . . ." I shut down the screen.

"You just can't get the hang of this sharing stuff, can you?" Luke reaches across and drags the mouse from my hand, pulling up the e-mail. His expression darkens. "A fake e-mail address." He shakes his head. "Why isn't this person coming after me too?"

I pat his arm. "Now's really not the time to get your feelings hurt. Maybe someone will threaten you next week, okay?"

Luke's expression holds me in place. "I don't like you being in danger. And it makes no sense—why just threaten you?" He shoots off a copy of the e-mail to Officer Mark.

I force a smile, despite the fact that I'm more than a little creeped out. "This person probably knows I'm the better sleuth."

Luke doesn't laugh. "In the meantime, you need to still make sure someone's with you at all times. I'm serious, Bella. Go nowhere alone."

~~~~~~~~~~

"All I gotta say is, I *better* get some sympathy votes out of this." At lunch Anna's arm hangs at an angle in a sling. "How's a girl supposed to eat a burrito with one arm?"

"Just lean over it and gnaw."

Ruthie's suggestion has me smiling.

"Hey, Anna." Felicity Weeks stops at our table. "Sorry to hear about your arm. I hope it heals quickly."

"Um. Thanks." Anna tries cutting into her burrito with a plastic fork. "I hear Callie Drake's back today. Word is she's *still* denying calling the hotel."

I watch Felicity's reaction to the mention of her best friend. "Yeah. Oh, speaking of that—Daddy is interviewing two caterers this week."

"Make sure they know how to make those cocktail weenies." Ruthie rubs a napkin over her face. "Man, I love those things."

Felicity wrinkles her nose. "I hardly think either one of them even know what that is."

"We can't afford a caterer right now," Lindy says. "*Especially* a fancy one. Felicity, you can't go making decisions for the junior class like that."

Ruthie jerks her head toward Lindy. "Yeah, *she's* the president."

Felicity claps her hands. "But that's the best part—Daddy's going to pick up the tab!"

Smiles break out across the table. Except for Lindy. "We don't need handouts. I was working on getting the catering donated."

Felicity pats Lindy's back. "I'm sure you're a great class president. But this is my senior prom. I want it to be *perfect*. I've got my dress, my shoes, the photographer, a limo."

"Yeah, too bad you won't have a crown," Anna teases. "Oh, did I say that out loud? Must be the pain meds talking."

As we laugh, Felicity struggles with a smile. "Such the kidder, Anna. Well, I must be off. I have to study for a trigonometry test, and I promised my tutor we'd review. I'll let you know about the caterer."

As she saunters away, Anna frowns. "She took the lead for queen after she got us the new prom location. And now a caterer? That is not even fair. I want that crown. Maybe I can get my uncle to deejay the event. He's Funky Freddie on 105.7 from midnight to four a.m." She glances around the table. "What? Y'all don't know him?"

"Maybe I could ask my third cousin Eugene to deejay." Ruthie fixes one of her hair spikes. "He just got out of prison, so we could probably get him for cheap."

"I'll arrange the music," Lindy says. "Maybe Budge could do it. He was the deejay for one of our student council dances last year."

"Budge?" *My* stepbrother?

Ruthie sighs. "Yeah, as in the boy who was *not* on my Match-and-Catch results."

"Like *those* mean anything." Lindy tears into an apple. "Speaking of that, I still have your results, Bella. You and Luke forgot them in the hall the day I handed them out."

"I don't even want them now." Like I need more confusion in my life. "Ruthie, are those stupid results why you've backed off on chasing Budge?"

"No. I found out some discouraging information. Turns out your stepbrother is not down with JC."

Sometimes conversations with Ruthie McGee remind me of the time I went to Italy, and it took me thirty minutes to communicate I needed a bathroom.

"You know," she says. "He doesn't have a membership card to Club Saved. He doesn't ride the God train. Your stepbrother does not have his passport to the Pearly Gates."

"He's saved." Who would've thought I'd be defending Budge? "He's just struggling right now. But he hasn't skipped church in a couple of months, so don't give up on him."

"So if he wasn't saved, you wouldn't go out with him?" Anna asks.

"Hey, I am a rule follower." She sniffs and runs a finger under her dog collar. "Plus my dad would cut off my hair-bleach allowance."

"I think it's good," Matt chimes in. "We talked about this in FCA just last week."

Last Wednesday at the Fellowship of Christian Athletes meeting, our speaker broke out the Bible and showed us God's big N-O on dating nonbelievers. I can't help but think of Hunter. I dated him *knowing* he wasn't saved. And now what am I doing? Sure, it's just a friendship. But I think Hunter and I both know there could be more simmering beneath the surface.

After school I meet Budge at the hearse, and we pick up Robbie at Truman Elementary down the street.

Robbie steps out of the car rider line and walks toward us, his backpack dragging the ground behind him.

"School is sucking the life out of my little brother," Budge says as Robbie hops in the back and buckles himself in.

I twist around my seat and smile at Robbie. "Good day?"

"Yeah." He doesn't even look at me. "The best. I'd love four more just like it."

I nod to a piece of paper in his hand. "Did you have art? That's a great looking picture of a dog."

"It's Betsy." Robbie's pet cow. "And I already know it's ugly. Billy Simpkins told me so, like, fifty million times."

"What did I tell you to say to Billy Simpkins?" Budge's face is intense as he drives.

"I can't tell him his momma's uglier than anything I could draw. He's a giant. He's a mutant of genetics."

How Robbie even *knows* the word genetics is beyond me. At his age, I think I was still trying to figure out why the left shoe couldn't go on the right foot.

"What grade's this kid in?" I ask.

"Second. For the third time." Robbie leans on the door like the life has left his bones.

"Have you told the teacher?"

"No!" Budge and Robbie yell.

"Dude, that totally breaks man-code." Budge turns on the street that takes us to the industrial park. "If you're a man, you take care of it yourself. Robbie just needs to get some backbone. Outsmart Billy Simpkins."

Robbie says nothing.

I dig into my purse and find my last two dollars. "Stop and get him some ice cream on your way home."

"Um . . . thanks." Budge tosses the money in the console as we pull up to Summer Fresh. "You know when you've been a pad packer here for sixty days, they give you free samples." He grins as I step onto the pavement. "Just something for you to look forward to."

I slam the door.

The ugly building stands before me like my own Billy Simpkins, taunting me and making me feel icky. I do *not* want to go in there. I mutter a quick little prayer and roll back my shoulders. I can do this. But before I go in, I might as well get one thing over with.

I turn around and wave to a distant van. "Yes, I'm *really* going to work here! Get your shot now!" A long telephoto lens sticks out of the window, and I give them a few complimentary poses before running inside.

The gray-headed receptionist gives me a badge, then leads me back to the factory and passes me off to another woman. Her badge reads *Earlene.*

"I'm the assistant line manager for this machine." She pats a big metal contraption. "This here thing is old, but recently rebuilt. It's been a little testy lately, but I think she's fixed." Earlene's hair is so gray it's nearly purple, and I find it hard to focus on her instructions for studying the lavender hue.

"Now, Bella, the feminine napkin will come off that conveyor belt, sticky side up. Your job is to place the adhesive sheet on it and pack it in a box."

Earlene flips a switch, and the conveyer belt lurches and chugs. Within a few seconds pads begin to slowly roll out in a line like little sanitary soldiers. Earlene's Velcro shoes squeak as she leans over the belt and easily puts the slick paper in the right spot.

"Easy stuff, little lady." Her drawn-on brows seem to point to heaven and keep her in a constant expression of surprise. "Now you try."

I step up to the conveyor, snap on some gloves, and repeat Earlene's motions.

"Good job. You just gotta go with the flow." She barks with laughter. "Get it?"

"Yeah." *I need a prom dress. I need a prom dress.*

An hour later I'm listening to my iPod and sticking the thingies on the pads like I was born doing it.

At a tap on my shoulder, I find Earlene. "Guess what?"

I force myself to look away from her mustache. "What?"

"We just got new rush orders, and we need to double our output. I'm going to have to crank up the speed on this baby. Can you handle that?"

"I think so." Considering I could do my calculus homework *and* work the line at this pace, I believe going a little faster would be a welcome change.

With a knobby hand she turns a dial. "Okay, it will speed up gradually so you can adjust. When it gets to double time, it will stay at that constant speed. If you need to stop the conveyor for any reason, push that big red button over there." She points to a glowing circle at the opposite end. "And whatever you do, do *not* let anything touch the floor because it has to be thrown away. *And* it comes out of your paycheck." Earlene's smile reveals overly large dentures. "Are you ready for your break yet?"

"Maybe later." I'd hate to tear myself away from all this fun.

"Okay, but if you get in a *sticky* situation, just holler!" She chortles all the way to the other side of the factory.

I plug my earbud back in and get a rhythm going. Swipe, stick, grab. Swipe, stick, grab. This really isn't that bad. The belt speeds up, and I stand ready with my adhesive papers.

"Are you Bella?"

I throw a pad in a box and pause the iPod. "Yes." Swipe, stick, grab.

"I'm Newton Phillips's mom." She holds out her hand. "Janice."

I shake her hand quickly, careful not to miss a beat.

Small eyes blink behind oversized safety goggles, and I have to wonder what part of the plant she works in. "I just wanted to thank you for arranging his prom date. Newt may be brilliant at designing games, but he's not the most socially advanced boy."

I try to compose a look of surprise.

"And I know this Lindy Miller is a good girl, so I'm hoping this is the beginning of a new phase in his life."

"Ms. Phillips, it's just two people going to prom together." I throw some pads in a box. "They're not really dating."

Her smile is slight. "I know. But it's still a move in the right direction for my Newt. He needs to know there's more out there than these fantasy worlds he creates. Good luck with this machine. It can be a little—"

"Sticky. Yes, I know." Doesn't anyone in this building have some original jokes?

Ms. Phillips acts like she's going to hug me, but then seems to think better of it. She leaves me to my work and my music. I mentally take notes for the *Tribune* article. This will definitely provide some comic relief, I guess.

Sometime later it occurs to me that I totally need a tinkle break. I speed to the red button and push it. The conveyor shudders to a stop. I grab my red Chloé bag and scan for a bathroom.

Reeeeeeeek!

I drop my purse at the shrill sound of gears moving. Standing in frozen horror, I watch as the conveyor belt begins to move like a locomotive, gaining in speed and noise. Pads begin to sail out of the chute like bullets from a machine gun.

It comes out of your paycheck . . .

"Noooooo!" I dive for the conveyor, grabbing adhesive papers and sticking them on like I've got four arms. Swipe, stick, grab. Swipe, stick, grab.

Swipe, swipe, stick—

Stick, stick, grab—

No! I can't lose any. But the pads are building into a mound at the base of the conveyor. I rake them upwards with my arm and sit on the belt. I pull up my legs and rest them on the sides, making a wall with my body. There must be no pad casualties!

As if a dam breaks, the pads only come faster and faster. I jump all over the machine, slapping papers with my feet, chin, and hands—everything I've got.

It's too much! It's a tsunami of supermaxis! I'm running out of strength. Out of hands. Out of sticky-on-thingies. Is this what Noah felt like when the rains came?

I've got to work my way back to the red button! I have to stop this deranged machine. It's possessed.

The pads pelt me like an endless hailstorm. Somewhere in my brain the sound of a wailing alarm registers. Maybe it's the ambulance. Maybe I've suffocated in this sea of lady products and I don't even know it. My hands refuse to stop moving though, and I reach out blindly and just keep grabbing. The pads pile all around me until I'm lost beneath them, like a skier trapped under an avalanche.

"Bella? Hellewww? Bella?" A familiar voice. Eula . . . Eunice . . . Earlene!

With my remaining strength I cry. "Save me!"

"Hold on! I'm going to pull the plug!"

Can't. Breathe. Must get out. I have a cat to raise.

I feel the conveyor belt stop beneath me, and the alarm's cry goes silent. My butt's on fire like I've ridden a treadmill on my tush.

"Where are you?" Earlene's hands wade through the pile. "Don't let me grab anything inappropriate. I can't afford a sexual harassment suit."

"Just get me out of here!"

Pads go flying until I finally have a hole to breathe in. Then I can move my arms. And now I see Earlene's face, frozen in shock. Or maybe that's just her brows.

"My stars, little missy. I thought we'd lost you!"

I drag in air in gulping gasps as Earlene begins to rip pads off my body right and left. "Ow. Ouch. Hey!"

"You're covered in them." She snickers. "They're like cockleburs. They're stuck everywhere!" She tears one from my hair. My face. There is no spot on my body that does not have something glued to it. "You look like a maxi-pad mummy."

Earlene can hardly remove the pads for laughing so hard. She lightly touches a few spots on my face and neck. "Little missy, you're going to have what we call around here sticker burn. It will be a little red. A little whelpy. No big deal."

"Makeup will cover it up, right?"

She looks at her shoes. "Uh. Yeah."

"Earlene . . . this was very, um, educational. I think I have enough information for my article. And this really isn't my thing." I'm so weak!

"Are you saying this job doesn't make your heart extra-absorbent with happiness?"

I close my eyes and pinch the bridge of my nose.

"Hon, if this place isn't a *super* fit for you, then by all means don't *stick* around."

As Earlene continues her zippy double entendres, I walk away, the sound of her guffaws in my ear. This day could not get any worse.

Out of the corner of my eye I see a guy with a palm-sized video camera trained right on me.

Well. I stand corrected.

Knowing your most embarrassing moment in life will soon be on national television is bad. But knowing it's going to be on YouTube in ten minutes? A *hundred* times worse.

chapter twenty-five

~~~~~~

*S*ome girls dream of Jake Gyllenhaal or the boys from *Gossip Girls*. Me? Every night this week, I've had nightmares about drowning in a deluge of feminine protection.

I shut off my alarm this Thursday morning, and Moxie hops onto the floor—promptly tripping over a pair of boots. After my shower, I mosey to the kitchen. Mom sits at the small table, biting into a bagel and turning the page of a textbook.

"How's philosophy?" I kiss her cheek and pour myself a glass of juice.

She sticks the bagel in her mouth and grabs her pencil. "Interesting. I had hoped to find some insight in here on Robbie's strange behavior."

"Like how he TiVo's all of Anderson Cooper's specials on CNN? Or how he's memorized every word of the Superman TV shows, cartoons, and movies?"

"No." Mom scribbles some notes. "I meant his strange behavior *lately*."

"Oh. You've noticed too?"

"He was up before I was this morning. He went to his quiet place. Why don't you go check on him?"

This means he's out in the pasture with Betsy the cow. Betsy's his pet. And she licks me. I don't want Holstein slobber on me this morning.

Mom turns tired eyes to me. "Bel, I was up late last night talking to Dolly. Please help me out here."

"What's up with Dolly?"

Taking a sip of coffee, Mom shakes her blonde head. "She got word yesterday that the baby's father *just* found out about him. He's been stationed in Iraq and had no idea the girl was ever pregnant."

"But Dolly is Mason's mother now. He can't have him back."

"Yes. He can, and he wants his son. Dolly's got a lawyer on it, but with the dad in the picture, this could nullify the adoption. It will probably go to court."

My heart hurts for Dolly. This will make three children she's lost. "I'll go check on Robbie." I go to the back door and grab my coat off a peg. But what I need is a rain slicker or one of those suits like the astronauts wear. Maybe Betsy will keep her tongue to herself today.

With little light, I tromp through the grass and open the metal gate that leads to the pasture. Bundling my coat around me, I walk until I reach the pond. Robbie sits Indian-style with a flashlight, throwing rocks into the water. Betsy lounges beside him.

"Hey, buddy." I sit down. "Kind of a cold morning to be out."

His eyes stay fixed on the pond. "Betsy wanted some company."

The cow looks at me like I'm a giant lollipop. "Robbie, is someone picking on you at school? Has someone hurt you?"

"Nobody's hurt me."

"Well, something's wrong. Please tell me what's going on."

"I'm a big boy, Bella. I have to be strong and take care of myself."

"Says who?"

"Superheroes don't depend on other people. My dad doesn't let anyone get the best of him."

"Yeah, but that's Hollywood. And wrestling . . ." How to put this? "It's not as real as it looks either. Why don't we talk to your dad tonight? You can tell him everything that's going on."

"Nothing's going on, and I don't *need* anyone's help!" He rubs Betsy's wet nose then stands up. "I have to get ready for the bus."

I'm almost sure I see the glisten of a tear as he runs past me and back toward the gate.

Betsy rises as I do. "Oh, no. You stay put—ew!" One French kiss in the face. She bats her big black eyelashes and takes a step closer. And like Robbie, I take off in a sprint.

In journalism class I write a rough draft of another teen job article. I'm calling it "I'd Rather Be Shopping: My Thoughts on Child Labor." I guess I need to interview some other student workers and get some pics of them on the job. I'm so sick of seeing pictures of *me* on the job. Everyone knows about my Summer Fresh disaster by now. As soon as Wednesday it was splashed all over the tabloids. And I'm currently number one on YouTube and Google Video. I knew God was working on my humility, but I didn't know torture would be involved.

Abbie and Tabbie, identical twins and fellow reporters, sit at the computer in front of me. They laugh over something on the Internet, and I double check that it's not me.

Luke makes the rounds to all of his staff and checks everyone's status, answers questions, and offers help. When it's my turn, he doesn't even look at my screen. "Did you find out where Callie Drake's boyfriend was on the night of the basketball game?"

"No. I've been working." To his credit, Luke doesn't even crack a smile. He hasn't made *one* single snarky comment about my run-in with a million maxis.

"The prom queen voting site did have Anna in the lead by a nose." He sits in the empty seat next to me. "Then last week after Felicity came through on the new location, she pulled ahead."

"And after Callie got busted for the phone, *she* plunged to the bottom." I've gotten in the habit of checking it too.

"What do you think—did Callie make the phone call or—"

I finish Luke's sentence. "Did her boyfriend? Luke, I have to be honest. I've asked around a bit and found nothing. I don't know how to approach Callie to find out if her boyfriend has an alibi for Saturday. Everything I've come up with sounds lame."

He smiles. "Think outside the box. What do you know about Callie?"

"Her boyfriend's a jerk. He's the jealous type. He doesn't like her friends, and I overheard him say he wishes she's get some new ones." I ramble off a few more useless facts.

"So ask her to hang out with you."

"Is this an attempt to make sure I'm not alone? How about *you* ask her to hang out." Okay, I know how stupid that sounded. "Fine. I'll work on it." Eventually. I hate awkward situations—which pretty much sums up every minute of my life right now.

"Bump into Callie, tell her you're going to the movies or something Saturday night, and invite her. You're not going to Vegas with your parents, right?"

"I'm going to New York this weekend." While my family whoops it up at the semifinals in Vegas. I feel kind of left out.

"Then Monday night." He stands and gives my shoulder a squeeze. "I have absolute faith in you."

"You're just saying that so you don't have to take care of this yourself."

His grin makes my heart flip. "Maybe I just like to watch you in action."

It's an even larger crowd tonight that gathers at Mickey Patrick's gym for *Pile Driver of Dreams*.

"Take a bite of this chocolate tart and tell me that isn't the flakiest crust you've ever had." The Oklahoma wrestler known as Breath of Death holds out a platter. "My secret is buttermilk and egg whites."

I pop one in my mouth and chew. "Perfect. The crust is airy, yet substantial." I have no idea what I said, but the six-foot-seven Breath of Death claps his hands in giddy joy. If he weren't married, I would seriously wonder about him.

Through the crowd I see Luke slip in through the double doors. He has Ruthie, Matt, and Lindy in tow. I lift a hand in greeting and work my way to the back to talk to my mom.

"Does Dolly need any help?" I ask.

"You might check. Breath of Death handled the desserts tonight, but Dolly insisted on doing the rest. She said it would keep her mind off things."

Tonight's party theme is Western, with beans in a kettle,

barbeque chicken individually wrapped in bandana paper, and all the side items somehow served in cowboy hats. Dolly may be queen of cooking, but my mom knows how to make it all look pretty. I reach past a lasso and sneak a bite of fried potato.

I walk through a group of men making animal noises and taking turns with headlocks, toward Mickey's office. I see Mickey's back and start to ask him where Dolly is.

"Hey—" I immediately swallow the rest of the sentence as Mickey steps to the left, revealing Dolly. The two don't even notice me.

"I just wanted to tell you that I'm here." Mickey runs his finger across Mason's cheek. The baby sighs and nestles deeper in his mother's arms.

I step back a bit so they can't see me.

"Thank you. It will be fine." But Dolly's voice cracks.

"I know a great lawyer in Tulsa. I can make some calls. His firm is the best."

"I don't think that's going to be necessary, Mickey."

"Let me help you."

She shakes her head. "No."

"Dang it, Dolly. Let the past go just long enough to let me help you. When we get this settled, you can go back to hating me."

The silence in the room is a sharp contrast to the noise in the gym.

When Dolly finally speaks, her voice is barely a whisper. "I don't hate you."

"Then don't shut me out of this."

"I've met with Mason's father." She sniffs and rocks her son.

"He's a good man. He served his full term with the army. Fought in Afghanistan. He has supportive parents who are going to help him. Parents who want their grandchild."

Mason squirms in her arms and begins to whimper. Tears well in her eyes as she transfers the baby to her shoulder and pats his back. Mason's crying only intensifies.

Dolly's grin is watery. "Neither one of us can seem to quit crying the past few days."

Mickey reaches for Mason and brings him to his chest. "That's a good boy. Mickey's got you." He hums a low tune and sways. "Go take care of your party, Dolly. Mason's not going anywhere tonight."

Dolly stares at the man who was once her husband. The man she's barely spoken to since the night her girls were killed many years ago.

"What exactly are you doing?" a voice breathes near my ear.

I swallow a yelp and turn away from the office. "Luke!" I hiss. "You scared me to death."

Dolly sails right past us and joins my mom at the food table.

"Budge and Ruthie are talking." Luke jerks his head in their direction. "Well, Ruthie's talking and your stepbrother is just kind of standing there, mouth open like a hooked fish."

"Poor guy. Hey, have you tasted the chocolate tarts? Breath of Death made them."

"Have you ever noticed how giggly that guy is?"

"Have you ever noticed his initials spell BOD?" We laugh, and I notice I've gravitated even closer to Luke.

His smile slips. "Bella, promise me you'll be careful with Hunter."

This is getting old. And confusing. "You tell us to trust our instinct all the time in journalism. I think I know Hunter."

He glances at Breath of Death, who's rearranging the decorations. "Sometimes people just aren't what they seem."

chapter twenty-six

"We're thinking a June wedding. Something small since money's a little tight. No more than five hundred people."

I bite into my steak and try to pretend like I give a poop about Christina's wedding details. I had to listen to them all the way from the airport. I used to bring Lindy with me to Manhattan. But now that Dad has swapped Mr. Chow's for Chili's and is doubling up on nose jobs, it's just me. And them.

"We're going to be bridesmaids." Marisol announces this like she's won the lottery.

"You know, I was in my mom's wedding." I reach for a crusty roll at the dinner table. "Maybe I could pass on this one and just enjoy it like a normal spectator."

Christina's forehead wrinkles. "Kevin?" she whines.

Dad reaches across his dining room table for my hand. "Bella, we want you to be involved. I'm not just marrying Christina, I'm marrying you."

"Ew."

"No!" He shakes his dark head. "What I mean to say is, I'm marrying Marisol. Wait—um, Christina is my bride, but I, er, I mean she and Marisol are a package deal. And you and I are a package deal, and together we're all this big two-for-one special getting married and—"

I hold up my hands. "I think I get the idea." Though my head hurts.

"Yeah, so it will be great. But honey, it is kind of turning into a big wedding." Dad smiles at his fiancée. "Perhaps we could tone it down just a bit." He turns to me. "There are ten other bridesmaids besides you and Marisol."

"I'm the maid of honor," Marisol says with a smirk. As if I'd *want* that title.

"So . . . twelve bridesmaids?" And I battled the dangers of maxi-pads just so I could buy a prom dress? "Sounds expensive. Dad, do you even have twelve good friends to be your groomsmen?"

He takes a drink of water as Christina answers for him. "Some of my family will be his groomsmen."

"I thought you were an orphan. And your family was all in Brazil."

"Bella!" Dad gives me the *Are you on drugs?* look.

Christina's smile is as fake as the collagen in her lips. "I also have family in the United States. In my culture, we embrace anyone into our family. And we treat them with love and respect. At all times."

I nod my head. "Neato."

"I'm going to ask Luisa to bring in the ice cream for dessert now." Dad brushes off his Armani slacks and stands.

"I'll help you!" Get me out of here. This woman brings out the Sharpay Evans in me.

"No, you stay here and talk."

"I'm not going anywhere, you know," Christina says as Dad is out of earshot. "I've done everything I can think of to be your friend."

You could buy me an alternator. "Christina, I just need some time to adjust. Within the last six months both my mom *and* dad have found me a new stepparent. That's all." *Oh. Plus I don't like you.*

She purses her full lips. "I'm sure you want your father happy. And *I'm* what makes him happy."

I glance at her sister, and she's sitting back with her arms crossed like she's the stinkin' queen of my dining room.

I nearly shout a hallelujah when Dad returns, carrying bowls of ice cream on a tray. Luisa waddles behind him with her famous hot fudge sauce.

"Darling," Christina purrs. "I just had the most marvelous idea! Why don't we take Bella to that therapist we've been seeing?"

"Bananas?" Luisa leans over and cuts some fruit into my bowl.

"I do *not* need a shrink."

Dad's face lights up. "Yes! Brilliant idea, sweetheart. We could all go tomorrow for a group session. Bella, this man works wonders! I've learned things about myself I never knew. Why, did you know I was a midget goat farmer in a past life?"

"Nuts?" Luisa chunks a few on my ice cream and winks a warm brown eye.

"I'll call and make the appointment right now." Dad pulls out his cell, ignoring my string of protests.

"I think I'll take my ice cream upstairs. I want to watch *Pile Driver of Dreams* and work on some other stuff." Like drool over the latest *Vogue* and pray for my dad's midget soul.

I flick on the TV just as the announcer gives a replay of the last episode. I watch the first few contestants as they battle well-known professional wrestlers. Jake is the last to enter the ring. I say a prayer and smile when the camera pans to my mom and stepbrothers. I wish I were there. Sometimes this visitation business barely seems worth it. I spend more time in an airplane than I do with my dad.

By the end of the hour, I feel as jittery as Moxie on catnip.

"The time has come when we must say good-bye to one of our wrestlers. America, you have voted, and tonight we're putting the smackdown on the dreams of . . ."

Please don't be Jake.

"Cinnamon, you're going home." The redheaded lady with cantaloupe boobs buries her face in her hands and cries. I stand on the bed and dance and sing. Before I get to the second verse of my made-up song called "Jake Is Better Than Cinnamon Big Jugs," my phone rings.

"Do you need rescuing from your dad yet?"

"Hunter." I smile. "How did you know?"

"We have a deep connection, Bella. When you hurt, I hurt. When you crave a mocha, I crave a mocha. *And* there's the fact that the last three times you've been to your dad's, you've begged me to get you out of the house."

I fall back onto the bed. "See you in fifteen?"

"I'll be there."

By the time I get to Starbucks, Hunter's already seated with three coffees waiting on the table.

"Are you drinking double tonight?"

He grins. "This one is mine." He taps the smaller one. "The two supersized ones are all yours."

I fill Hunter in on the wedding plans. "My dad is in this weird place right now. I don't think he should just jump into marriage. It wasn't that long ago he was dating every sorority girl in New York state. And now he'll have a child in the house again." The thought of Marisol conjures icky feelings.

Hunter reaches for my hand and twines his fingers with mine. "Things change. We have to roll with it and make the best of the bad."

"I guess. How is your dad's business? Has he been able to recover any since the accountant took off?"

Hunter absently strokes my hand. "My dad will never be the same. I don't think my life will be either."

His sickness. "Hunter, I'm sorry. I know the last few months have been hard on you. And I am rambling on about a stupid wedding." At least I'm healthy. At least my dad's business is still operating.

"Do you have your prom dress yet?"

Speaking of painful subjects. "No. I found this red one at Bergdorf's last month. It's by a new designer named Bliss. She's amazing. It's strapless and red." I sigh. "And heaven." I could totally see myself dancing in it all night long.

We talk a little longer before Hunter offers to see me home. The brakes of the taxi squeak as he stops at my house. Hunter walks me to the door, and for a second I think he's going to hold my hand.

"I'll see you next month for prom," he says under the glow of the porch light.

"Thanks for going." I smile into his face. "And thanks for being my friend again."

His arms wrap around me and he pulls me close, tucking my head under his chin.

"Hunter?"

"Yes?"

"Do you know what my favorite color is?"

"Black." Though he didn't say pink as well, I'll give him partial credit. But every New Yorker lives in black.

"Do you know which side I usually part my hair on?"

He runs his hand over hair that is pulled straight back in a ponytail. "Is this a trick question?"

"Okay, what's my favorite dessert?"

Hunter frames my face in his hands. "Bella, when you're near me, all I see is your face, your eyes. Your smile. I'm sure there are lots of things I don't pick up on, but all I know is when I'm with you"—he presses his lips to my cold nose—"for a little while my world is just right."

chapter twenty-seven

o then the therapist was like, 'Bella, imagine you are a French poodle. Now how would you communicate to your father and Christina?'"

"I hope you didn't say you'd pee on them." Ruthie slaps the lunch table, her belly laugh projecting across the entire cafeteria.

While my forced therapy session with Dr. Moonbeams and Incense wasn't funny Saturday, now that it's Monday and I've got some distance, I'm starting to see the humor.

"And then he lights this candle and asks me to watch the flames and imagine them as my negative feelings eating at my mind." I cover a giggle with my hand. "And then makes me, Dad, and Christina shape our thoughts into Play-Doh."

My laughter dissolves as I spot Luke headed our way.

Anna nudges me with a pointy elbow. "Mmmm. That boy is yum-ee. I would be writing him all *sorts* of articles if he were my editor."

Luke greets everyone but focuses his attention on me. "Can I talk to you?"

He turns on his heel, and I follow him outside into the courtyard. We wind around to the parking lot where Felicity Weeks and

Callie Drake stand next to a black BMW, the very car I had picked out for myself once upon a time. That was before my mom and dad decided I needed to live more Wal-Mart and less Saks.

"My tires are *ruined!*" Tears spill down Felicity's fake-baked cheeks. "Daddy is going to be so ticked! And I do not have time for this right now." She all but hisses at Callie. "I have a voice lesson immediately after school. And a ballet class following that!"

"I'll take you," Callie offers.

"You." Felicity sticks her manicured nail in my direction.

"Me?"

"Yes, you're the little crime-solver around here. Can you find out who did this?"

I stoop to inspect a tire. "Yeah, I can just dust for prints and find out within seconds who slashed your tires."

Felicity blinks twice. "You—you can?"

"No." *I'm not the CIA.* I catch Luke's small eye roll.

"I'm really sorry, Felicity." Callie puts her arm around her friend.

"Don't touch me!" Felicity stiffens and steps away. "You did this. I *know* you did. How could you? We're best friends."

Callie's face registers shock. "What?"

Felicity looks at Luke. "Do you see the pattern? *All* of the prom queen candidates have had something happen to them—Anna and the check, Ruthie and the pictures, and now me and my car. The only one who hasn't had any big catastrophe . . . is Callie."

Luke steps between the two girls. "Now, I don't really think that—"

"You want to win this just so you can turn the prom into some Greenpeacey, feminist liberal circus!" Felicity swipes at stray tears.

"Well, I won't let you. My mother was a Truman prom queen. And my grandmother was a Truman prom queen, and unlike you, *I* respect the title!" Felicity's voice elevates like she's defending her right to breathe.

"Felicity, you *know* I would never do anything like this!" Now Callie's yelling. A small crowd begins to gather around us.

"Know you? Ever since you've been dating Joshua, I barely recognize you." Felicity returns her attention back to me and Luke. "Do I call the police? The principal? The mayor? Who?"

He barely hides a smile. "Yes to the police and principal."

"And the president," I add. This earns me another frown from Luke.

"My Beemer and I will have justice!" Felicity stomps off in patent leather flats.

I watch her sashay into the building. "Please tell me I was never like that."

Luke lifts a dark brow. "You were slightly more tolerable." His wink is slow and chill inspiring. "But you've grown on me."

"Look, I didn't do this. I don't slash tires and steal money." Callie's voice matches her forlorn face.

Luke gives me the eye, like *do something.*

"Um . . . of course you didn't, Callie." I smile encouragingly. "You know what you need?"

"A new best friend?"

Pretty good guess, actually. "What you need is a girls' night out." I nod once. "Yep. A Monday night out with the girls."

"What girls?" she asks.

"Um . . . well, me." Who else can I drag into this? "And . . . Lindy Miller, Anna Deason, and Ruthie McGee."

"I don't know."

I lower my voice so the crowd of students around us can't hear. "Ruthie's harmless. I'll make her leave her nunchucks at home."

"And her pocketknife."

Ruthie would rather saw off her own arm than be without it. "I'll see what I can do."

"I'm in."

~~~~~~~~~~

"You hit my arm one more time, Ruthie, and I'm pushing you out the car door."

I glance in the backseat and wonder again at the stupidity of this plan. I could've just messaged Callie on Facebook.

"Well, excuse me, Anna. I guess you got a total BOGO at the emergency room. You went in for a broken arm and came *out* with a crappy attitude."

"Ladies!" Lindy shoots them both a mom look in the rearview. "Don't make me pull this car over."

"Why are we doing this again?" Ruthie asks. "Don't y'all know there's a new episode of *American Chopper* on tonight?"

"I just want to expand Callie's circle of friends."

Anna leans forward in the seat. "I don't know why. This is the girl who cancelled the caterer, right? And *probably* the banquet hall too. I say if we hang out with anyone, it ought to be Felicity. She's the one who's saving prom."

Lindy turns left onto Main Street and huffs, "I had prom under control before she butted in."

"Let's just show Callie a good time tonight, okay?" I stare down all three girls. "Maybe invite her to church or FCA." Or a few coun-seling sessions so she'll detox from her boyfriend.

Lindy pulls into the restaurant and turns off the car.

"Here?" Ruthie opens her car door. "You didn't tell me we were eating at the Wiener Palace."

"Is that a problem?" *Please don't break out the brass knuckles hid-den in your sock.*

"Problem? I love this place!" She runs on ahead of us.

I swing open the glass door and wave at Callie Drake, who sits in a corner booth. We all squeeze in and join her.

"Welcome to the Wiener Palace. I'm Budge, your sultan of—"

I drop my menu and stare at my stepbrother.

"Bella?" A crimson blush starts at his neck and spreads upward. "Ruthie? W–W–What are you girls doing here?"

Ruthie narrows her eyes to snakelike slits. "I didn't know your stepbrother worked here."

"Oh, yeah." I say brightly. "See those feathers in his hat? You have to earn those. And the bigger the plume, the higher your ranking."

Ruthie's eyes continue up the line of his hat. "You must be like king of wieners or something."

Budge shrugs then looks away. "Some call it a gift."

I bite back a smile. "I'll have the Frankly My Dog, I Don't Give a Chili."

Ruthie only has eyes for Budge. "What do you recommend?"

"I . . ."

Please don't say yourself with a side of relish.

"Our special is the Drop It Like It's Hot Dog. It's exceptionally tasty tonight."

She nods her head. "I'll take four of those."

Budge gets the rest of the orders and disappears into the kitchen.

"Ruthie, you could just ask him to the prom, you know," I suggest. "Just as friends, if nothing else. Would that make it easier?"

"Yeah," Lindy agrees. "My prom date isn't a date. He's just a friend of Budge's."

The conversation takes on a life of its own as we wait for our food. Soon Callie is piping in like she's one of us.

"Here are your meals, ladies." Budge balances a tray on one hand and passes out our food. "And here are four hot dogs for you, Ruthie." He takes off his hat and does a sweeping bow in his vest and balloony pants. "Enjoy your stay at the Palace, where everyone is hot, I mean royalty!" His hat slips from his hand, taking flight like a Frisbee. It slices over our table and heads straight for Ruthie's hot dogs.

Splurt! Two hot dogs splatter on her shirt and slide down. Budge grabs napkins in both fists and heads straight toward Ruthie's—

"Hey!" She pushes his hands away, and before I can say *relish*, she has Budge pinned in a headlock.

He swallows hard, sweat beading on his forehead. "I'm sorry," Budge croaks. "Didn't mean to."

She stares down into his reddish purple face. "Bring me another hot dog."

" 'Kay." Without air, his voice is strained, his eyes bulging.

"You're gonna pay for my dry cleaning bill, Budge Finley. You got that? *And* I've decided you're gonna take me to prom. But no funny business. No lip action in the backseat of your hearse, as totally romantic as that would be." She releases his neck, and Budge's gasp for breath nearly sucks in the walls. "My dress is pink by the way."

Budge staggers backward and escapes into the safety of hot dogs and buns behind the counter.

An hour later we've covered nearly every topic imaginable. The conversation is winding down, and my dinner sits like a twenty-pound blob in my stomach.

I decide to get down to business. "So . . . Callie. Your boyfriend seems nice." For a control freak.

She smiles. "He is. We've been going out for about a year. He supports me, he supports my causes, and he's always looking out for me."

Ruthie licks mustard off her hand. "My ex-boyfriend could light a firecracker with his farts."

I think this is probably considered romantic on her planet.

"Don't you hate it when your boyfriend uses your cell phone though?" That didn't sound so lame in my head.

Nobody really says anything. Big help.

I try again. "So what did everyone do this weekend?" I stir the straw in my Sprite.

"I can't remember what I did," Anna drolls. "Oh, wait. I broke my arm. I highly recommend it for some weekend fun."

"What about you, Callie?" *Please take the bait.*

"Joshua was in Tulsa at his dad's all weekend, so I stayed home and babysat my little brother."

Interesting. I prod further. "I'm sure he could hardly eat his lunch when you told him that Felicity blamed you for her slashed tires."

Callie twists a napkin in her hand. "Actually, I didn't get to tell him about it until after school. He stayed home *sick* today."

Quotey fingers. She totally did quotey fingers when she said "sick." Joshua was unaccounted for Saturday night *and* has no alibi for today.

"Did he hang out with anyone at home?" My playful grin is wide—and hopefully believable. "You know, play some Guitar Hero or Halo?"

She shakes her head. "No. Just him. His mom would've killed him if he'd had friends over."

I let this information marinate in my head. I must say, not a bad night out. Mission accomplished.

"This conversation bores me." Ruthie yawns and picks at some chili on her shirt. "Can we talk about *me* some more?"

chapter twenty-eight

On Thursday morning I sit in the kitchen ignoring two camera guys. My head rests on the old table. It's very difficult to eat oatmeal that way. But I'm not giving up.

Budge stomps into the room. "Do you know you have a blob of brown stuff on your nose?"

"My life is in the crapper."

"I think it left a souvenir on your face."

Sitting up, I wipe the oatmeal off my nose and glare. No job. No money. No prom dress. No idea what I'm going to do about Hunter. And I'm still getting to school riding shotgun in a car once used to transport dead people.

"Do you have any openings at the Wiener Palace?" Budge looks at me like I just asked if he'd like to light his computer on fire. "What? You wouldn't even know I was there. I'm a good worker."

"You're a walking catastrophe, is what you are. Every job you've touched has exploded—some literally—in your face."

I stare into camera one. "None of those things were my fault." Okay, maybe a few. But when you find yourself putting antibiotic ointment on your face because a swarm of maxi-pads attacked you, it's easy to get a little depressed.

Mom sweeps into the kitchen in black yoga pants and matching jacket. "Where is your brother, Logan?" She lowers her voice until it's barely audible. "Lately we play this ridiculous game of hide-and-go-seek every morning before school. He hides, and I spend my time looking for him and running late."

I stir my lumpy oatmeal. "I think he hates school."

Budge smirks. "Who doesn't?"

"Doesn't anybody care that something's going on with Robbie?" I whisper, hoping the cameras won't pick it up.

Mom grabs a water and stands behind my chair. "Honey, we've had three meetings with his teacher. We've tried talking to him countless times, but he just says nothing's wrong. I don't know what else to do. I've consulted every parenting book I know."

Before she started her community college classes, Mom read a *lot* of parenting books. She wasn't exactly a major player in my upbringing. But I have to admit, she's doing pretty well in her new role as mother. Except for the fact that she and her husband are totally striking out with Robbie. Something is up with him.

Thirty minutes later, my little brother is accounted for and ready for the bus. And I'm belted into the hearse, my head pounding with the music volume, and hoping my ears don't bleed from the screamo. No wonder teenagers are so violent these days. I know *I'd* like to hurt someone. Budge swats my hand as I reach for the radio controls. I roll down the window, letting in the March breeze and sharing with all of Truman a little ditty called "Care Bears Wear Beards on Tuesdays."

In journalism, Luke makes his rounds, then sits beside me. "Last week's article on teen jobs was good."

"Thanks. The research has been . . . memorable."

His smile is oddly warm. "I think everything about your life is just crazy right now. It will settle down when the reality show is over. It has to be hard living with constant video cameras and seeing your picture on the cover of tabloids. I saw Budge's picture in *People* last week."

I mentally groan. In that same issue was yet another photo of me and Hunter. This one was from my last visit to New York, and Hunter looks like he's about to kiss my face off.

"Luke, Hunter and I are still just—" Friends.

"None of my business."

What if I want it to be your business? "How's Taylor?" I haven't heard him mention his girlfriend in forever.

"She's fine." He drums his fingers on the desk. "Bella, I think we need to talk to Victoria Smith again."

I think about our last visit with the bank teller and cringe. "Are you hoping someone will run us off the road again? Maybe hit the other side?"

"I want to ask her about Callie's boyfriend. Maybe she feels like sharing information now. I've contacted her and arranged a meeting."

"What?" I squeak. "We agreed, Luke. We're a duet. *Not* a solo."

"I didn't hide it from you. Can you ride to Tulsa with me after school?"

I twirl my hair around my finger. "Fine. Pick me up at the house. If there's a chance of being run off the road again and dying in a ditch, I need to change clothes." I don't have good underwear on.

When Budge and I get home, Jake is in the living room with Robbie. The big man paces the floor while Robbie sits like a statue in a chair.

"Do you know how *scared* I was when the teacher called to say you hadn't made it to school yet?"

Budge and I don't even pretend like we're not listening.

"Robbie, you are never, *never* to walk to school. I know you don't like the bus, but unless you can give me a reason you shouldn't ride it, that's our only option right now. Now I'm asking you for the last time, is someone picking on you at school or on the bus?"

I can barely hear his answer. "No."

Jake gets down on his knees, eye level with Robbie. "Son, I don't know what's going on with you, but you know I'd butt drop anyone who tried to hurt you. Please talk to me."

We all lean in, balanced on tippy-toes of hope. Is Robbie going to talk?

He opens his six-year-old mouth. "Nothing's going on at school. No one's picking on me on the bus."

Jake pinches the bridge of his nose and sighs. "Go upstairs. And no TV. You're grounded—again."

As Robbie runs to his room, I notice a hint of red under his shirt.

"His cape." I point to his retreating back.

"I know." Jake flops into a seat. "He doesn't wear it anymore."

"Yes, he does." I glance back at the stairs. "It's under his clothes."

~~~~~~~

Luke and I sit across from Victoria Smith in a Tulsa McDonald's. She eats from the package of fries Luke bought her and keeps one hand on her triple-thick shake. It's like she knows I'm totally lusting after her ice cream.

She looks like she's lost ten pounds and is in need of more than a Happy Meal.

"I don't know what more I could possibly tell you." Her jittery eyes focus on the Playland behind us. "I've told you about the day I cashed the check at least ten times."

"Okay, we won't talk about that anymore." Luke's voice is as soft as puppy fur. "Victoria, do you know Joshua Day?"

"Joshua Day?" She bites on her straw. "Like, the senior from Truman?"

"Yes." I nod.

"No, I don't really know him. Why? What'd he say about me?"

Luke rests his hands on the table and tells Victoria what we know so far. "People are getting hurt at school—the girls running for prom queen. We just don't want to see anything bad happen, and I'm sure you don't either, right?"

"Right." She drawls the word out.

I lean closer to Luke so I can talk. *Ignore his cologne. Don't stare at his jawline.* "We think Joshua might know something about the incidents. Victoria, we would never reveal you as our source, but was he in the car the day you cashed the check? Did he threaten you to be quiet?"

"I—" She sets her shake down with a thud. "I have to pee."

I look at Luke as she leaves. We're, like, nose to nose. I slide down a bit and pretend to wipe some crumbs off my pants.

"You were breathing on my neck."

I glance up. "Was not."

His mouth curves upward. "If you had been any closer, we'd have been PG-13."

"I guess I was just getting into the discussion." My face must be as red as Ronald McDonald's hair. "Sorry."

His finger sweeps across my hand. "I didn't say I didn't like it."

A few minutes later Victoria returns. "I . . . um, have to tell you something."

Luke and I both move to the center of the seat and lean in. If she came back to tell us the toilet paper was scratchy, it's going to be a huge letdown.

Victoria stares at her hands. "I can't say much, but I think you're on the right track with Joshua Day." Her voice seems to gain strength. "You *have* to keep me out of this for my own protection, but Joshua is the one who was behind those calls to cancel the caterer and banquet room. And Joshua . . . he's been harassing the girls."

"Have you been helping him?" I ask.

"No!"

Luke grips his Coke. "Was he the one who transferred the junior class's money into Anna Deason's account?"

"Yes. He's brilliant at computers. He writes all sorts of programs." Her eyes grow distant, as if she's seeing him. "He's great at fantasy. It's reality that he has trouble with. But I love him anyway. Even if he won't stop chasing her and—" Victoria clamps her mouth tight. "I have to go." She jumps out of the seat, doubles back, grabs the shake, and bolts out the door.

We get back to Truman just in time for the opening of *Pile Driver of Dreams*. The crowd has expanded and somehow an even bigger flat screen has appeared.

Dolly sits with Mason in her lap and laughs at something he does. From a distance Mickey watches, his face impassive.

Luke and I grab the two vacant seats next to Lindy and Matt. Not that they notice we're there.

"I just don't see why I have to hear about your prom date from someone else, that's all," Matt says.

"So that's what you've been so pouty about lately?"

"I thought maybe—"

"What?" Lindy barks. "That we'd go together? As friends. Like we *always* do things together—as friends."

"*Best* friends. And I don't even know this Newton guy."

Lindy crosses her arms and jerks her head away. "You can meet him at prom."

"You've been acting weird ever since you got that Match-and-Catch form back," Matt says. "Does it bother you that it paired us together? It's not like I'm your brother or a cousin."

She rolls her eyes. "Aren't you?"

Luke's whisper dances on my neck. "Lindy likes Matt?"

"You're just *now* putting that together?" I tsk. "Clearly *I* have the sharper reporter's instinct."

Of course, right now my instinct is saying, *Luke, back up before I get the urge to do something crazy like feel your biceps or run my fingers through your hair.*

With many of Jake's coworkers, friends, and fellow wrestlers, I tune into *Pile Driver of Dreams.* When the show turns to Jake, it shows him at work in the early morning hours. Some footage of him with Budge and Robbie. The family at church last Sunday. And Jake in his pirate garb taking someone to the mat.

"You're on the screen, Bella." Mom grins from across the room. Images flash of me having a one-woman fight with the pad machine.

Me on the front steps with Hunter, staring intensely into his eyes. Mickey's gym erupts into whistles and *ooohs*.

I shake my head and laugh it off. "It's nothing!" I look up and find Luke watching me. He averts his gaze and returns his attention to the TV.

And it *is* nothing with Hunter. Nothing more than friendship.

And I've decided that's all I'm going to let it be.

I think.

chapter twenty-nine

The week passes by so easily, I'm just waiting for the sky to fall. Though lots of March rain, there's no prom queen calamity, and Jake made it through again. Now it's down to just him and Sanchez the Snake. In less than three weeks, the two wrestlers will go head to head. Or spandex to spandex. Wedgie to wedgie.

On this Wednesday morning, I sit Indian-style on the floor of the library at our Fellowship of Christian Athletes meeting. Callie sits beside me, looking a little uncertain.

Today the speaker, a football player from Oklahoma State, spoke on forgiveness and letting things go. It started out kind of boring, but when he started playing the YouTube clips, I began to tune in. And Callie showed up, surprising us all.

". . . And God tells us to forgive as he forgave. You know, Jesus didn't hang on that cross just for you alone and just so you could forget it. We are to be Jesus to others. Are you still holding on to a grudge?"

About ten possibilities pop into my head.

"Are you still withholding forgiveness for someone who deserves it? How's that going for you? Is it accomplishing anything?"

I think of my dad. Maybe I don't like Christina because I'm still hurt he left my mom. Maybe Marisol isn't *totally* awful. I guess I can't show them Christ if I'm catty all the time. And Christina has made an effort with me.

"Think of family . . . friends . . . *former* friends . . ."

Ew. Mia. My BFF who stole Hunter. Okay, so Hunter was just as guilty. And I did forgive him.

I need to call Mia. Tell her it's okay and just let it all go. Or I could talk to her when I go to Manhattan for spring break next week.

And maybe I should forgive Budge for flushing my MAC eye shadow down the toilet last month.

Nah. Let's not go crazy.

After prayer, we're dismissed. I stand up and stretch my arms. "How did you like it?" I ask Callie.

"It was good." Her eyes flit over all the people in the room. "Thanks for asking me. It's like after I got with Joshua, all my friends forgot about me. Except for Felicity." She steps closer. "Bella, you know I didn't do all those things, right? I would never hurt anyone."

"I believe you." And I do. I don't even think she knows about her boyfriend's misdeeds. But she soon will if Luke and I have anything to do with it.

Later in journalism, I stand behind Luke at his workstation. "Did you want to see my final draft?" I ask.

He minimizes an e-mail message, but not before I see his girl-friend's name. "Um . . . yeah." Luke takes my work from my hand. "Bella, this is good," he says after some time. "Just like the job features, every article you've submitted about living with a reality show has been top-notch."

I try to wipe the big goofy grin off my face, but fail.

"I've learned a lot about the wrestling business from reading your work." Luke takes off his glasses. "Learned a lot about you."

"Well..." *Inhale. Exhale.* "It's been fun working on this together. I really liked having you around on Thursday and Friday nights." I replay the words in my head. "Er, and everyone else! Yep. Matt. Lindy. Breath of Death. That guy *totally* livens up a party, eh?" *Why am I still talking?*

"I guess since the show is taking a few weeks off before the big finale, our standing date at Mickey's is off."

I swallow. "Yeah." The show will still film the families, but it won't go back on the air until the Thursday night before prom. "Too bad the paper won't send you to Vegas with us for the final show. But then there'd be two of us rushing around like mad Saturday morning trying to get back in time for prom." *He's smiling. What does that mean?*

"There's a class meeting at lunch. Are you going to be there?"

"Yes. Can't wait." *Can't wait for a class meeting? Did I really just say that?*

After calculus I take my rumbling stomach straight to the cafeteria to pick up something to eat. I bump into Anna. "What's your hurry?" I ask.

"Class meeting. Felicity's going so she can make some big announcement. I can't wait to see what it is this time." Anna rolls her eyes. "Maybe her daddy's arranged for horse-drawn carriages for all of us."

"Did you say there's a class meeting?" Ruthie stops. "Will my prom date be there?"

I shrug. "I guess it's possible."

"I'm in. Let's go."

The girls wait for me as I grab a sandwich to go. When I rejoin them at the cafeteria doors, Callie Drake stands next to them along with her boyfriend.

"Oh, and here's Bella," Callie says. "This is my boyfriend, Joshua."

I force a smile. "I feel like I already know you." *Seriously, dude, I mean that.*

"I had a great time at the Wiener Palace last week." Callie looks at all of us expectantly.

"Sorry Felicity's still giving you the cold shoulder," I say. "You can hang out with us anytime." *Just don't bring Psycho Joshua.*

"I'm gonna go get in line. I don't want them to sell out of pizza." Joshua steps away, then turns around. "And Callie, don't be long or I won't hold your place."

She laughs nervously. "He's pretty serious about lunch. I better go."

We say our good-byes and then head to the library for the meeting. Lindy is just calling it to order when I take a seat beside Luke.

"Okay, guys. Next week is spring break, and then . . . prom. We've had a few fund-raisers and now have enough money to pay the deejay and—"

"I have an announcement! Excuse me!" Felicity Weeks makes her way from the back of the room.

From my spot, I see Lindy tense, like she totally wants to tell Felicity to shut her yapper.

"I am here today as a representative of the senior class." Felicity beams like she's found the cure for cancer. "And as you know, I have provided us an alternate location for prom." She stops as a few people hoot in support. "And now I am pleased to tell you that my father has secured the top caterer in Oklahoma, OK Kibbles—all free! My daddy will be picking up the tab as a donation to Truman High."

Half the room cheers in response. The other half just stares, knowing there's more.

"Man, her popularity rating is going to be off the chart," Anna grumbles.

"*And* as a favor to my daddy, Big Cool from KLRC radio has agreed to emcee and deejay the event!"

"Wait!" Lindy yells over the crowd. "Wait! Felicity, you can't step in and take over prom. We have class officers, and we have to vote and—"

"All in favor, say aye!" calls Brady Malone, the secretary.

"Aye!"

The whole room shouts agreement, and Lindy knows it's over. "Fine. Felicity, please give us more details."

Anna raises her hand. "And don't fear because I'm bringing balloons!" She looks around the now silent library. "Fine. I see how you are. You'll have a balloonless prom. That's what you'll have."

After the meeting I spend the rest of my classes thinking about Luke. And thinking about Hunter. Both guys are, like, putting something out there. I don't know what. But Luke has Taylor, and my ship with Hunter has already sailed. Hasn't it? It's just that he's so different. I really like the new version. A lot. But . . . he doesn't make the butterflies bungee in my stomach like Luke does.

After school I hop in the hearse, and in a blaze of shrieking lyrics, Budge takes us to Truman Elementary to pick up Robbie.

"Can you find a ride to tutoring tomorrow morning? I don't have my gamer meeting."

I stare at Budge. "What? Your army of dorks isn't meeting? Did someone die?"

He answers by cranking up his hideous music just as Robbie gets to the hearse.

"Hey, buddy." I ruffle Robbie's hair as he climbs in back. "Did you eat any paste today?"

"Just a little." He shoves some papers into his half-open backpack.

"Did you have art?" Budge asks. "Let's see what you drew. Maybe a symbolic representation of global warming?"

I think of his past artwork. "A picture depicting your feelings on the cruelty of petting zoos?" I wrap my arm around my seat and grab a paper. "Let's see."

"No!" Robbie yells. "Give it back."

"Robbie, it's in two pieces. What happened?" I hold up two halves.

"Nothing."

Budge inspects the paper. "A dog? You painted a dog?"

My older stepbrother and I share a concerned look.

"Maybe it's a metaphor for his need for world peace?"

Budge snaps his fingers. "Yeah, or a symbol of man's inner struggle with—"

"It's a dog." Robbie snatches the paper back and clicks into his seat belt. "Can we just go home?"

"Did someone rip your paper?" I ask.

His short legs kick against his seat as he stares out the window.

Another thought occurs to me, one that makes my heart hurt. "Has someone been making fun of your drawings?" Still no reply.

"If so, Robbie, that's just stupid. You have the best artwork I've ever seen. Like, museum quality."

Budge turns into Sugar's Diner. "Total Smithsonian material."

The car stops and we all pile out. "We'll talk about this later, okay, Robbie?" He ignores me and walks on into the diner.

The three of us sit at the counter on red barstools. I hear a plate clatter to the floor and without looking, know it's my mom.

She scurries by us. "Be with you in a jiffy. I have a chicken-fried steak emergency."

A few minutes later she reappears, her hair wilted to her head. "Shakes all around?"

We all nod. "Crazy day, Mom?"

"Yeah." She looks across the restaurant. "Dolly's had the last few hours off."

I follow the trail of her gaze and find Dolly in a booth, sitting across from a guy who could be her son. Her face is drawn, and even her hair seems deflated.

Mom swipes the counter with a rag. "Mason's dad. This is their third meeting. His parents just left a bit ago."

I can't tear my eyes away from the restrained pain on Dolly's face. "What does her lawyer say?"

"Dolly's already made up her mind." Mom's hand stops mid-swipe. "She's giving the baby back to his father."

chapter thirty

Webcams are so weird. It's like watching a movie where the sound is a split second off from the film.

"Dad, speak up toward the mic, I can't hear you." I glance in my handheld mirror and feather my lashes with mascara. Running late for school as it was, and then dad *had* to talk to me.

"Bel, I just can't believe it's already Thursday. This week has totally gotten away from me."

"I know. I can't wait to see you Saturday." A whole week in New York.

"Yeah, babe . . . about that. I know you're going to be devastated, but I've cancelled your flight."

"What's that? I don't think I heard you right." I tap my finger on the computer.

"Bel." He sighs big. "This amazing opportunity has come up. Christina has found a cable channel in Brazil that wants to interview me for a TV show. It's what I've always wanted. It would be me and my life and—"

"Butt implants."

"More than that. It's a chance of a lifetime."

"So not only are you cancelling our spring break plans at the last minute, but you could be moving to Brazil?" I lift my laptop and smash it to my face. "Do you see how unhappy I am?"

"Don't do that, honey. A frown today, a wrinkle tomorrow."

"This week was important to me." I hear the catch in my voice and rein it in. "I wanted to spend time with you. Get my dress for prom. See some Broadway shows and be the girl on your arm—like we used to do."

"I know." His pixilated face appears contrite. "I hate that I'm letting you down. Again. It seems like I'm always doing that. But I have to go to Brazil. *E! News* doesn't use me for commentary much anymore, and the offers are fewer and fewer these days. If I'm going to get back on track financially, I have to make some sacrifices. And it will give me an opportunity to meet some of Christina's relatives." His eyes plead with me through the computer screen. "I'll make it up to you—some way, somehow."

"Dad . . ." I take a deep breath. "I've been thinking about some stuff, and I wanted to tell you that I forgive you. For what you did to Mom. And me—for leaving us." His head jerks like I just declared my love for Kmart.

Dad thinks about this. Finally he gives a half smile. "Thanks, Bel. Do you forgive me for bailing on spring break?"

"I'm only doing one pardon a day." *But tomorrow doesn't look so hot for you either.* "Bye, Dad. Have fun." *Without me.*

As long as I'm in the forgiving mood, I might as well call Mia and get it over with. I briefly consider sending her a postcard or e-mail. *No. Suck it up and do it in person.* I pull up her number and hit Send.

"Hey! This is Mia. Please leave a message . . ." Voice mail. Score.

"Mia, it's Bella. I know this is random but, um, just wanted to tell you that I'm sorry for how things went down last fall. I guess you've figured out by now that I've forgiven Hunter, and I wanted you to know . . . I've forgiven you too." I try to think of something else mature or inspirational to say, but come up with nothing. "I hope one day we can be friends again."

Wow. Being responsible sure takes it out of you. This calls for a Pop-Tart.

"Mom, my ride's here! I'm leaving!" I grab a light jacket and head out the front door where Ruthie sits in her mom's Volvo station wagon. I turn my head so she won't see me laugh. If there was ever a girl who did *not* belong behind the wheel of a wagon, it's Ruthie McGee.

"S'up?" she says, squirting ketchup on some Dairy Barn hash browns.

"Wow. Nice pink hair." She turns her head to give me the full effect. "I like it."

She starts the car, licking her fingers. "With spring on the way, I thought I needed a change."

As we drive down the dirt road, the school bus passes us on its way to pick up Robbie. Poor guy. I hate to see him have to get on that thing. I think it petrifies him.

Ruthie sings along to the music, her face scrunched with emotion.

"Celine Dion?" I ask.

"Yeah." She belts out the chorus. "She sure sings some deep crap."

A couple of miles down the road we pass a group of kids huddled together waiting for the bus.

An idea unfolds in my head. "Stop the car." Ruthie brakes and we both jolt forward. "I didn't mean in the middle of the street." Total seat belt burn.

As she turns into a driveway, I fill her in on Robbie's weird behavior. "It's just a hunch, but I think the kid who's harassing him probably rides this bus. So if you'd just let me out, I'm going to get on the bus. Oh, and I'm going to need your hoodie."

Without a word she yanks off her black sweatshirt and passes it over. I pull it down over my head and secure the hood.

A minute later I unbuckle. "Here's the bus. I'll see you back at school."

"Wait!" she yelps, as I climb out the door. "What about calculus tutoring?"

"I'll just skip it today." I hear the engine turn off and look back. "What are you doing?"

"I can't miss this!" She runs to catch up with me.

I wave my arm toward the car parked in someone's driveway. "You're just going to leave the station wagon at this person's house? Blocking the drive?"

"Oh, my mom won't need the car. She'll have my bike to ride." She pushes up the sleeves of her t-shirt. "If we're gonna rough up some little kids, then I totally want in on it."

"Ruthie, I'm not going to rough up any—never mind. Just stand behind me and look mean."

We climb on the bus and walk right past an elderly woman at the wheel. "Good morning, sweeties! It's a great day to do some learnin'!" Granny pulls the door closed with a *whoosh*. I wonder if she can even see me behind glasses that are thicker than my hand.

"Don't stop at the Ford's because they're at Gerald Flatt's," a short kid says in passing.

"Super dooper!" Granny's dentures clickity-clack. "Don't stomp on the Lord just because it's raining cats." She nods and adjusts her hearing aid. "Those are words to live by, little man!"

Oh, wow. Robbie could've been screaming for help every day on this bus, and Granny No Ears would never hear.

With Ruthie following, I make my way to a vacant seat toward the back of the bus, keeping my head down. I spy Robbie four seats up, his head also lowered. I point him out to Ruthie. She gives me a rock-on sign.

Just as I'm about to tell Ruthie her rock-on privileges have been taken away due to her love for "My Heart Will Go On," the bus lurches to a stop again. The door opens and kids spill up the steps and into the aisle. I study the faces. Do any of these kids look like thugs? Who would pick on Robbie anyway? He's the sweetest kid ever. A little weird, but who isn't?

"Oh, yeah, little short one." Ruthie's turned around talking to a middle schooler. "On episode three-hundred-and-twenty-seven, I thought I was gonna pee my pants when Raven got stuck in that tree!"

I swat her shoulder. "Would you turn off the Disney channel and *focus*? Don't draw attention to us."

Two stops later, nobody is even talking to Robbie but the white-haired girl in pigtails sharing his seat. And she looks like she's about to sprout angel wings, not two fists.

Thirty minutes later the bus chugs to a stop at the edge of the elementary school.

"Have a joyous day, sweeties!" The driver opens the door and everyone trickles out.

Shoot. That was a total—wait a minute.

I press my nose to the grimy window and see three kids standing there, arms crossed, scowls in place. They're waiting for someone. I look up the aisle in time to see Robbie file out, his face pasty white.

"Let's go." I bump Ruthie with my hip and nudge her out.

She cracks her knuckles, then her neck. "Lead the way. I got your back."

I slide past her and down the steps. "No weapons, Ruthie. I want to talk to some kids. *Not* get arrested." I hear her sigh.

Robbie walks down the sidewalk toward the school, his backpack hanging low. He doesn't make eye contact with the three boys, just keeps going.

"You owe me money, Red."

The kids look like they might be all of ten. I immediately have the urge to smash their faces in now and ask questions later.

"Red, I'm talking to you. You got my money?"

Robbie sidesteps one, only to run into another. A tall brown-headed kid grabs him by the shoulders. I put my arm on Ruthie to hold her back.

"I want your lunch money, and I want it now."

Robbie stares at the grass. "I—I don't have it. I brought my lunch again."

The kid gives him a small shove. "That's not good enough."

"Maybe you can fly away and get it," another chides. The three laugh heartily as they circle in on Robbie.

"I warned you what would happen if you came to school without my money again."

"And what is it that will happen?" I step forward.

The kid doesn't release Robbie. He looks at me, then Ruthie. "Who wants to know?"

"We do." I smile. "I'm Mary Cline." I flash my driver's license. "I'm with playground security. This here is my partner—"

"Drew Barrymore." Ruthie flexes.

"Right. And Drew and I have gotten quite a few complaints about a group of boys who are such sissies they have to pick on little kids instead of anyone their own size. Would you happen to know where I could find those boys?"

"No." A snot-nosed blond in a flannel shirt spits on the ground. "Why don't you go look for 'em?"

Ruthie and I step closer. I glance at Robbie, who stands there motionless, his mouth a perfect oval.

"Drew Barrymore, I think our search is over, don't you?"

She pops her knuckles again. "I think we've found our sissy boys. Shame too. I was hoping we wouldn't have to get the police involved."

"Wait a minute!" I point to Robbie. "Isn't that the wrestler's son?"

"I think it is, Martha."

I cough. "*Mary.*"

"It is indeed, Mary. I heard that Captain Iron Jack is as mean in real life as he is in the ring. Do you remember what happened to the last bunch who were picking on his kid?"

I whistle low. "Those girls were never heard from again."

I continue to ignore the boys and move closer to Robbie. "Young man, I'm going to have to ask you *not* to do your kung-fu moves on them. I believe we were present for your last tussle, and it took us two weeks to scrape the blood off the sidewalk."

Ruthie shakes her pink head. "Totally ruined the hopscotch area."

"This kid don't know how to fight," Blondie says.

Ruthie and I both chuckle.

"Why do you think we're here?" I ask. "They only alert us when something big's going down. And word on the street was that Robbie here was getting ready to administer some pain."

Brown hair snorts. "Whatever." But his voice isn't quite as strong this time.

"Robbie," Ruthie says. "I would be honored if you would show me your famous dancing tiger block."

Robbie just stares.

"No, no, we can't ask that of him. It's too much." Yikes. What have we gotten into?

"Maybe the peaceful turtle block?" Ruthie does not feel my eyes lasering into her and keeps going. "Or the fiery rat slam. That's a good one."

The boys stare for a moment before dissolving into whoops of laughter. Again.

Robbie lifts wounded eyes to me.

"I would be honored, Robbie, if you would show them your moves on me. I can take the pain." I look at him hard. "Like *now*." I give the smallest of nods.

"I'm not sure . . ." his small voice whispers.

"What a baby."

Come on, Robbie. Read my deceptive, devious mind and work with me!

"Listen, puke-face, we've wasted enough time," pops the tall one. "Double the money tomorrow or we'll take it out on your face."

"*Hiiiiiii-yay!*" Robbie squats into some crazy stance, his green eyes intense on mine. With well-timed grunts, he moves into a series of poses, each one crisp and . . . very believable. This guy has been watching a *lot* of kung fu.

Again I give just a hint of a nod. With a warrior's yell, Robbie charges, his left foot airborne. I take it right in the gut.

"Oomph!" My coat pads the blow, but not before my eyes cross. Purposely I stumble backward groaning with pain. He throws a few *Kung Fu Panda* punches to my side, and I collapse on the ground moaning.

Robbie jumps over my thrashing body. He looms over my face, holds up chopper hands, and I catch his wink.

"*Heeee-yah!*" Pulling a wrestling move from his repertoire, Robbie brings down a hand, and a centimeter before impact, I jerk away as if hit. I wail in agony and look at the boys through slit eyes. It's quite possible they're buying it. At least they're not laughing anymore.

"Oh yeah?" Ruthie stomps forward and roars. "You think you can take me?" She kicks a perfect Tae Bo roundhouse. I see Robbie hesitate . . . then run right for her gut. "Feng shui!" she yells as he attacks.

Robbie lands before her in a cartwheel, pivots, then jabs both elbows into her stomach.

"Aughh!" Ruthie yells. She taps her stomach, sending him a signal. "Hit me again, short one. I can take it."

He clotheslines her neck, and her head bobs roughly to the

right. Ouch. That one was real. She motions to her stomach again—
just a small movement.

Robbie faces out toward the boys, then goat kicks Ruthie with
everything he's got.

She cries sharply and falls, but not before a red stain oozes
through her shirt.

"She's bleeding!" Brown hair boy yells.

"He killed her!" From thug number three.

Robbie freezes as if someone pushed pause on his remote. His
eyes are bigger than the tire swings on the playground. His little
hands shake.

"We're not worthy to fight you," I croak. "Doctor . . . I need a
doctor."

Ruthie lies still, spit dribbling out of her mouth.

While the boys move closer to inspect my friend, I tug on
Robbie's pants. "It's okay," I mouth.

He turns on the three bullies. "Next time . . . it's going to be you.
I've let you push me just because I didn't want to hurt you. But know
this—my dad's a wrestler, I'm a warrior in training, and not only do
I land a lethal kick . . . but I eat paste and live to tell about it. If you
ever pick on me *or* anyone else again, I'll come after you. And I'll be
bringing help."

Like something out of a movie, the leader hesitates for only a
second before running away. His coconspirators all but trip over
their own feet to catch up with him.

Ruthie peels open an eyeball. "They gone?"

I see Robbie instantly relax. "You're okay?"

She laughs and reaches her hand into her shirt, only to produce
a squashed ketchup packet. "It was a great day for hash browns."

"But now you're all gross." That's so Robbie. He's been problem free for less than a minute and already found something else to worry about.

Ruthie taps the red spot. "For you, I'll wear the stain with honor."

I pull myself upright. "Robbie, you did a great job. I'm proud of you, buddy."

He sniffs his nose, swipes some dirt off his hands, then clutches my waist with all his might. "Bella, you make my whole face smile."

My throat constricts as I wrap my arms around him and squeeze. "I love you, little brother." A tear plops onto my cheek. Right before I'm tackled by Ruthie.

"I love you, too, guys." She snorts into her sleeve. "That was the best!"

"Robbie?" I say with smushed lips. "You'll always be a warrior to me."

"Thanks, Bel," comes his muffled voice.

"But seriously—the paste thing? You've got to give it up. Your breath smells like Elmer's."

chapter thirty-one

After school, I have Budge make a pit stop at Pancho's Mexican Villa. "I'll be right back," I say.

"Can I have a taco?" Robbie starts to bail out too.

"No. They stunt your growth." And I shut the door.

I plow toward the door and fling it open. "Welcome to Pancho's Mexican Villa!" a girl chirps. Her smile is nearly wider than her face.

Wow. "You're new here, aren't you?"

"Yes!" she beams. "First day!"

Tomorrow she'll sound like the other zombies.

I bypass her gleaming counter and hang a right to Manny's office.

At my knock he wrenches it open. "What do you wa—" His hand goes to his largest gold chain. "What can I do for you?"

"Um . . . I just wanted to apologize for losing my cool and starting a food fight."

"How sorry?"

"This much?" I hold out my hands the width of a taco.

Manny chews on a toothpick. "Do you want your job back by chance?"

Let me think about this. "No."

"Look, two kids just quit, and I'm in deep trouble with spring break coming on. You could just work that week for me and then see how it goes."

Well, gee, at one point I had plans to go to Manhattan, but . . . "I could be persuaded."

He smiles, his gold caps gleaming. "I'll up your hourly wage by a dollar."

Not bad, but I have a car to fix now. "Can I have a two hundred-dollar advance?"

His eyes pop. "What?"

"I'll mention Pancho's in my next newspaper article."

"It's a deal. But I'm hiding the refried bean shooter."

"It's probably for the best."

When Budge pulls the car into our driveway, we're singing three-part screamo harmony. Life is pretty good, and Robbie is back to being Robbie.

"I'm off to watch a documentary on the Japanese dung beetle." He skips into the yard, a red cape fluttering behind him.

My phone vibrates in my purse, and I scrounge for it. "Hey, Luke."

"How fast can you get back to school?"

"Five minutes. What's up?"

"Meet me in the school office. And bring Budge with you." The line goes dead.

"Budge, can you take me back to school?"

He rubs a smudge on the hearse. "No way, freak job."

Yes, we are definitely back to normal. "Two words: Hannah. Montana."

"Let's roll."

The twin doors leading into the high school are open, and we walk on through straight to the office.

"Hello?" I call.

"Back here." Luke steps out from the secretary's office. "We have a new development."

Mrs. Norwood sits behind her desk, her face illuminated by the computer screen. "Yes, the grades have definitely been altered. But just for those four."

Luke looks from me to Budge. "This afternoon someone got on the school server and changed some grades. Felicity, Anna, and Ruthie all suddenly had one F each."

"And the fourth person?" I ask.

The secretary taps a few keys. "Let's just say Joshua Day went from academic distress straight to the honor roll."

Budge nods his head. "*Niiice.*"

"Does the grading program tell you what time the grades were changed?" I step over to the computer. Mrs. Norwood's Avon perfume overrides any chances of my sniffing Luke. Plus I think it's killing some of my brain cells.

"Yes." She pulls up another screen. "This person would have to have special access—like administrative codes—to change these grades. Even a teacher's password wouldn't allow for editing a student's grades in all classes."

"What do you need from me?" Budge asks, primed to dig into high-security files.

"All of our tech crew are at a conference." Mrs. Norwood chews on her lip. "I guess I can let you into the grade program. Budge, I need you to tell me who was logged on between one and one thirty."

Luke and I take a seat on the floor. My back rests against the wall in the small office.

"Thanks for calling me." I twirl Budge's car keys in my hand. "I'm glad you didn't leave me out of the fun."

"I think we're about to solve another one." He holds up his hand, and I slap mine to it. "Bella, did I mention Taylor and I broke up?"

A giddy thrill spirals through my body. "When?"

"Christmas."

The thrill swan-dives. "As in December?"

"We're still friends."

"But we're friends too. So why didn't you tell me?"

"I just—"

"We got it!" Budge yells. "Take a look. Check out this list of people who were logged on," Budge says as we gather around him. He reads off a list of twenty names. All teachers. But two secretaries. And one student.

I stare at the name. "Joshua Day."

chapter thirty-two

On Friday morning the parking lot is crackling with spring break energy. Somehow I didn't wake up with it. Maybe it's because my dad dumped me for his Brazilian sugar, and I'm going to be spending every day working in a restaurant known for producing greasy tacos and deadly farts.

Walking up the steps to the school, Mark Rogers, my friend from the Truman police department, intercepts me.

"Hey, Bella."

Behind him two other men in uniform escort Joshua Day, his hands behind his back. "But I didn't do anything! I have no idea what you're talking about! I'm innocent!" Callie runs along behind him, crying as he's stuffed into a squad car.

"You and Luke Sullivan did a great job investigating this case, you know." Mark watches the car drive away. I can hardly hear him over the gathering crowd. "But next time, leave it to the professionals."

"Anything for a prom queen." I scan the parking lot for Luke.

"I'll keep you posted." Mark pats my shoulder and ambles away. A local news reporter follows him. As does a camera guy for *Pile Driver of Dreams.*

I spy Luke talking to Anna, Ruthie, and the gang. Lindy stands awkwardly between Newton and Matt. Luke catches my eye and smiles.

"The Sullivan-Kirkwood team do it again." Anna hugs me to her as I join them.

"And Budge," I add and wave him over.

"My prom date's a smartie." Ruthie high-fives my blushing stepbrother. "Like the smartest computer geek on the planet."

Budge shuffles his feet. "Not *the* smartest. That's Newt."

"So *my* prom date is the smartest computer geek on the planet." Lindy laughs, but sobers when she sees Newt's face. "I meant smartest person. You're totally not a geek."

Newton's left eye twitches.

"Ugh, thank goodness they apprehended him." Felicity joins our circle. "That Joshua was a menace to society. But now we can all go to prom safely."

"Hi, Felicity." Newt brushes the long hair out of his eyes. "You didn't show up for physics tutoring this morning."

Felicity flips her blonde hair and looks at Newton like he's a Payless clearance shoe. "I was busy. I have a lot of prom details to attend to now that it's at my house."

"You could've called," he says.

"Newt, unlike you, I don't have a lot of free time. I'm kind of dealing with some important things right now that someone like *you* wouldn't have a clue about. I'm *sorry* if you cut your stupid gaming schedule short to meet me."

Newt's face is redder than my patent leather bag.

"Do you have a date?"

Felicity laughs at Ruthie's question. "Well, of course I do. My new boyfriend goes to OSU. His daddy's the district attorney in Oklahoma City."

I look at Luke and cross my eyes. Seriously, I was *never* like Felicity. Right?

"I must run off, but don't forget today's the last day the voting results for prom queen will be up on the class Web site. Cast your votes!" Felicity walks away, waving over her shoulder. "Tah-tah!"

"That girl . . ." Anna seethes. "She's totally bought the crown with daddy's money. She's so far ahead, it won't matter how many votes I get between now and prom. Everything she does just makes her votes quadruple. Last week I gave out pencils. No change in the poll. Yesterday I passed out cookies to everyone—all for nothing."

Ruthie nods. "I've been campaigning too. Wednesday I told a girl I hated her shirt."

I frown. "What was that supposed to accomplish?"

"Nothing. But it made *me* feel better."

The first bell rings, and we gradually migrate inside to the lockers. The halls buzz with the news of Joshua's arrest.

Luke stops at my locker. "Are you okay?"

With the news that he's been single for months? "Yeah, why?"

He examines my face. "I don't know. You just seem down. I mean, we just cracked another major case and you weren't even that excited."

"I have to stay here for spring break. I guess I'm just bummed." And I'll be smelling like tacos all week.

"I'm sorry." He leans on the locker beside mine. "I know you were looking forward to seeing Hunter."

I nearly drop my book. "Hunter? No, I wanted to spend the

week with my dad. We had plans." I shut the door, absorbed in one single thought: I hadn't even *thought* about not seeing Hunter. Not only was I not sad about it, but when dad cancelled, Hunter never even crossed my mind.

"Bella?"

"Huh?" I realize he's been talking.

"I asked you if you wanted to get together over break and work on our *Pile Driver of Dreams* articles."

Get together? I stare into his blue eyes. What does that mean? "Um . . . uh . . ."

Luke pushes off with his foot. "It's okay if you don't want to work on break. Not everyone does." He smiles and pats my shoulder. Like Mark Rogers did. Yet different. "I'll talk to you later."

Shoot! Did I just mess up? What if he was asking me out? And all I could say was *uh*. But no. He said it was to work. And this is Luke. The guy keeps his nose to the grindstone. Whatever that means. Why would anyone ever want to put her nose to a grindstone?

After school Budge chauffeurs me, Robbie, and Newt. We drop his friend off first.

"Dude, what is *that*?" Budge puts the hearse in park and bails out. There in front of Newt's garage is a tricked out Honda Civic. "Check out those rims!" Budge runs his hand over the purple paint-job. "Where'd you get this?"

Robbie and I get out and inspect the car.

"Online." Newt smiles with the kind of satisfaction that only comes from having some wheels. "Can't drive it until I get it licensed."

Budge gets behind the wheel. "Where'd you get the Benjamins?"

"Tutoring." Newt points out something on the stereo.

"Tutoring paid for this?" I ask. "That's *gotta* be better than wearing a sombrero."

Budge snorts. "Or getting attacked by a pad machine."

"Nobody asked you."

"Or diving nose first into a wheelbarrow of horse poop."

"Newt, have you ever heard of Hannah Mon—"

"I'm shutting up now."

On our way home, we pass Jake running on the dirt road. A camera crew rides in front of him in a truck bed.

"Dad's really ramped up the training lately." Budge wheels the hearse into the yard.

"I heard him lifting weights at three thirty this morning." Which qualifies as crazy in my book.

Later in my room, I lie sprawled on my bed with Moxie on my stomach. I pick up my phone for the millionth time. No call from Mia. No text. I've forgiven her! She should be sobbing with gratitude.

God, I am so down. Luke's totally thrown me for a loop. Did he not want me to know he'd broken up with Taylor so I wouldn't pursue him? And Hunter's . . . complicated. And Dad totally dumped me. I should be on my way to New York right now. I should be getting ready for shopping, Broadway, and guilting my dad into buying me something. Instead, I'm stuck at home all week working for Manny "Tacos Make the World Go Round" Labowskie.

Knock. Knock.

"Bella?" My mom pokes her head in my room. "Will you come downstairs?"

I roll onto my back and sigh heavily. "Do I have to?"

"I think you want to."

As soon as I hit the kitchen, a guy with a camera jumps out. "Oh!" I yelp. "You little—" Just a few more weeks of this. I compose myself and find a smile. "You little booger." I wag my finger. "You scared me." I turn around and roll my eyes all the way outside.

Following the sound of my mom's voice, I walk into the backyard. Where Jake sits in my Bug. My beautiful *running* green Bug! The engine purrs like a happy cat.

Clapping my hands in glee, I jump into the passenger side. "Oh, car! I've missed you! But who fixed it?"

"Jake did." Mom holds out my door. "Well, he paid to have it fixed."

I turn to my stepdad. "You did that? For me?"

He shrugs a meaty shoulder, making his neck almost disappear. "It was nothing."

Out of the corner of my eye, I see the camera guy move to get a better angle. "Oh. You did it because of the show." I swallow back a lump of sadness. "Well, whatever the reason, I'm grateful. Thanks." I kiss him on the cheek and go back inside.

"Hey."

I lift my head out of the fridge to see Jake. "Yeah?"

"I wanted to ask you—" He turns on the camera guy. "Could you give us a moment?"

The guy shakes his head. "No way. This is good stuff. Ought to get you a ton of votes."

"I said, *please* go away." Jake draws himself up to his full height. "Now."

The camera guy skitters out.

"Bella, I didn't get your car fixed to make myself look good for the show."

"You didn't?"

"No way."

"Then you got it fixed so I wouldn't have to endure anymore screamo in Budge's car, lose my mind, and possibly hurt innocent people?"

His mouth curls into a grin. "Exactly."

"Thanks. Um . . . I'll pay you back."

"I know you could, but this one's on the house. I would've gotten it fixed sooner, but your mom wouldn't let me."

"Isn't she sweet," I deadpan.

"Thanks for saving Robbie—with those bullies. I should've been more on top of it. I never should've believed him when he said no one was picking on him."

"It's okay. That's what big sisters are for, right?"

"I have something else for you." Jake reaches into his jeans pocket and pulls out an envelope. "I know you're upset that you're not going to be spending time with your dad and doing all your usual Broadway stops."

I put on a brave face. "Oh, who needs to see *Wicked* again? After thirty-seven times, I guess I've got the plot by now."

He hands me the envelope. "Open it."

I peel it open. "Two tickets for the Tulsa Performing Arts Center?" I read the print. "*Wicked?*"

"I was hoping for time number thirty-eight, you'd see it with me. Just you and me—no cameras, I promise."

Tears prick the back of my eyes.

"I know it's not New York. And we won't eat anywhere fancy. Probably just grab a burger at—*oomph*!"

I wrap my arms around this giant of a man. "Thank you! Thank you!"

I blink back the wetness. I do *not* cry. Ever.

Sniff.

Well.

Maybe for *Wicked*.

chapter thirty-three

The alarm on my phone chirps right into my dream just as I'm diving into a sea of Versace dresses. I struggle to stay there as lifeguard Zac Efron waves to me from the shore, but the incessant beeping won't go away. I'm forced to open my eyes.

Monday morning. How is it a school week is so much longer than a vacation week? Though the play in Tulsa with Jake was amazing, the rest of the break was just one burrito after another.

Moxie mewls and covers her eyes with a paw. At least somebody gets to sleep in.

Sitting up, I flick on my lamp and grab my Bible. I pull the ribbon bookmark and open to where I left off yesterday. When I finish, I get out my prayer journal and write a quick letter to God.

"Bella?" My mom taps on my door twenty minutes later. "You awake?"

I put the cap on my pen. "Barely."

"I'm taking Jake to the airport, so you need to make sure Robbie gets ready for school. Don't let him pick out his own socks."

I slide off the bed, grab my robe, and follow her downstairs. Everyone is gathered at the kitchen table.

Last week Jake received word that he had an appearance on *Regis and Kelly* in New York City. I wish I could go with him. I lived there all my life and never went to the show.

Jake cuts a banana for his youngest. "Now Robbie, if anyone gives you a second's worth of trouble, you go straight to the office and have them call me or Jillian. No more secrets, got it?"

Robbie nods his head, his eyes all for the Cheerios in his bowl.

"I'll see you guys in Vegas Thursday." Jake kisses his son on his head, then fist bumps Budge. "This house better still be standing when I get back." He pats my back then heads for the Tahoe with my mom.

At school everyone is just as lethargic as I am.

"Hey, Bella." Lindy intercepts me after English class. "Any word on Joshua Day?"

"Not yet. I'm hoping Luke's heard something," I say. "Is Matt still giving you the cold shoulder?"

She frowns. "He didn't call me once on spring break."

"Maybe his raging jealousy has rendered him mute."

She rolls her eyes. "Nice try."

I hustle down the hallway and into journalism. The class is empty except for one. Luke sits in the chair next to my workstation. A smile crawls up my cheeks, and I'm helpless to stop it. His expression says he's happy to see me, and my stomach wobbles like Nickelodeon slime.

"Mr. Holman wants us to cowrite an article about what led us to Joshua Day."

I set my stuff down. "Good morning to you too."

"If it's good enough, the *Tulsa World* is interested."

I raise my head. "Seriously?"

He nods his dark head. "For real."

I squeal and launch myself into his arms. "Omigosh! That's amazing!" His arms wrap around me just as I realize what I've done. I step back as if I've touched lightning. "Sorry." I clear my throat. "Um . . . you can let go of my hand now."

But he keeps it. "Do you realize what a big deal this could be?"

"You holding my hand?"

His grin is slow. "The paper." He brushes his thumb over my skin then releases me.

I struggle to remain neutral. Unaffected.

"We have to make sure we have every fact straight, so we need to put our heads together and map out the story." He pulls out my chair and motions for me to sit.

"So what's the latest on Joshua?"

"He's still in jail. His family couldn't afford to post bail."

"Callie must be going crazy."

Luke pushes up the sleeves of his Abercrombie henley. "Joshua still insists on his innocence."

"So do most ax murderers."

Since I have the day off from Manny's House of Indigestion, I call Mom after school to see if she wants to run to Tulsa to help me shop for some new heels. I need something to snazz up my old last-year's model of a dress. Though I could get a new dress with my money for bringing Ruthie's harasser to justice and my job advance, I think I'll just save it.

"I can't, Bel. I have to get to Dolly's. The family is coming for the baby. I need to be there with her."

"Today? Now?" But I didn't get to say good-bye to baby Mason. "Can I go?"

Mom's hesitation crackles over the phone. "I don't know . . ."

"Budge can watch Robbie. I'll pick you up at Sugar's." And I disconnect before she has time to argue.

I drive my key-lime-green Bug to the diner. When I swing open the heavy glass door, the overhead bell jingles. And mom stands there waiting just a foot away.

"Let's go." Her mouth is set, her face pinched.

She buckles into my passenger seat as I start the car. "What's with the bag?" I ask.

Mom rests a big plastic bag at her feet. "It's a care package—an entire chocolate pie from Sugar's, smothered chicken fried steak, some Kleenex, a new push-up bra, and a romance novel."

"A bra?"

She shrugs. "Your dad always said perky boobs make everyone feel better."

"He also said thin thighs could bring world peace."

She flings the bra into my backseat. "Good point."

Ten minutes later the Bug eases into the driveway. Mom grabs her bag and we slip into the front door without even knocking.

"Dolly?" Mom calls from the living room, where we tiptoe around suitcases and boxes of Mason's things.

She steps out of the kitchen, Mason in her arms, her eyes red and puffy. "He's been asleep for an hour, but I can't seem to put him down. It's like we're two magnets . . . stuck together." A tear slips down her cheek only to be chased by another.

The doorbell bongs a short melody. All three of us jump.

Dolly's eyes widen and zip to Mom. "He's here." She swallows. "I can't believe this day has come already."

"Are you sure you want to do this?" Mom grips Dolly's shoulders. "We can fight this."

She pats the baby's back. "This is Mason's father—his family." More tears free-fall. "I know I don't go to church and stuff. Haven't stepped foot in one since the girls' funeral. But I do pray. And this is what I'm supposed to do." Her voice breaks on a sob. "It's just so hard."

Mom glances toward the door. "Are you ready for me to let him in?"

Dolly wipes her nose and nods.

Mom pulls open the big oak door. Mason's father stands in the entryway, his parents and attorney behind him.

"Hi, I'm Jonathan." He holds out a hand and Mom shakes it. She puts on her best fake smile and ushers the family in.

The door swings open again, and Mickey Patrick walks in. "Hi. I was . . . um, in the neighborhood."

Dolly keeps her attention on the young father. "These are his things." She gestures to the mountain of boxes. "I did some shopping for him just yesterday. Spring is coming soon, and I wanted him to be ready. There's a really cute Easter outfit in the red suitcase." She sniffs. "You may not want it, of course."

Jonathan stares at his son. "He'll wear it. I'll send you pictures."

"That'd be nice." Dolly's breath shudders in her chest. "The blue bag has his favorite toys. He likes to have his froggy rattle as soon as he wakes up. But that's on the instructions I wrote out for you. Those are in the brown suitcase."

"Yes, ma'am," Jonathan says calmly, like he has all the time in the world. And I guess he does. He now has a lifetime to spend with the son he didn't even know he had. But that still leaves Dolly alone. With a gaping place in her heart.

"And I packed up his crib set and all the décor because he really likes looking at his cowboy things. He loves his horse mobile, so be sure and turn that on for him. Sometimes when he's—"

"Dolly—" Mickey steps from the behind the family and wraps a big arm around his ex-wife. "Let him go, babe."

Her face seizes and she breaks down, clutching the still-sleeping Mason. "I love you, sweet boy." She presses a kiss to each of his cheeks. "You're going to be so happy with your daddy." Her watery words are a struggle to decipher.

Mickey runs a knuckle across the baby's hand. "When he gets fussy, he enjoys a little AC/DC too."

I look at Mom, and she's just as teary eyed as me. This is majorly sad—like *Fox and the Hound* sad. Like *Bambi* sad.

Dolly pulls Mason from her shoulder and kisses him one last time. She whispers words for his ears only, then offers the baby to Jonathan. Slowly. Carefully. Hesitantly. Her arms stretch out to meet his.

Jonathan's face transforms as he holds his son. His parents move to either side of him. He looks to Dolly. "He's going to be my everything."

Though it sounds a little dramatic to me, it seems to be just what she needs to hear. Dolly attempts a smile and nods her weary head.

When the last box is packed away, Jonathan hugs Dolly. "Thank you. God brought Mason to you for a reason. Whatever that is, I'm grateful."

Jonathan holds his sleeping son, and together with his parents, disappears into the van, down the driveway, and out of Dolly's life.

The ride home is a quiet one. No radio. No talking. Just me and my mom silent with our own thoughts.

It occurs to me that something was missing out at Dolly's. "Where was the camera crew? Do they have the day off?"

"I asked them to stay away. This was private." Mom parks the Tahoe in the front of our house. "And it was nice while it lasted." She gestures to two men in the yard, one of them wielding a large camera.

Ignoring the *Pile Driver of Dreams* crew, I follow Mom onto the front porch and almost trip over a large UPS box.

She leans over it. "To Bella Kirkwood."

Fun! "For me?" I pick it up and carry it with me into the house. Too big to be diamonds. To small to be a new Mercedes.

I drop the box on the ugly orange couch in the living room. Peeling off tape with my nails, I lift the flaps. "It's my dress!" I reach in and grab the red strapless piece of art. "It's the one I wanted from Bergdorf's. Is this from Dad?" I didn't even look at the return address.

Mom picks up a small white card from the floor. She reads it, then passes it to me. "Not your dad."

Bella,

Can't wait to see you at prom. I hope this dress is just one of many things that will make the night perfect.

Counting the days until I see you again,
Hunter

I run upstairs, clutching my fabulous new dress. Shutting my bedroom door, I rip off my clothes and ease the dress over my head. I stare into my full-length mirror and peel up the zipper.

It's perfect.

I spin around the room a few times before breaking into a waltz with an invisible partner. Breathless from turning, I collapse onto my bed and call Hunter.

He picks up on the fourth ring. "Hello?"

"Simply amazing."

He laughs. "But enough about me. Tell me how you feel about the dress."

I run my hand over the smooth material. "Oh, Hunter. Thank you. I don't know what to say."

"Don't say anything. I'm just glad to make you happy."

"Happy? I'm delirious! I love the dress. And I love that you did this for me. But Hunter . . . it's so expensive."

"Don't even think about that. Just enjoy it."

I look at the skirt fanning around me. "I will. I don't ever want to take it off." Something beeps in the background. I hear voices in loud conversation. "Where are you?"

"Um . . . at the hospital."

"What?" Here I am gushing about a dress and he's in the hospital. "Are you okay? What's wrong?"

"It's nothing. I came in this morning, and I'll be out in a few hours."

"Please tell me what's going on."

"Bella, forget about it." His voice is weak, but stern. "Just a little flare-up with my stomach. You know the routine—more tests."

"Hunter, I realize this isn't the time. But this weekend we are sitting down, and you are telling me every detail of your health situation. I want to know everything."

He draws a deep breath. "There're are a few other things I want to talk to you about when I see you."

I think of Luke's hand on mine this morning. Then I think of Hunter hugging me the last time we saw each other. Our long talks. This fabulous dress. If Hunter wants to discuss us getting back together . . . I believe I know what my answer will be.

"Hunter, I have something to tell you too."

chapter thirty-four

know, Lindy. I'm really sorry I can't be there to decorate today and tomorrow. I'm sure you will have plenty of help. I think it's nice that Felicity got the helium for the balloons." I watch the final passengers board the early morning flight to Las Vegas. "No, I don't think she wants everyone to think you're an incompetent, do-nothing class president who doesn't know a streamer from a shrimp roll. Look, I have to go. I'll see you Saturday night."

After a quick call to Hunter to check on his progress, I power off my phone and stick it in my bag.

"The teenage years are difficult and trying ones," Robbie says from across the aisle.

Mom licks her finger and flips a magazine page. "Tell me about it."

In a few minutes the plane taxis down the runway. Then with a lurch that never fails to make my stomach drop, we become one with the clouds, birds, and smog.

Three Sprites, two *Teen Vogues*, and one iPod movie later, we touch down in Vegas. I look over at the boys, and they're head-to-head asleep—Budge with his mouth wide open.

"This is going to be so exciting." Mom lifts Robbie's suitcase from the conveyor at baggage claim.

"Hey, it's Dad!" Robbie scampers away from us and runs straight into Jake's waiting arms. Jake sweeps him high in the air.

"You guys ready to go to the hotel?" With Robbie on his shoulders, Jake wraps an arm around Mom. "It's something else."

Yeah, the WWT hotel. Of all the cool places to stay in Vegas, we have to stay at the one dedicated to wrestling. Why not the ritzy Bellagio? Or the cool one that looks like Paris?

Outside a stretch limo waits for us. Robbie and Budge *ooh* and *ahh*. Even though I've ridden in one many times, I can't help but run my hands over the buttery leather seats.

We all find a window to press our nose to as we drive through town. This Las Vegas place is unreal. It's like we're on a different planet.

The limo glides to a stop at the hotel. We climb out and take in the sight before us.

"It's in the shape of a big wrestling ring." Robbie's head is cranked all the way back to get the full view.

Jake escorts us to the front desk where we're greeted by a staff of men and women in tight Lycra shorts and tank tops.

"Welcome to the WWT hotel," a pert blonde says. "After you get settled in your suite, we hope you'll explore the Spit and Spandex Museum, the Rope Burn Buffet, as well as the Chop Drop Casino. And we also have a virtual gaming room where you can experience a computer generated wrestling match and know the thrill of having a karate chop to the larynx or your arms broken in two."

The guy beside her smiles. "And Clay Aiken will be performing in the Head-Butt Lounge tonight."

None of us move. We all just stare.

"Okay, guys!" Jake hustles us away. "Let's go see your rooms."

We ride the glass elevator to the fifteenth floor. Robbie holds his hands over his head and makes whooshing noises like he's flying. Budge listens to his iPod and openly gawks at all the hot ladies in skimpy uniforms below.

"Here you are." Jake opens our door.

We walk past the bathroom into a living room. On either side of us are two bedrooms. Per *Pile Driver of Dreams* rules, Jake and Mickey each have their own rooms on a private floor, so I pick out a bedroom for me and Mom.

Peeking into the room, my jaw drops at the king-sized bed in the shape of a wrestling ring. Microphones hang over the bed in some sort of freakish attempt to be a chandelier. I think this might be tackier than my bedroom at Dad's.

I check the bathroom. Behind the door hang two velvety robes like a wrestler would wear after a match. The sink is a giant wrestling boot. I reach into my purse and click away with my phone. No one will *ever* believe this place without photographic proof.

When I rejoin the family in the living room, Mickey Patrick sits on the couch, his arm playfully crooked around Robbie's neck. Is it weird that headlocks are an acceptable form of greeting in my family? Dogs sniff each other's butts. Most people handshake. But us? We grab you in ways that make you think your neck is going to snap off.

"Are you nervous?" Mom sits on the opposite couch next to Jake, her hand resting on his knee.

He blows out a long breath. "It's big stuff tonight. For the next two days, we're paired with professional wrestlers from WWT and had just today to plot out a storyline and choreograph the wrestling matches. So this is the big leagues, you know? Tonight's about pleasing the viewing audience for the votes, but tomorrow is about pleasing the judges from WWT."

Jake kisses Mom's cheek. "I hate to duck out so soon, but I have to get back. Lots of work to be done yet."

"I need to go too." Mickey stands up, his gaze averted. "I want to call and check on Dolly."

After dinner we have time to walk the strip before returning to the hotel. Al Gore would *seriously* not be pleased with this town's electricity bill. As night falls, we walk back through the hotel and the clanging casino to the WWT arena.

God, please let Jake win. And keep him safe. It would be really cool if he came through this without anything broken. Like his spine.

An usher guides Mom, Budge, Robbie, and me to our seats near the floor. A camera across the room is trained on us, but I don't care. I'll be through with cameras by next week after the wrap-up show airs. Through with America occasionally seeing my face on TV and in the tabloids. Through living *la vida* Lohan.

Some time later the *Pile Driver of Dreams* host walks to the center of the ring. He wears a tuxedo, and the crowd roars when he's handed a microphone.

"Ladies and gentlemen! Welcome to our two-part finale of *Pile Driver of Dreams.* As you know, our contestants are working with the familiar faces of WWT. Tonight you'll see them in action with the wrestling heroes. After the show, we'll post the numbers, and that's when you call or text your vote."

I don't have unlimited texting, but I think Mom will understand five hundred or so over my limit.

"And tomorrow night the two remaining contestants will go head-to-head for the judges. The scores will be averaged, and we will announce our winner of the WWT contract. Are you ready, America?" The yells and applause of thousands thunder in the arena. "Live from Las Vegas! This . . . is . . . *Pile Driver of Dreams!* Our first contestant will be Captain Iron Jack!"

A door on the center stage opens. Smoke billows out as Jake saunters toward the ring. He poses and works the crowd. As his professional opponent enters the same way, Jake takes the moment to slip through the ropes and step into the ring. Before thousands in the arena and millions at home, he drops to one knee. And bows his head. Oh, my gosh. He's praying. On national television.

I think I'm kinda proud. A good portion of the crowd shouts their approval. I just hope he doesn't split his pants while he's down there. Wouldn't be anything holy about that sight.

I spend the next hour biting my nails. Just another reason to get a manicure before prom. Jake is seriously good, but will it seal a victory? I'm not exactly sure how you measure the quality of a choke hold or a leg squeeze. And his competition, Sanchez the Snake, is the one who dreams of being a professional wrestler just so he can send money to Mexico for his mother's liver transplant. How do you compete with that?

I tried to talk Budge into stepping in front of a bus for some sympathy, but he wouldn't go for it. I guess he doesn't want his dad to win as badly as I thought.

When the show is over, we all walk back to the hotel room with a security escort like our last name is Cyrus. Fans snap Jake's picture and beg him for autographs. It takes us forty-five minutes just to get through the lobby.

On Friday we go to another buffet for breakfast. With such easy access to pancakes, I eat them like I'll never see another.

We spend the rest of the day rotating between sightseeing, finding Robbie when he flies away, and doing interviews for the media in the pressroom, which is the weirdest thing ever.

"Bella," the reporter for *E! News* begins, "all of America has followed you through your public relationships."

"You mean my friendships." Would it be impolite to growl here?

"Has it been hard having your life documented on television while you sorted out your feelings for Luke Sullivan and your ex-boyfriend Hunter Penbrook?"

I feel my face flush with desert heat. What if Luke sees this? "As I have said all along, both of these guys are my friends. I would hate for anyone to make more out of it just for the sake of a story." *Wa-pow!* Take that!

My entire family fields questions like these for hours, as does the family of the remaining contestant. When I walk by one camera fixed on Robbie, I smile as he tells them how his cape helps him save the world on a daily basis.

As Mom finishes up with CBS, I gravitate toward some brownies and snacks on a table.

A woman in airbrushed jeans and a halter top grabs two. "This stuff is crazy, isn't it?"

"I hope you don't mean the brownies," I say. "Because I really need one right now."

She laughs with a Marlboro-laced huskiness. "I mean the months of cameras, the interviews, the gossip magazines."

"Are you Sanchez the Snake's wife?"

She cackles again. "I still can't get used to that name." She wipes her black-lined eyes. "I call him Louie Heine. Though I've certainly called him a snake plenty of times too." She sucks in a fuchsia pink lip. "I'm Frannie, and I am *not* Louie's wife. I'm his *ex*-wife."

"Oh." I crunch my teeth on some nuts. Why do people have to destroy a perfectly good brownie with nuts? "That's too bad about his mom. I hope she gets her liver." Just not with winnings from the show.

She snorts loud enough to turn a few heads. "Right. His dying mom. In Mexico."

Okay, well, her bitterness is putting a downer on my snack time. "I'll see you at the show, Frannie." I stuff some chocolate chip cookies in my purse and walk away. Somewhere there's a buffet calling my name.

Later in the hotel room, after I'm glossed, CHI'd, and sprayed, I join the rest of the superprimped family in the sitting area. We all look ready for our close-up.

Mom has us say a quick prayer for Jake, then we're out the door, walking down the hall on carpet so busy it makes my eyes hurt.

Once again we are escorted to our seats in the WWT arena. Chills break out on my arms as music swells and the host begins his intro.

"Hello, America! We're coming to you from Las Vegas at the World Wrestling Television Hotel, and we are down to the final night. This evening our contestants, Captain Iron Jack and Sanchez the Snake, will have two matches—against each other. We will combine your voting results from last night with the judge's scores at the end of this hour. The winner will walk away from here as the new professional wrestler on the WWT team. Live from Las Vegas . . . it's *Pile Driver of Dreams!*"

The crowd goes wild. Robbie and Budge hold up signs for Jake. I scan the crowd for more just like them.

Giant screens play highlights of the last few months, giving the overview of Jake and Snake's lives.

"Captain Iron Jack gets up before dawn to train, then reports to work at a local factory to help support his wife and three kids. Jillian Finley and Bella Kirkwood, once Manhattan princesses, now live the Wal-Mart life on Jake's income . . ."

Eek. No need to make us sound like we're one paycheck away from living out of the Tahoe.

"Sanchez the Snake works three jobs . . . to pay for his five children . . ."

The person behind me kicks my seat, and automatically I turn around. It's Frannie. Her arms are crossed, her eyes narrow slits. "Pays for his five kids." She does her snorting thing again. "And I'm Reese stinkin' Witherspoon."

I return my attention back to the screen.

"Sanchez the Snake also supports his mother, who will die soon without the money for an organ transplant." They show pictures of Snake's kids and a pitiful shot of his shriveled up mom. The entire arena *awwwws*.

"*Aw,* my tush!"

This lady is worse than high schoolers in a movie theater. "Frannie"—my voice snaps a little too harshly—"can you keep it down?" I dig into my purse. "I have some cookies if you want them."

"Sorry, kid." She smacks on a big wad of gum. "This whole

thing is about over, and I'm officially at my breaking point." She points toward the screen. "They're making him out to be some stinkin' saint. That man's never paid a dime of child support to my five kids." She blinks rapidly as if holding back tears. "And little Tommy needs . . ."

I hand her a Kleenex. "Shoes?"

She sniffs. "A Wii."

"But if your ex-husband hasn't paid you in all these years, why are you here?"

"Because I want that money. He owes me." She blows her nose. "But now . . . my tummy hurts, you know?"

"From all the brownies?"

"No," she whines. "From keeping his secrets."

The heavens open and angels sing above me. "What are you talking about?"

"And tonight he tells me he knows he has it in the bag—and won't be giving his kids their share."

I'm so in her space, I've all but leapt over the seat. "Frannie, what secrets?"

Her dark brown eyes lock onto mine. "Sanchez the *Snake* does *not* have a mother in Mexico. She lives in Scottsdale, Arizona, in a condo on the ninth green."

"But the little old lady? The video footage?"

She waves a hand. "I did some acting in my skinny days—small parts in sci-fi movies. We don't even know that lady. I spent *weeks* Googling to find someone in Mexico who needed an organ or something. I found one other lady, but she was Chinese and spoke clear English."

"So Louie, er, Sanchez the Snake just went and filmed this woman in the hospital?"

"That lady don't speak no English. Apparently neither do any of the reality show crew because nobody's called Louie's bluff." Frannie digs in her purse and pulls out some Maalox. She opens the bottle and chugs it like water. "I ain't proud of this. And I haven't slept in, like, six months since he hatched this plan." She grabs her cheeks and pulls. "And I'm getting wrinkles from the stress."

I glance at my mom and my stepbrothers. The first match has started, and they are so in tune with that, they haven't heard a word of this.

My heart pounds in my chest. "Frannie, wouldn't you feel better if you came clean?"

"I know, right?" She tightens the lid on her Maalox. "I tried to talk to the producer this afternoon, but he told me that Louie had warned him about his 'bitter, delusional ex-wife.' I'm not bitter! I'm furious! And *I'm* the one who showed Louie all those wrestling moves. Who do you think he's been training with? And those pants he has on? Mine!"

Ew.

I move to the empty seat beside her. "If you want, I could go with you to try and convince them to listen to you again."

"It's no use. The producer kicked me out of his office. He had security tailing me all day."

I stare at the ring where Louie has Jake pinned against the ropes. See, the dirty secret to wrestling is that it's all planned and choreographed. So while the moves are real, your opponent knows exactly what's coming so he can minimize the hurt if possible. Jake is supposed to win the first match and Sanchez the Snake the second, to keep it all fair.

But nothing's fair now! How dare Sanchez the Snake pull the old dying-mother card?

"Security may be following you, but not me. I'll be back." With no time to lose, I don't even bother filling my mom in. I run down the steps and sprint toward the ring.

"Mickey! Mickey!" I stop right in front of Jake's manager. "You have to listen to me. Louie, er, Sanchez the Snake—he's a fraud. His story about his mother—"

With his eyes zoned on the ring, Mickey moves me aside. "Later, Bella."

"No, you have to hear this!"

He walks away, yelling toward the ring at an illegal move.

Augh! *Think, think, think.*

I spy the black-haired camera guy who has followed me around like my own personal paparazzi. "Hey! You!"

"Don't block my camera! Are you nuts?" he yells.

"Crazy camera guy, I have urgent news. Sanchez the Snake—he's no good. He's been playing you guys from the beginning. His mom—"

"Beat it."

I tug on his shirt. "Look, if you don't listen to me—"

"You'll what?" His look is withering. "Shoot me with some more refried beans?"

Sheesh, a girl starts one teensy-weensy food fight. "Dude, the contract the wrestlers signed—that we all signed. It said something about being disqualified for misrepresenting the facts."

"Look, I don't have time for your chitty-chat, but I will tell you that it's too late. We can't do anything about it now. The votes have been tabulated, the judges are set to make a decision after the second match. This is a live show, and we have twenty-five minutes left. It's over."

But this is Jake's dream. He can't lose out to some lying snaky scumbag.

I glance up at Frannie and shake my head. But I'm not going to give up.

Everyone stands and claps as the first match is over. The referee holds up Jake's hand as the winner. After a small break, they begin the second round. I'm losing time here. Where is the producer? I finally spot him behind another camera crew, but he's surrounded by security.

God, what do I do? I need help!

WWWD. What would a wrestler do?

I watch Frannie walk down the steps and stop at the bottom rail. "What do you need me to do?"

I think for a second. "Provide a distraction."

She nods. "Done."

In four-inch heels, Frannie goes running in front of security, screaming wild insults against her ex-husband. Her arms are waving like windmills. I take the opportunity and shoot straight for the ring. I make a flying leap toward the mat, heaving my legs over and rolling until I'm on.

Just as Jake falls right next to me.

"Bella?" His eyes widen like he can't believe what he sees.

"Hey." I smile. "I just thought I'd drop by."

As Jake holds out an arm to shield me, he yanks me up. The ref breaks through, yelling at the top of his lungs.

"What the heck are you doing?" he screams. "Are you insane?"

I feel five thousand faces turn to me. The arena is eerily quiet. Security has dropped Frannie like a dirty diaper and is headed straight toward me.

"Uh . . ." A hundred words pummel in my brain, but none of them will make sentences. Mom stands with Mickey, her face white. I clear my parched throat. "This man is a phony." I point my shaking finger at Sanchez the Snake. "He—he. Mother. Golf. Not. Mexico." Oh, crap! "No, I mean, his liver needs child support!" *Oh, Lord, something has a hold of my tongue and won't let go!*

Jake pulls me to the side and holds up a rope. "You need to leave." A vein throbs at his temple as *boos* come from every direction. I barely dodge a Coke bottle.

Security rushes the ring and climbs up.

"Come with me, ma'am," one says as he grabs my arm.

"Don't hurt her." Jake removes his hand. "She'll go with you."

"No!" I jump back. "I won't! Sanchez the Snake has been lying to you all!" My voice grows in volume and strength. And if I'm not mistaken, I think what I said actually sounded like English. "He pretended to have a dying mother to get the votes. But his mom is alive and well. And he has five kids and has never paid a dime of child support to Frannie." I flail an arm toward his ex-wife below. "She needed the help, so that's why she went along with it. But she couldn't do it anymore and nobody would listen to her." Two beefy guys in black bump Jake out of the way and wrap their hands around my arms like shackles. "Listen to me! There is some lady in Mexico who needs a liver, but Sanchez found her just so he could film—"

The rest of my sentence is drowned out. My eyes are filled with the sight of Sanchez the Snake leaping off the ropes, his body soaring like an eagle. I'm powerless to move as his shadow covers me.

Somewhere I hear Jake's roar. A security guy shrieks like a girl.

And I go down.

Pain and shock register in my back, my head, my face.

Sanchez hits me like a missile, and I'm on the mat, collapsing under his massive weight. My arms. My legs. My head. Pain.

There's a stinky, sweaty man on me.

My eyes roll back in my head. I shudder for breath.

I give into the pushing darkness in my head.

And everything goes black.

chapter thirty-five

I put down the *USA Today* as Mom packs up my things. "The WWT owner was able to find the doctor and get you an early release." She feels my head and winces at the bruises. "I called Hunter and updated him. He'll meet you at prom. But honey, are you sure you're okay? I would feel better if you stayed here today. Maybe even another evening."

The hospital nurse takes away my lunch tray as I down some Tylenol. "No. One night in this place is enough. Plus this gown is scandalous!" I mean, every time I go to the bathroom, everybody sees my business.

Mom pulls a brush through my wild hair. "I don't know *how* you didn't break something. It's a miracle."

Budge tears his attention from the TV. "A miracle *and* Frannie Heine. That was awesome when she did a swan dive for Sanchez right as he was about to land. If he had hit you dead center, we'd be calling your dad for plastic surgery right now."

"That was a brave thing you did, Bella, but stupid. You should've told me what was going on," Mom says.

I run my fingers over my split lip. "I just didn't want Jake to lose—not like that."

Robbie runs around my bed, his cape flapping. "And thanks to you, he won!"

Mom smiles. "Life is going to be very different from now on."

"Great," I droll. "I need some more change in my life. Moving from Manhattan just wasn't enough."

"Bella, please think about—"

"No." I swing my feet over and put on my shoes. "I am *not* missing prom. And neither is Budge."

Jake enters the hospital room and holds the door shut, muffling the sound of cameras snapping outside. He looks at me and winces like my mom.

"Stop doing that! You guys are making me feel like I need to go to prom with a bag over my head."

Budge lifts his brows. "I suggested that months ago."

Jake sits on the edge of my bed. "Good news and bad news. The bad news is since you and Budge missed your flight this morning, I couldn't get you guys on another flight."

I drop my shoe. "Get to the good part."

"The WWT president has scheduled his private jet to fly you and Budge to the Tulsa airport."

"Oh, my gosh. That's awesome!"

He lays a hand on the part of my arm that isn't blue. "*But* the plane doesn't leave until three thirty this afternoon."

The panic I felt when a psychotic wrestler took me out is nothing compared to this. "But that's five thirty Oklahoma time. We'll be late for prom! I wanted the day to get my hair done. To get a pedicure. To at least have time to zip up my dress!"

Mom's eyes grow big. "Do we need to call the doctor?"

"No!" I squeal. I must get control or else they'll strap me to the bed and make me stay here. "I mean, I'm grateful for the ride. If we have time to get ready, then that would be nice. But if not, I guess we'll go as is."

"You could wear your hospital gown," Budge snarks. "Show your best side."

I lunge for my stepbrother. "I'm about to kick your best side—"

~~~~~~~~

Standing at the base of the airplane, I carefully hug Mom.

"I can't believe I'm letting you go. Alone. After something the weight of a refrigerator landed on you." She runs her hand down the back of my head. "I'm going to get the worst-mother-of-the-year award."

I pull away before she drags me back to the car. "I'll be fine. Budge will keep an eye on me."

She rolls her blue eyes. "Actually, Dolly will. She'll be at the house waiting for you to help you get ready. Dolly will also be spending the night, so don't try anything funny like coming in past curfew."

"How about sneaking my date up the trellis to my room?"

Mom's lips form a firm line. "Very funny." She carefully kisses my cheek. "Be careful. And call if you need anything."

Jake tosses Budge the keys to the Tahoe, and we board the plane.

Feeling stressed and nervous over the time crunch, I check my seat belt three times, consulting my watch between each tug. The pilot said it would take us almost three hours to get back home. Then there's the hour-long drive to Truman. Time to change. I guess Budge and I will have to settle for being fashionably late.

My stepbrother reclines his seat. "Ruthie is going to kill me for not showing up on time."

"Does she know you're picking her up in the hearse?"

He adjusts the headrest and closes his eyes. "She told me she was a modern woman and didn't need a man picking her up."

I laugh at the picture in my head. "So she's wearing a dress and riding her motorcycle?"

"You got it."

Hope she has bloomers.

I spend the next two hours watching TV shows on my iPod. Needing to stretch, I get up and grab a Sprite from the refrigerator at the wet bar.

"So is Newt picking up Lindy in his pimped-out Civic?" I hand Budge a Coke.

"Nah," he says. "He's driving his mom's clunker. She won't let him drive his until he pays to get her Chevy fixed."

"Can't be any worse than your death wagon."

He holds up a finger. "*Au contraire.* Lindy will have to climb in on the driver's side because Newt's passenger side is so bashed in."

"I'm sure Lindy will be totally impressed. She'll spend the rest of her life thanking me for this setup."

Budge pops the top on his can. "He told his mom he hit a deer, but there's no stinking way."

The faintest notion tingles in the corner of my mind. "What kind of car does she have? Two-door? Four?"

"Four. It's some sort of grandma sedan."

I lean on the armrest toward Budge. "When did he have the wreck?"

"I don't know. What difference does it make? Sometime before Christmas break, I guess."

My pulse begins to speed. "Like the same time Luke and I were run off the road?"

Budge opens his other eye. "Don't be ridiculous. Newt can barely see to drive at night. Plus he works in the evenings."

"Tutoring?"

"That's after school. Most nights he works as a janitor."

Warning bells ding in my already throbbing head. "Where, Budge?"

"The Truman National Bank."

My mouth falls open. "I think I'm going to puke." My step-brother holds out his barf bag. "Budge, what if Joshua Day had help in all those things he did? Or what if he didn't *do* any of them?" The facts race through my head, and I try to focus and line up every detail like Post-its in my mind. "Whether Joshua was involved or not—Newt was. He *had* to have been."

"That's insane. Newton Phillips is the wimpiest guy I know. He *couldn't* hurt anyone. He's perfectly capable of shutting down the world with his computer, but *not* harming people or threatening anyone." But as Budge says this, his expression shifts. Like the possibility is suddenly not so far-fetched.

"When I was working at Summer Fresh—"

"Is this before or after the maxi-pads attacked you?"

"—I talked to Newt's mom. She said she was glad I had arranged the prom date between him and Lindy because she was worried about what she called his 'fantasy world.'"

"She just meant the games he creates," Budge says.

I grab my stepbrother's arm. "And she said she was glad he was going with Lindy because she was a good girl, and that it was a step in the right direction for him—like he had been messing with some bad stuff. Or bad people." What does this mean? I can't think fast enough! And the gaps—there are too many holes in what I know. "Did Newt date anyone recently?" Did he date anyone—*ever*?

Budge rubs his hand over his stubbly face. "No . . . not really." His eyes close as he thinks. "Wait—he would talk about this girl he tutored. He would always say how hot she was and stuff—how he'd do anything for a girl like her to like him."

"Who was it?"

He sticks a finger in his ear. "Dude, yelling is not going to jog my memory. I don't know. He never told me her name."

"Newt tutored Felicity." The fact explodes in my mind. "It has to be her! He acted weird around her the other day—reminded her she'd skipped tutoring. I've never even seen him *talk* to a girl before that morning."

Budge's eyes grow wide. "All along Newt's been sabotaging the prom queen race."

"And setting up Joshua Day to take the fall." Get me off this plane! I'm seriously about to jump out of my skin. I need a phone. I have to call Lindy and tell her to stay away from Newt!

"Wait a minute." I hold up my watch. "We're descending. What's going on?" We've only been in the air a little over two hours. Did God provide a miracle and speed up time?

The copilot sticks his head out of the cockpit. "Hey, guys. I don't know if they told you, but we're making a pit stop in Denver. We have to drop a small shipment off."

"What?" I shriek. "You can't!"

He smiles. "I heard you guys were excited about some dance." He shakes his head. "Ah, to be young again."

"Um, can you maybe step on the gas a little? You know, break the speed barrier or something?" I force a laugh. "Wouldn't that be so much fun?"

The copilot just grins, then goes back to business.

"I'm on the verge of a screaming freak-out here." I tap my fingers on the armrests.

"Do you think Felicity was in on it?" Budge asks.

I consider the possibility. "I don't know. She was desperate to be prom queen, but her tires got slashed too. Would she do that to her own car? She was leading the race, especially with her dad funding, well, everything."

"If Newt's behind all this, there's no telling what's he's got planned. He's, like, freakishly brilliant. You should call Lindy."

My ears pop as we finally land.

After we roll to a stop, the copilot opens the exit door. "We should be heading back out in thirty."

Thirty whole minutes? "Do you want me to run the package?" I offer. "I'm awfully fast." At least when a psycho-maniac is taking my friend to prom.

The guy gives me another weird look, then exits the plane.

I rip out my cell and call Lindy.

No answer. Just as it goes to voice mail, the line goes silent. I check the bars on my phone. Only one? *Please, God. I need some holy cell reception!*

I try Luke's number.

"Hello?"

My breath releases in a whoosh. "Luke, I have to talk fast—"

"Bella? Hello?"

Are you *kidding* me here? "You have to stop Lindy from going to prom with—"

"Hel*looo*? Hello?" *Click.* Dead line.

I thrash back into my seat. "Try your phone, Budge."

He holds it up. "No reception here."

I pace the short length of the plane until an eternity passes. Finally both pilots are strapped in again, and we're in motion.

"Just an hour and a half," the pilot calls.

I glance at my watch. "We're not going to get to Truman until, like, nine thirty." Rummaging in my purse, I wrap my fingers around a Snickers. This moment calls for chocolate.

"Hey, I'm stressed too." Budge holds out his hand, and I grudgingly give him half. If I've learned nothing else this year, I've learned sacrifice.

He eyes the candy bar. "You gave me the smaller part."

What? I didn't say I was a saint.

My heart stays lodged in my throat during the entire flight. At one point I reach for my phone again, intent on sending Lindy a text.

"You don't want to do a thing like that." The pilot walks toward the wet bar and grabs some pretzels.

"No. I was just . . . um . . . er . . ." Oh, I give up. I toss the phone into my purse.

"Maybe you should do some of that prayer stuff or something." Budge waves a hand around like he's trying to conjure some Jesus.

"You could do it, too, you know."

He turns to look out the window. "I have."

I pray and pray as the plane seems to move at turtle speed. *Please keep Lindy safe. Please let me get in touch with her. Please let Newton split his pants and have to go home.*

For the rest of the way, I divide my time between pleading, praying, and watching the seconds tick. I'm about ready to promise the Lord I'll never say a snarky thing to Budge again when the pilot announces we're landing. Eight fifteen local time. Everyone is at prom by now. What if Newton's hurt Lindy? Or Felicity? Or gone postal on every girl there?

I don't realize I'm holding my breath until the wheels make contact with the runway. When we stop, the pilot lifts a lever and the door whooshes open.

"Thank you. Great flight. You're the best." I heave my suitcase, letting it *thunk* down every step as I pull it behind. "Let's go, Budge!"

I sprint like someone's holding a blowtorch to my butt. My body aches from last night's beating, but I push through it. Budge struggles to keep up. My lungs are burning when we reach the Tahoe. Budge fumbles for the keys.

"Open the car!"

"I'm trying!" he yells. "I can't take this pressure!" His hands shake. His fingers become tangled with one another.

I run to him and latch onto his shoulders. "Pull yourself together, man!"

"I've got them!" Budge holds up the keys like he's found the Holy Grail. "I've got them!"

As he screeches out of the parking lot, I furiously dial Lindy. Straight to voice mail! I try Luke. Same thing! I leave desperate messages.

They're all doing the cha-cha slide, *meanwhile* there's a lunatic among them!

I try one last number.

"You have reached Hunter Penbrook. I can't come to the phone right now. Please leave . . ."

"Hunter, it's me. Call me when you get this. You remember Lindy, right? She's possibly in danger. You have to find her and tell her to stay away from Newt Phillips. Call me!"

Budge drives like a maniac. I check my phone every five seconds. Why isn't Hunter checking his? Shouldn't he be waiting for my call anyway?

"Ruthie's going to kill me when she sees me dressed like this." Budge swats at some chip grease on his jeans.

And my totally amazing dress from Hunter. Wasted. I'm going to my prom wearing my cutoff Abercrombie sweats and hoodie! Can't *wait* to see those pictures.

I hit redial a million times as the miles fly by. I want to shout when I see the Truman city limits sign.

The tires squall as Budge navigates the turns. Felicity's driveway is longer than any street in town. Fancy landscaping lines either side of the path.

Finally I see lights. Cars. Tons of them. Limos. "Park at the front," I say, even though it will block people in.

My head pounding and my side hollow with a dull pain, we run the rest of the way. Through a gate. Straight to the large canopy.

Budge breathes like a rhino. "I'll get Newt."

"And I'll find Lindy."

We throw open the canvas doors and step inside, splitting into

two directions. I blink to adjust my eyes to the dim lights. I walk
toward the pulsing music.

A hand covers my eyes.

Arms grab my middle.

And I scream.

chapter thirty-six

B ella, it's me!"

My eyes struggle to focus. "Hunter?" I lower my fists and bend at the waist, my bruised ribs begging for rest. As I breathe in and out in my jogging togs, he stands there regal and flawless in his tux.

"Always a trendsetter, aren't you? I think I'm overdressed." He smiles.

"I'll explain later."

"Hey, how are you?" He steps closer, his fingers reaching toward my face. "Let me see what that idiot wrestler did."

I shoo his hand away. "I'm fine." Okay, I'm not. I'm tired, I'm sore, and I really need an ice cream fix. "Hunter, I have to take care of something, but I'll find you in a little bit. We need to talk."

He reaches for my hand. "We definitely need to talk. Bella, I—"

"Not now." I walk backward. "Eat some quiche! Have some punch! Do the Worm!" I put some speed into my steps, my eyes scanning for my friend. "Have you seen Lindy?" Empty, clueless faces stare back at me.

I move to the dance area and weave through the maze of class-mates. "Lindy! Lindy! Anyone seen Lindy Miller?"

This is bad. Very bad.

"Bella?"

I pivot at the deep voice. "Luke!"

His eyes flash fire as he reaches out, his hand sweeping across my cheek much like Hunter's. Yet so not like Hunter's touch. Goose bumps skitter across my skin.

"It looks worse than it is."

His fingers still on my jawbone. "I'd like to tear that man apart."

Oh, any other time I would totally appreciate his macho-protectiveness. But *not now!* "Luke, I need to find Lindy—or Newt Phillips. We were wrong about Joshua Day. Newt was the mastermind behind all of this. We've got to get Lindy away from him. Help me find her."

He doesn't even question me. "Let's go."

"No, we need to split up." I point to the other side. "I'll go that way. Call me when you find either one of them."

"Bella, when this is over, we need to talk."

"Yeah, yeah, get in line." I shoot through a swaying couple and continue my urgent search.

A few minutes later I stand at the back exit of the canopy. No Lindy. No Newt. And I would *kill* for some ibuprofen.

Three girls walk by in a cloud of perfume and giggles. "Don't worry about your lipstick. We'll fix it in the bathroom."

"Wait!" I grab one by her tiny dress strap. "Where are the bathrooms?"

She looks at me like I showed up to prom in sweats or something. "Um . . . in the house. Just follow the Chinese lanterns to the back door."

I butt my way in front of them and zoom out the exit. The path takes me past the pool and some couples making out. I step into the house and into a kitchen the size of our yard.

"Lindy?" I yell her name. Moving down the hall, I find a bathroom and set my fist to the door.

"Just a minute!"

Was that her? "I need to talk to you!" I bang some more. "Hurry up."

The door wrenches open. Ruthie stands there in a pink frothy dress, accented with a black leather spiky belt and dog collar. Combat boots rise to meet her calf-length hem. I sag against the wall and consider giving into hysterics.

"What?" she asks. "Is it my hair? It's too pink tonight, isn't it?" She pats her size XXL updo that's somewhere in the color range of Pepto and Hello Kitty.

With as few words as possible, I fill her in. "Go find Lindy. I'm going to search the house." Ruthie doesn't budge an inch.

I roll my eyes and give her a shove. "Yes, your hair looks fabulous."

With a nod, she disappears.

The kitchen begins to fill with people mingling. Unnoticed, I pass through and follow the gleaming wood floor into a massive living room. Hideous pieces of art hang on every wall. A life-size portrait of Felicity holding a poodle looms above the fireplace.

"Lindy?" I call as I search the first floor. "Lindy Miller!" *God, please-oh-please let me find her.*

Peeking over my shoulder, I make sure I'm alone. Then I open every door I find. Nothing. No one. I climb up the grand staircase, my ribs throbbing with every step.

On rubbery legs, I reach the top and open a door and find a sparsely decorated guest bedroom. Double-checking the closets, I move on to a bathroom that could swallow our living room. The knob on the next room sticks, and gritting with pain, I push 'til it gives.

I'm emptied into a large office. I step inside and—

The door slams behind me. I jump and spin.

"N–Newton." Not good. Not good at all.

His back is pressed to the door, and he looks at me with a wild gleam in his eyes. I've seen that look—on Budge when he's gunning down the enemy on Halo.

"Hey . . . um, have you seen Lindy?" My voice is as high as a ten-year-old boy's. "Nice tie, by the way. Like the tux. And your shoes sure are shiny. How do they do that, huh? I see you didn't wear white socks. That's always a good choice." Oh, my gosh. Am I still talking?

Newt twists the lock on the door, his eyes never leaving mine. "So you figured it out."

"Yes, I was dying to know whether Felicity's dad was a Mac man or preferred the PC." I tap his PC. "I'm more of an Apple loyalist myself." My fake laugh sounds more like a drunken sheep. "Now that I found out, I'll just be going."

"I don't think so."

I drop my act. "Just open the door. Don't be an idiot."

He laughs. "I have an IQ of 170. It's a waste of time to question my intelligence."

Crazy and cocky. Perfect. "Why, Newt?"

He looks into the space above my shoulder. "I would've done anything for her."

"Felicity?"

He nods. "When she presented the idea, it was like a gift had just fallen into my lap. Like destiny."

"*She* was with you in the car when you cashed the check at the bank. And you made it appear as if Anna had signed it."

"I'm a good forger. I can copy anyone's signature."

"And the teller—Victoria Smith? Obviously she was in on it."

His grin is predatory. "Let's just say I had some dirt on her she didn't want anyone to know about. And we dated for a bit—before Felicity."

I scan the room for something to use as a weapon. "Why frame Joshua Day? What did he ever do to you?"

"Why, Bella. *You* provided that little detail. Victoria called me from McDonald's that day you met. She mentioned you were hinting about Joshua. Everything had all fallen into place so nicely. This story has simply written itself."

I can't hide my smirk. "Why don't you just ask Felicity out? Why do you care if she gets prom queen? Is it really worth hurting other people?"

"You know nothing about me!" he roars. "I've been in this school since kindergarten and no one ever acts like I even exist! I *love* Felicity. She promised me we'd be together for prom when I had taken care of everything. And I warned you to stay out of this. You're all alike—always in my way."

Hmm. So psycho boy has a small dislike for the female population. "So you did all this—snuck into my house, doctored the photos, transferred the money, got Callie's phone, and—"

"And had Felicity call the caterer, yes. She cared about me." His mouth twists. "As long as she needed me. And by the way"—he shakes a finger at me—"you really should look at getting a new lock for that back door."

I wait a few seconds. Wait for his wave of crazy to ebb. "Then why go to prom with Lindy?"

"To make Felicity jealous."

Somehow I manage to keep a straight face. "And then Felicity broke her promise."

"Like I was a nobody," he snarls. "She never cared about me. And after *all* I did for her. But revenge"—his eyes lock onto mine—"is definitely worth the price of admission."

I force my voice to remain low and calm. "Where is Lindy?"

"When I saw you'd arrived, I sent her on an errand outside. I've been waiting for you, Bella. Because nobody gets the best of me. But now we're through talking." With strength I didn't know he possessed, Newt shoves me and I hit the wood floor, my head barely missing the desk. I am *so* getting a massage after this weekend is over.

He looms over me, his hands fisted. Something shifts in my brain, and my pulse calms. *God, we can do this.*

Last year I survived an entire football team. I've survived an airborne wrestler with nothing to lose. And now *this*? I am *not* letting this dork get the best of me. I scramble to stand.

"Do you see my face, Newt?" Now I'm the one advancing. "I had a little tangle with a man who weighs more than both of us put together. And I *won*." Sort of.

I close the distance and stick my finger in his chest. "Now you're going to let me out of this room or I'm going to tear you apart, limb by stinkin' limb."

His chuckle drips of demented evil. "You know what's cool about being a geek, Bella?"

I tense my muscles, ready to spring. "You always have your Friday nights free?"

"No one really knows anything about you." His leg shoots out in a kick that hits me straight in the ribs. I feel something give and double over, bile rising in my throat. "Like I'm a black belt in *tae kwon do*." He laughs. "I like comic books." He lands a chop to the top of my shoulder, and I sink to my knees. "I've recently learned a lot about explosives." The base of his hand smashes into my temple. "And I'm really great with a computer."

I don't even have time to move as he swings the keyboard like a bat.

Not again.

The floor rises to greet my face.

My eyes cross.

And I'm out.

chapter thirty-seven

I don't feel so well. My mouth tastes like rusted yuck.

Did someone drive a bulldozer into my face? Where am I?

Omigosh.

Lindy! Felicity!

How long have I been lying here?

Ohhhh, Newton Phillips.

I gingerly move one arm. Ow!

Wait—why can't I see? I run my hand over my swollen eyes. I'm blind! *Help me, Jesus, I'm blind!*

The door creaks, and I tense. A shock of pain ricochets through my limbs.

"Bella?"

My mouth hurts to move. "Luke?" I choke back the tears. "I—I can't see. That karate-chopping nerd must've hit my optical nerves and—"

He flips on the light and rushes to me.

"It's a miracle!" I reach for him. "I can see!"

Luke digs into his pocket and calls 9-1-1.

"Why are there two of you? Aw, you're both so cute." I close my eyes again. My head is so fuzzy.

His hands roam over me as he talks.

"Ow . . . Ow . . . Ow . . ."

He snaps his phone shut. "We have to get you to the hospital." Grabbing a Kleenex from the desk, he presses it to my bleeding forehead.

"Story of my life." I clutch his lapel. "Luke, is it too late? How long have I been in here?"

"You've been out of my sight for fifteen minutes."

"Maybe you shouldn't let me out of your sight anymore."

"I don't intend to." He frowns at my wounded face.

Some of the fog dissipates. "Newt—he's going to hurt Felicity. I don't know what his plans are, but they involve explosives. We have to get everyone out of the tent."

"They were winding down the music to announce the prom king and queen when I left."

"Where's Lindy?"

"Budge has her."

I go limp with relief. "We have to go. The police might not get here in time."

Luke scoops me up slowly, as if he's afraid I'll break.

I bite my lip on a yell as I'm lifted into his arms. "When this is over I'm going to have a glass of punch. And a bottle of Tylenol."

His blue eyes sweep over me and rest on my face. "I'm so sorry this happened to you." He runs his hand across my battered cheek, then stalks out the door. Every step down awakens a new ache.

"Wait," I say when we reach the bottom. "I can walk."

"Are you sure?"

Tempting, but yes. Clutching my side, I follow him through the living room and into the empty kitchen. Everyone is outside for the big announcement.

Luke pushes through the crowd in the tent and clears a path. I struggle a few steps behind, as my woozy head jerks from one side to the other looking for Newt. The king and queen candidates form a line at the front of the tent.

The deejay stands on a small stage and pulls a piece of paper from his jacket. "And now, juniors and seniors of Truman High, your prom king is Jackson Feldman . . ."

"We have to get Felicity off the stage!" I yell.

Luke nods and keeps moving toward the front.

"And no prom would be complete without a queen!" the deejay says. "The Tiger prom queen is . . ."

A fake electronic drumroll rattles the tent. The noise escalates as everyone starts to clap.

The deejay holds up the crown. "Felicity Weeks!"

"Bella!" I stop as Lindy grabs my sleeve. "What's going on?"

"We have to get Felicity out of here. Newt's going to hurt her. We need to evacuate the whole place."

Lindy stares toward the stage. "That's not the crown I bought."

The prom king lifts a giant, sparkling tiara over Felicity's head. She sheds big dramatic tears. *Sister, spend an hour in my shoes, and you'll have something to cry about.*

I catch sight of Luke's back. He's headed toward the stage. "Lindy, get out of here. Now."

Pushing past the pain, I rush up the steps to the contestants. Luke stands on the other end of the platform.

I grab the deejay's mic. "We need everyone to clear the tent. Leave immediately!"

Nobody moves. Idiots!

Felicity rips the mic from my hands. "Get off of here, you lunatic! I've waited my whole life for this."

Her tiara bobbles on her head, and I catch sight of a tiny red flicker. A light. "A bomb!" I scream. "It's on her tiara!"

That does the trick. The floor turns into a stampede. People run in every direction, shooting out exits, diving under tables, and crawling under the plastic walls.

One person stands in the middle. He holds a small device.

"Luke, it's Newt!" I point to our villain.

Infused with adrenaline, I grab Felicity's crown, jump down, and run with it across the empty space. I glance back long enough to see Luke on the ground with Newt. They roll around in a scuffle of punches, kicks, and grunts.

Please God. Save us from the exploding cubic zirconias!

Police sirens wail in the distance. Time moves in slow motion.

"Get rid of that crown!" Luke yells. He punches Newt in the jaw then takes a blow himself.

I see my destination stretch out before me. I can't get there fast enough. Budge steps into my line of vision. "Leave!" I shout. "Go!"

He shakes his shaggy head. "I'm open. Pass it! I'll get it there!"

We both turn at Luke's victorious cry. "I have it!" He holds the detonator. "I've got it!"

Newt writhes on the ground, clutching his stomach. His shaking hand reaches into his pocket. I see the shine of metal.

"He has another one!" I cry.

Newt's bony finger presses into the detonator.

"Bella!" Budge calls, arms out.

Grunting like a tennis star, I heave the thing toward him, praying as it sails into the air.

On a yell, Luke charges my way, his body airborne and arcing toward me. I don't even have time to process the hurt as we go down. He turns to take the brunt of the fall, then rolls on top of me, his body shielding mine.

Budge plunges the tiara into the punch fountain. He ballet leaps away, his form a symphony of baggy pants and frizzed-out hair, and rolls under a table, pulling it on top of him.

Kablooom!

A spray of red liquid falls over us like rain. Shards of glass sprinkle everywhere, and I'm pulled tighter to Luke.

Luke rolls off of me and laughs. "We're okay." He pulls me up, picking a piece of glass from his tux. "Are you all right?"

I lick the punch on my hand and taste strawberry. "Yeah, but this totally needs some more sherbet."

He hugs me to him, still laughing. "I thought I was going to wet my pants."

I point to his red-stained trousers. "You sorta did."

Luke pulls away enough to plant a soft kiss on my forehead. "That seriously scared the heck out of me."

"You were amazing." With swollen eyes, I try to bat my lashes. "You're always like, saving me and stuff."

He quirks a brow. "It is getting old." He searches the faces around us. "We've got to get you to a doctor."

A crowd has gathered around us as the tent slowly fills back up. The police filter through, and Budge and Ruthie lead them to Newt, still curled like a snail on the ground.

"Oh, my!" Felicity fans herself with a napkin. "I could've died. You rescued me! I can't wait to tell my daddy about your heroics."

"I'd say you have a lot to tell *daddy*." I gesture to a cop. "Like how you and Newt robbed the class *and* the bank. And how you let Newt keep the money—if he'd sabotage the other queen candidates."

She gasps. "I don't know what you're talking about!" With manicured nails, she gestures to my face. "Clearly you've hit your head a few times."

"Oh, that is *it*!" With arms outstretched, I lunge for the girl.

Luke jumps between us, his mouth in a crooked grin. "I don't think so, Bel."

"No?"

"Nuh-uh," he drolls.

Ignoring my screaming limbs, I rest my hand on Luke's chest, but my glare is for Felicity. "But can't I rough her up just a bit? It would be a humanitarian deed. She needs to know how to defend herself—when she gets to prison."

Felicity blanches.

Luke laughs and wraps an arm around my waist and guides me toward the doors. "Let it go."

A woman in uniform grabs Felicity by the elbow, and I hear her sorry wail all the way outside.

"Omigosh, Bella!" Lindy crushes me in a hug, and my eyes cross. "Are you okay?"

"Easy." Luke pulls me back to him. "Bella's been knocked around a bit."

Matt Sparks stares in the direction of Newt in the patrol car. "I *knew* you shouldn't have gone out with him."

"It wasn't a date, Matt," Lindy protests. "But thanks for dragging me to safety. That was really . . . sweet."

Matt blushes and gives her an awkward side hug. "I just wanted you out of there."

I look at Luke and grin.

"Good catch, *brother*." I ruffle Budge's hair when he walks by. "You saved the night."

He rolls his eyes. "If I'd taken you home in bits and pieces, my dad would've totally killed me. So don't think it was about you."

"Isn't he the best?" Ruthie clutches his arm and sighs. "Oh! Your forehead is bleeding." She digs a tissue out of her cleavage and begins to daub. "My brave champion. If I had known it was going to be like this tonight, I would've brought my favorite knife."

The media covers the area and cameras flash like lightning. Even the familiar two goons from *Pile Driver of Dreams* are in the action.

My policeman friend Mark Rogers breaks into our group. He opens up a kit and commands me to sit on the ground. "Let me take a look at your face. The ambulance will be here shortly."

I let him swab and bandage some bleeding cuts, then beg him to leave. "I'm fine. Really. Go away."

"Only if you promise to have the medics take you in for observation."

Luke rests his hand on my shoulder. "She promises."

"Hey—where's Hunter?" In all the craziness, I totally forgot about him.

Anna Deason saunters by. "If it's the boy I saw you with on that TV show, I think he's over there with that girl."

Standing next to the pool, Hunter faces my direction. A girl has her hand going as she proceeds to gripe him out.

"Hunter!" I call.

The girl turns around, and for the umpteenth time, I'm dizzy. Mia.

I stomp over to them. "What are you doing here?"

"The reality show *paid* me to come out here." Mia snarls at Hunter.

Sure enough, the camera team has moved to a prime spot, their lenses focused right on us.

"What is she talking about, Hunter?"

He opens his mouth, only to snap it shut.

"Tell her," Mia barks.

Hunter's hands reach for me. I shrink away, warning sirens blaring in my ears. "Spill it."

"Bella, I care about you. Please believe that."

"But?"

He moves to touch me again but lets his hand fall. "The show has nothing to do with how I feel about you."

Mia jerks her hand toward the cameras. "Hunter broke up with me when *they* called him."

"What?" And I thought the hits were over. "You were just a prop for the show?"

"It's not like that." His voice is a plea. "Maybe at first, but not later. Not now."

The dark sky tilts, and I struggle to focus. I need to sit down. All these punches, kicks, and body slams are catching up with me. Oh, yeah, and the skanky lies of an ex-boyfriend.

"You don't understand, Bella." He runs a hand through his hair. "They went to my dad first, and everyone was pressuring me. My dad is on the verge of bankruptcy. He needed me."

My laugh is bitter. "Well, I hope you and your big fat check have a lovely flight back to New York."

"I'm sorry I hurt you. Please believe me."

"Believe you?" I laugh. "I can't even *look* at you right now."

Mia squints. "Your eye is pretty swollen."

I turn on her. "And I guess you were here to rub it in?"

She shakes her head. "No. The producer told me to throw a big fit, but I just wanted to warn you. I don't want him back either."

"And what about your disease?" I spit.

Mia snorts. "I'm sure."

"*That* was a lie too?"

Hunter reddens. "I do have a stomach condition. And it is debilitating."

"Irritable bowel syndrome," Mia snaps. "You know, like, when he gets stressed he has the runs."

"For a while they thought it was serious."

I close my eyes at the whine in Hunter's voice. And to think I thought he could've been dying!

"Bella, I'm so sorry. Please forgive me. But I have changed—that wasn't fake. I really did go to church." Hunter plants himself directly in front of me. "Tell me you weren't considering getting back together, and I'll go away without another word."

I look deep into his eyes and will the dizziness to abate. "Hunter, tonight I was going to tell you that I knew without a shadow of a doubt that I wanted nothing more from you than friendship." His face falls. "But you've ruined even that. I need reality—not some hyped-up TV version. Not someone *playing* my friend. Someone who's genuine when all the charm slips away. But I truly do hope you find Jesus one day. So I'll pray for you." I rub my temples and take my last look. "But this friendship is deader than a tiara in a punch bowl."

chapter thirty-eight

"Mom, quit staring at me. I'm not going to shoot lasers out my nose or anything else fabulous."

My mother takes a seat next to my hospital bed. "You have a concussion. The doctor did say to watch you."

"We're never leaving you guys alone again." Jake bounces Robbie to his other knee. "Last night was a close one."

I feel bad the big guy had to cut his Vegas trip short. They took the red-eye and got here this morning. Jake's missing out on lots of promos and interviews. Necessary things for the country's next big wrestling star.

"Yeah, well, you have to leave me alone," Budge says, patting the Band-Aid on his forehead. " 'Cause I'm meeting some friends at the movies tonight."

I lift a sore cheek and smile. "One of those people wouldn't happen to be Ruthie, would it?"

Budge suddenly finds his hands very interesting. "Yeah, her and some people from her church."

"Can we come in?" Dolly sticks her Aqua Net head in the room. Mickey follows her in.

Mom's face is a flashing question mark as she hugs her friend.

"We met in the hall," Dolly whispers. "No big deal." She rests a hip on my bed. "How are you, hon?"

"I'm alive, and none of my friends were blown up. What more could a girl ask for?"

All heads turn at the knock on the door.

I see the flowers first. Then Luke.

"Hey." He smiles and speaks to everyone in the room.

"Let's go get some lunch." Mom stands up and grabs her purse. "I could use something to eat."

"Bring me something back. They tried to feed me mashed peas a while ago. I need a burger." I *deserve* a burger.

Everyone files out, with Robbie trailing behind. He runs to my bed, crawls up, and plants a big one on my cheek. "You're my hero," he says and scampers out.

My eyes grow blurry, and I blink it away. Just fatigue, I'm sure.

Luke wears a dashing smile as he walks to my bedside and brushes the hair away from a bandage. He stares deeply into my eyes, and I wait for his sweet words.

"Kirkwood, you look awful."

Okay. That ain't it.

"Wow, Chief. Words like that just make my insides tingle."

He pulls a chair beside me. "So how are those broken ribs?"

"Bound tighter than a Victorian corset."

"I should've never let you out of my sight," he says.

Now these words I like. "Because you're crazy about me?"

"Because every time I do, you wind up in the hospital." He laughs. "Because the ER doctors know you by name."

"That's not true."

"They probably send you birthday cards."

"No, they don't." Just Christmas greetings.

"We're a pretty good team." Luke holds out his hand. I place mine in his palm.

"We saved the world." I smile into his eyes.

He reaches into his jacket pocket and pulls out an ice cream bar. "For my fellow crime-fighter. It's not from the Truman Dairy Barn, but it was the best I could do."

I unwrap it in one tear. "You're pretty good for me, I guess." I take a bite and sigh. "And face it, my coming on the newspaper staff was the best thing that ever happened to you."

He grabs my hand, drags the ice cream to his mouth, and takes a bite. "Since knowing you, I've been shot at, attacked, and nearly blown apart."

"Is this your way of asking me out?"

"Is it working?"

"I'll go out with you, Luke." I grab my ice cream back. "But just because you *obviously* need protecting."

He laughs. "You are pretty scrappy." His hand disappears into his coat again and pulls out two envelopes. "Recognize these?"

I take another bite. "No."

"Lindy apparently saved our Match-and-Catch results. She thought we might want to look at them." He hands mine over. "Time to see if you're my fated true love."

We both open the white envelopes.

I read the results and smile so big my bruised face hurts. "I'm afraid I must devote the rest of my life to Brian McPhearson. Maybe with my love, he will learn to blow his nose and wear his shoes on the right feet."

Luke nods. "And it looks like I'll be getting to know Tracey Sniveley and her thirty cats."

"I'm sorry. I guess there's just no chance for us." I reach for his hand and give it a friendly squeeze. "But we should totally double-date."

"Let's talk when you don't have a concussion." Luke leans close and presses a kiss on my forehead. "Oh, wait. That's never." And with a wink, he walks out of my room.

Sure. He talks big now.

But one day Luke Sullivan will need saving again.

And I think I'm just the girl for the job.

acknowledgments

As usual, I have a million people to thank. It is with a grateful heart that I acknowledge:

My Facebook friends. I owe you a lot for helping me name and rename (and name and rename) Luke Sullivan. I still don't see why Otis Sprinkledink is such a bad pick. To me it just reeks of hotness.

Editor Jamie Chavez. Book four together and you haven't kicked me to the curb yet! Thank you for your friendship, humor, intimidating intelligence, as well as your juicing tips. Please know I will never drink beets. Never.

Editor Natalie Hanemann. It's been a joy to get to know you and work with you. I can't wait to hang out and talk books even more.

Everyone at Thomas Nelson. To quote Queen Tina, "You're simply the best." It's an honor to be a Nelson author and see what loving care you give your books.

My blog family. Thank you for stopping by three times a week and reading, as if my insanity is entertainment . . . instead of proof I need heavy medication.

Chip MacGregor of MacGregor Literary. For traveling this road with me and for all the funny, encouraging e-mails along the way.

Erin Valentine. I couldn't do any of this without you, and so appreciate your friendship, support, edits, and "you can do it" advice. Are you *sure* you weren't a cheerleader?

Leslie and Kim. For putting up with me during "deadline lockdowns," when I turn into something a little less friendly and a lot more *Nightmare on Elm Street*-ish.

Mom, Kent, Michael, Laura, Hardy, and Katie Beth. I appreciate the love, support, and occasional meals-to-go. (You can't have too much of any of those.)

My readers, whose e-mails make my day. Thank you for giving up hours of your life to read my books, my blog, and the occasional witty line on airport bathroom walls. (Just kidding. I would never do that . . . and admit it.)

My students, who have to put up with a lot as I juggle teaching and writing. Forgive me for the times I stare right through you as a plot enters my head or scribble down your words verbatim because I want to steal them for a book. And I'm sorry for that one review game we did that drew blood. Okay, no. I'm not. That was funny.

The Father, Son, and Holy Ghost. I don't know that anything has stretched me more spiritually than being chained to a keyboard. Thank you for giving me a dream and blessing me indeed. Now as to those extra five pounds I've gained writing . . . we *totally* need to talk about that . . .

reading group guide

1. If *I'm So Sure* was made into a movie, who would you cast as the characters?

2. A reoccurring theme in the book is that things aren't always what they seem. Where was this theme evident?

3. In your own life, have you been in a situation where something or someone didn't match the first impression?

4. Bella Kirkwood really struggles in her relationship with her dad. Is she justified in her bitterness? What advice would you give her?

5. What would the perks be of living your life on a reality show? The drawbacks? Why is America so in love with reality TV?

6. What are some issues Bella has as a result of her parents' divorce? Describe some difficulties of being a child of divorce— either from a personal experience or from what you've seen a friend go through.

7. In what ways do Bella and other characters have a hard time with honesty—either in blatant lying or just not being able to share his/her heart? Why do you think it's so difficult to tell people how we really feel?

8. Bella's made a few mistakes in the boyfriend department. What advice would you give her? Can you think of a Bible verse that would apply?

9. Bella is learning to rely on family and friends in *I'm So Sure*. Describe the moments she needed them the most.

10. The character of Callie got so obsessed with winning the prom queen contest, she made some really bad decisions. Have you ever gotten so focused on something (one particular friend, a boy, a job, a test) that other things or relationships suffered?

11. How did Bella's "gift" of nosiness lead her into trouble? Do you have a dominant flaw that sometimes lands you in hot water?

12. Bella splits her time between Manhattan and Truman, Oklahoma. What are the perks of each? The downsides? What do you think God is trying to teach Bella with this contrast?

13. What do you believe the title *I'm So Sure* means? When you are making a decision or have a problem, how do you know for certain what the right answer is?

Follow Bella as she trades her Manolos for clown
shoes to unravel the secrets of the big top in . . .

So
OVER MY
Head

the next installment in *The Charmed Life* series.

♦ ♦ ♦ ♦ ♦ ♦

In stores May 2010

♦ ♦ ♦ ♦ ♦ ♦

Visit jennybjones.com

THOMAS NELSON
Since 1798

an excerpt from

So Over My Head

~~~

$\mathscr{I}$f my love life was the knife toss at a circus, I'd have Luke Sullivan speared to the wall with an apple in his mouth.

"Ladies and gentlemen! The Fritz Family welcomes you to the greatest show on earth!" A man in a top hat stands in the center of a giant tent, his curlicue mustache as delicate as his voice is strong. "Prepare to be amazed. Prepare to be wowed. Allow us to entertain you with sights you've never seen, horses whose feats will astound you, and death-defying acrobatics!"

On this first night open to the public, the crowd stands in a swarm of shouts and applause.

I stay seated and jot down some quick notes for the *Truman High Tribune.* Or at least that's what I'm pretending to do. In actuality, it's taking all my energy just to be civil.

"I just don't see why you had to invite her."

From his standing position, Luke glances down. "Are we back to that again?"

"You and I are working on the carnival story. Not Ashley."

Ashley Timmons, a new girl who joined the newspaper staff last week, has become my least favorite person on the planet. She's not quite as awful as those on the top of that list—namely the handful of people who've tried to do me bodily harm over the last year. But icky nonetheless. Fresh from Kansas City with her brother, Ashley thinks she is to journalism what Tiger Woods is to golf. She's disgustingly cute, and worst of all, she's Luke's ex-girlfriend. She only moved away for two years, but I can tell she's ready to rekindle anything they used to have. It doesn't take a keen reporter's intuition to see that. Just anyone with at least one working eyeball.

"We've hung out with them all week, Luke."

"I haven't seen Kyle in a long time, and he'll be leaving soon for college." Luke searches my face. "I've included you in everything. Have you felt left out?"

"No." I just want *her* left out. I don't mind the return of his friend Kyle at all. But where Kyle is . . . there you'll find his sister. "Tonight isn't about hanging out with your friend though. He's not even here. You invited Ashley for the paper."

"You've been ticked at me ever since your last article. But it was weak on verbs and lacked your usual creativity." He sits down and trains those intense eyes on mine.

"Yeah, and then you proceeded to show me some piece of writing wonderment your new recruit produced." Ashley came with glowing recommendations from her former journalism teachers. Everyone on our staff thinks she is, like, the greatest thing to writing since the delete key. Everyone but me.

"You know what your problem is, Bella? Number one, you're jealous and insecure—"

"Of her?" I toss my hair and laugh. "Maybe I just don't like the way she's thrown herself at you from the second she stepped into the classroom. I'm not insecure, but I'm also not stupid."

Luke's mouth twitches. "I meant insecure of your writing abilities. But now that you mention it, you probably are jealous of my talking to her. That would fit."

"Fit what?" A band of clowns ride unicycles in the ring, but I don't even bother to watch.

"It would fit with the Bella Kirkwood pattern." He lifts a dark brow. "You are completely distrusting of the entire male species. I guess one couldn't blame you, given your dad's history *and* your experience with your ex, but I have no desire to get back with an old girlfriend."

"This is outrageous. I do *not* have trust issues with guys! And you know what else?"

"I'm dying to hear more."

"I think you're enjoying all the attention from Ashley." All Luke and I have done is fight lately. While digging into other people's business might be my spiritual gift, I'm beginning to think arguing comes second.

"Ever since we've been together, you've balked at my every comment in journalism. You can't stand to be criticized—even when it's for your own good. And"—his blue eyes flash—"you're just waiting for me to cheat on you like Hunter. You think I don't see that?"

Hunter would be my ex-boyfriend from Manhattan. This past fall I caught him doing the tongue tango with my former best friend Mia. And then not too long ago I considered getting back with him. He swept me up with this new version of Hunter Penbrook, told me he had started going to church, said all the right things, bought me coffee. It's a little hard to resist a cute guy bearing a mocha latte with extra whip, you know? Luckily, at prom two weeks ago, I saw the light and let that rotten fish off my hook.

"I'm not worried about you cheating on me, Luke. I'm tired of you bossing me around and acting all 'I'm in charge.'"

"I *am* in charge. I'm the editor."

"Not of our relationship."

"I'm back!" Ashley chooses that very moment to flounce back to her seat. "I got you a cotton candy." She hands the pink confection to Luke. "Bella, I figured you're like most girls and need to watch your weight, so I didn't get you anything. What'd I miss?"

Luke holds me down with his arm. "Don't even think about it," he whispers.

The crowd *oohs* and *ahhhs* as the Amazing Alfredo begins juggling two long silver swords. I applaud politely when he pulls a third one out of his hat and tosses it into the air with the rest. I'd hate to think where that sword was *really* hiding.

Like a distant relative, the Fritz Family Carnival comes to Truman, Oklahoma, every April and sets up camp on land that, I'm told, goes way back in the Fritz genealogy. They stay at least a month—working on additional routines, training new employees, giving the local elementary teachers a nice afternoon field trip—and don't leave until they can ride out bigger and better than the year before. And while that might be odd, it's nothing compared to the fact that I'm sitting on the bleachers between my boyfriend and a girl who has been openly flirting with him. That chick needs to learn some boundaries.

"Bella, Luke said you might need some help with your article."

He holds up a hand. "I just thought it would be interesting to get our three perspectives. Bella will still handle the interviews."

"It's been so great to work with you again, Luke." Ashley's smile could charm the shirt off Robert Pattinson. "Just like old times, huh?" Her eyes gaze into his. Like I'm not even there. "Kyle's really enjoyed hanging out. Too bad he had a study session tonight."

Luke leans close, his mouth poised near my ear. "Just because we're dating doesn't mean I'm going to slack off on your writing. You're still a staff member. And you *know* I do not boss you around any other time. I have been nothing but respectful to you." He returns his attention to the ring. "Did you write down the fat lady's stats?"

"Of course I did." I scribble something illegible on my paper. No, I didn't get her stats. I'm too busy fighting.

"She's seven hundred and twenty-nine pounds, in case you missed it," Ashley chirps.

"Thanks." *Lord, help me be kind to this girl.*

"You always act like I can't handle the writing assignments," I whisper for Luke's ears only. "I think I have more than proven I can. Not only can I write, but I can crank out some award-winning writing *while* crime solving."

After I moved to Truman, I accidentally became the Nancy Drew of Oklahoma. Now that I'm known for my mystery solving skills, friends and strangers want me to help them out. Just last week I tracked down a stolen iPhone and did a little spying for a suspicious girlfriend who thought her boyfriend Buster was cheating. It's true he hadn't been going to football practice like he said; I found him at Margie Peacock's School of Ballet, lined up on the bar doing pirouettes and high kicks. I hear he makes a heck of a swan in Margie's recital.

"I'm not doubting your writing skills." Luke claps as the magician leaves, and Betty the Bearded Lady bows before starting her performance.

I'm transfixed by the hair on her face, and it suddenly makes me feel a whole lot less self-conscious about the fact that I didn't shave my legs last night. The audience claps in time to the spirited music as the woman's collie jumps through her hula hoop, then dances to the beat on its hind legs.

I shoot a pointed look at his old flame. "Let's talk about this later."

Ashley reaches around me and puts her hand on Luke's knee. "I forgot—I have my latest assignment on my laptop in the car. You told me to spice up my verbs, and I revised it. I wanted you to look at it." She returns to clapping for the Bearded Lady.

"Yes, Luke. She wants you to check out her spicy *verbs*."

"At least she takes constructive criticism well." His voice is just low enough for me to hear.

"That girl wants you back. Period."

"I'm not Hunter. And I'm not your dad."

"I have to go interview Betty the Bearded Lady." And I stomp down the bleachers to find her trailer outside. When I glance back, Ashley has scooted down. And taken my place.

The only thing scarier than living
on the edge is stepping off it.

A NOVEL OF LOSING FEAR
AND FINDING GOD

*Just Between
You and Me*

JENNY B. JONES

The new contemporary women's novel
from Jenny B. Jones.